by
Jason Pomerance

Also by Jason Pomerance

Women Like Us
Falconer (novella in four parts)
"Mrs. Ravenstein" - Writing Bloc Escape! Anthology
"Violet Crane" - Writing Bloc Deception! Anthology

I.

Celia's mother said, "Your fingers look pudgy, dear. Have they gained weight?"

Her older sister Bernadette said, "Well, not just her fingers, mother. Exactly how many pounds have you packed on?"

"And when was your last physical? You might want to look into an EKG and maybe even a stress test, or at least a chest x-ray, because in case you missed the news, heart attacks are killing more women than ever. *The silent killer*, they're calling it. And you know how old you'll be in, what? A matter of days?"

This came from Celia's younger sister, Rosalie, who, for as long as Celia could remember, felt it necessary to add a dose of doom and gloom to conversations about almost any subject. Polar ice caps melting? Rosalie had an opinion. That island of trash floating around the Pacific? Don't get her started. Rosalie's wife, Kim-Cuc, meanwhile, nodded along while nursing one of their twins, both girls. *As if this family needed any more of those*, Celia often thought, imagining a day in the not-too-distant future when they, too, would be nagging her or getting on her case about this or that.

Celia set down her fork. She didn't need that last bite of her mother's coconut cake, anyway, did she? Even though, like always, it was covered with a thick layer of the cream cheese frosting laced with shredded sweet coconut she adored so much it frequently invaded her dreams. She pushed the plate to the middle of the table so it was out of reach, or at least an effort to reach. She placed her index fingers at her temples and gently moved them in circles. She had recently read somewhere that even this sort of self-massage could reduce stress. Of course, you were also supposed to meditate—conjure up a soothing image and focus on it with clarity—but Celia always had trouble with meditation, unable to quiet her often-feverish brain or tune out all those work texts and emails.

"Here's a thought," she said. "Why don't we all just talk about something else? Why does every Sunday Supper have to be about what's wrong with me?"

"I'm good with that," said Bernadette.

"We can talk about whatever," added Rosalie.

They did change the subject. Rosalie and Kim-Cuc chattered about the twins. Bernadette went on a rant about some underling at the office who was giving her a hard time. But somehow, Celia knew, the conversation would veer back to how she might fix her life, which wasn't what these Sunday Suppers were supposed to be about, really. These dinners—which they'd plan, shop for, and fix together in a group effort, like tonight's roast chicken, mashed potatoes and long-simmered green beans—were supposed to be about family, about maintaining a weekly ritual that had been started by their mother's mother, so they could stay connected and pass the tradition on to the next generation. And, frankly, also so that Celia and her sisters could keep a closer eye on their mom, whose behavior was becoming frequently puzzling and sometimes even downright erratic. For instance, this very night, she had selected the menu after determining she couldn't find the water chestnuts needed for her infamous Oriental casserole, but hadn't Celia found several cans of water chestnuts right there in her pantry? Then, as they were prepping the meal, Daisy Bernhart reached for the salt and insisted on seasoning the chicken when all three of her daughters swore up and down she'd already done it. So the whole thing tasted too salty.

But were they examining their mother's latest lapse tonight? Had they discussed convincing their mother to see that neurologist a neighbor had suggested? No, like every week, everybody circled back to picking on Celia.

Oh, Celia knew her life was far from perfect. For instance, yes, sure, she had put on a few pounds recently, and, yes, she was on the verge of turning thirty-nine, and this was disturbing and distressful in so many ways. No, it wasn't the big four-zero, but thirty-nine felt even worse to Celia. There was so much she hadn't done, and, suddenly, it seemed like time might be starting to run out, or that some cosmic deadline was looming, and she was destined to miss it.

Also, long gone was her vision of what she'd be like as a grown-up. This vision—and that's exactly what it felt like, a sudden apparition—had come to her during the final leg of a family vacation to the mountains one summer when she and her sisters were small. It was the end of a long, hot week, so everybody was a little peevish and sluggish as they headed home: her parents up front, Celia and her sisters in the back seat of her parents' wagon. Usually, the girls sat in the order they were born, youngest on the left, oldest on the right, like little ducklings, Celia always thought, which meant she was forever stuck in the middle, on the uncomfortable hump between the two better window seats. Occasionally, she'd consider fighting for a window, but usually, she accepted her place. It just seemed easier.

On that particular day, Rosalie and Bernadette were so engrossed in some argument that Bernadette simply followed her sister into the car and took the middle, leaving Celia the prized window. She gazed out of it dreamily, lulled by the motion of the car and the rhythmic bopping jazz their father liked to listen to, and sometimes sing along with, on the radio. Eventually, Rosalie fell asleep, Bernadette stuck her nose in a book, and their mother and father lapsed into what often felt to Celia like tense silence.

They had just crossed over a bridge. Celia noticed a sign—'*CAREFUL: BLIND CURVE AHEAD*'—she remembered it warned somewhat ominously before the wagon picked up speed as her father merged into heavy traffic. She had the window open and could hear the throaty roar of the approaching car before she saw it. It was a classic old Camaro, a convertible, fiery red, with the top down, the radio blasting pop, a girl group singing something about loving and losing a boy.

At the wheel was a woman. She had long, streaked blond hair blowing in the breeze, a small delicate nose, and a perfectly straight line of dazzling white teeth. Celia could make out a peasant blouse and some sort of exotic turquoise jewelry around her neck. The woman's lips were painted a frosty pink, and she may have been smoking a cigarette. Celia could never be sure if she invented that detail. But it was like an image on a movie screen: a woman who seemed confident, powerful, free, and at peace, without a care in the world. Celia couldn't take her eyes off her.

Then the woman turned, and for a second, they locked eyes. Celia could swear she detected a mysterious smile, like this woman was coming from somewhere important or was harboring a significant secret. As fast as it had approached, the convertible passed, and this apparition was gone, replaced by an ashy grey old couple in a rusty sedan staring stonily at the road ahead.

Celia thought: *that's what I'll be when I grow up, self-possessed and cool, the kind of girl who'd light up a room the second she walks in or be the center of attention at a party.* She even created a whole persona for this futuristic alternate-universe version of herself and christened her with a new name: Lisa. Lisa was a bolder and more assured sort of name than Celia, which seemed to indicate a kind of wishy-washiness, really.

But along the way, something went wrong, and she never found that future version of herself.

Well, a lot went wrong.

This kind of thing didn't happen with her sisters, who always had a flair for setting goals and reaching them. Bernadette, for example, always talked—without a hint of reservation or modesty—about being rich, having scads of money, so she could travel and buy fancy cars and such, and here she was, a top executive with a hedge fund, raking it in. She always looked fabulous, her hair expertly cut and colored, always outfitted in something that was perfectly tailored and, Celia suspected, extremely pricey. Rosalie, conversely, had been helping the less fortunate since toddlerhood, taking in strays—people and animals—and insisted she'd do just that when she grew up, somehow make the world a better place. Now she was a social worker, dedicated to the needy, and she looked the part, Celia thought, always wearing something that might have come from a thrift store, eschewing make-up and hair products. For a time, when she was younger, Rosalie seemed to even ignore or look down on bathing and basic hygiene.

But Celia never turned herself into something self-possessed and cool. She generally considered herself awkward and ill-at-ease, uncomfortable in her own skin most of the time. Also, somewhere along the line, her life had taken some strange detour. When she was a kid, she envisioned that she'd do something colorful and interesting when she grew up. Certainly, Lisa would have. Lisa would have been the curator of an art gallery, or she'd have a job in fashion. She'd live in a funky part of Brooklyn, and she'd have a closet full of short skirts and stiletto heels. She'd have a cool child, too, on her own even if the right man hadn't come along, one of those artsy kids she'd see around the city, kids with whimsical names always making pretty sketches or sculpting something interesting out of clay. Celia didn't have the loft, the clothes, or the child. The truth was, she looked terrible in short skirts, and stilettos made her ankles ache.

When she was younger, though, she did have something of an artistic bent, a genuine interest in photography. This she attributed to a friend of her mother's she always admired, who was a true talent. This woman traveled the world and photographed life wherever she saw it. Once, she had a showing at a gallery, of pictures mostly in black and white that fascinated Celia, some so etched in her mind she could still see them to this day. Like one of a small Asian girl with severely-cut bangs, gazing heavenward after letting go of a balloon, or another of a young woman in a polka dot dress in a field of white flowers that seemed an extension of the dress, so that at first all Celia could see was an almost ghostly face.

In fact, this friend had taken Celia into the darkroom she'd put together in her basement, and she demystified the process of turning a blank sheet of paper into a picture. Celia watched, fascinated, under the soft, eerie glow of the red lamp as an image was projected from the enlarger and, as the paper moved from one developing bath to the next, it came to life. She learned you could manipulate colors and shadows and shadings. She begged for her own camera on her next birthday, and when her parents came through and gave her one – okay, well, it was only a little Instamatic—she carried it everywhere because she never knew when she'd find something interesting to capture. She took out books from the library and read up on famous photographers. She carefully studied their work. Then came junior high and high school, and her interest waned. Too many other distractions – first gymnastics, which she gamely tried out for but failed to win a spot on the team – then debating club, then, well, boys.

But the photography bug cropped up again when she left for college. During freshman year, she loaded up on courses in art history. She took classes in photography alongside girls who wore mostly black, or refused to shave their underarms or sit in the sun for more than two seconds, who were vegan or at least vegetarian and who heavily lined their eyes with kohl, and the serious boy versions, guys who had unconventional facial hair and wore funny-shaped glasses. Some even had tattoos, mostly in spots where their parents wouldn't see them. They'd all argue noisily and for hours about Diane Arbus and her freakish subjects or Ansel Adams and his awe-inspiring landscapes and nature shots and Edward Steichen and his innovations.

But a few harsh critiques from her professor on the composition of her photos, and sometimes on the subjects themselves, eventually did her in. She had always adhered to the idea of photographing people when they weren't expecting it, naturalistic photos that told the story of the human condition. But she hadn't yet learned the trick of disappearing, this professor insisted, and her eye on the human condition attempts wound up forced and artificial. Or her subjects, often strangers, looked shocked and sometimes even outright angry. She could remember to this day, more than twenty years later, exactly what the professor said. Her work lacked depth, was insubstantial. She had potential, he admitted, but she'd have to buckle down and do the work. Meanwhile, there was no support or encouragement from her mother ("You know what's always awfully useful, dear?' Daisy Bernhart would say on her nightly calls to check in, "A nursing degree. Just in case.") or from her sisters, that was for sure—and Celia had a crisis of confidence. She dropped all the art classes. She switched to a business major.

Not that Celia Elizabeth Bernhart was all that interested in business, although she did appreciate the courses were largely about numbers, which acted in predictable ways, unlike people. In college, she was interested in Todd Murdoch, who was a business major. Todd was tall and lanky with an athletic build, sandy blond curls, and eyes the color of a pale sky. He was from California, and he surfed, and so of course that seemed exotic and alluring. Plus, he reminded her of one of her childhood crushes, Christopher Atkins from the movie "Endless Love," which Bernadette had gotten on tape for a birthday and Celia watched, well, endlessly until the tape actually broke and Bernadette forced her to buy a new one.

She first encountered Todd sophomore year, and Celia, who had put on well more than the freshman fifteen, had dieted herself back down over the summer. She had begun an exercise routine—running (okay, super-fast walking) and had stuck to it, determined to tone the excess flab and dimples on her thighs. Also, she had managed to tame her reddish-brown hair, which, in good times, tended toward curly in a nice way but in bad times, usually depending on the weather, progressed to an outright unpredictable and embarrassing frizz, which somehow only accentuated her freckles and made her slim little nose seem awfully sharp. Oh, people – aunts and uncles and other relatives mostly – had been giving Celia that lame line for as long as she could remember, that she had such a 'pretty smile', that her eyes—a deep, interesting shade of olive—practically twinkled when she was excited or happy. Still, she rarely felt even remotely attractive to boys. Not in grade school or high school, though there were of course all kinds of mad crushes and nervous fumblings at parties in friends' clammy basements; somehow, she always was left feeling let-down or disappointed, unsure of what it meant to be in love or how it should actually feel.

So it was surprising when Todd approached her, even though she'd been secretly watching and tracking his moves forever - always on the sly, she was certain. Until one day, she was in line in the cafeteria and she realized Todd was standing right next to her, so close she could feel the warmth of his skin. Maybe this was fate! So of course, she nixed the idea of the tuna melt and curly fries she was considering, asked for a bowl – no, a cup – of plain broth, and planned to head to the salad bar, all the while hoping Todd wasn't noticing the line of sweat starting to break out on her brow or that her hand trembled when she accepted the broth from the lady behind the counter, so that the cup jiggled on the saucer with a mortifyingly loud clatter.

"Don't you want your crackers?" had been Todd's opening line.

"Um," Celia had said, "What?"

He pointed to the cafeteria lady, who was holding out a couple of packages of Saltines for the broth. "Oh!" Celia said.

She could still feel how her cheeks burned red. "No, thanks," she managed and hurried off, nearly taking out the dweeby math nerd in front of her. At the salad bar, she found Todd next to her again.

"Just in case you change your mind," he said, pointing to the Saltines, now sitting on his tray. "They are free, you know. But if you don't eat them, I will."

He smiled. Celia was lost.

They wound up eating together, Celia carefully picking at lettuce leaves and taking dainty sips of the broth to avoid slurping, determined to ignore how the fine blond hairs on his arms made her stomach do flip-flops. But why, she always wondered, did the boys she liked express interest in her and then seem to lose it? She had made it all the way through high school, unlike many of her friends, a virgin. Oh, she had begun all the preliminary explorations, but sealing the deal had eluded her. With Todd at that lunch, she had fast developed an easy rapport, which Celia decided would mean they'd be buddies and nothing more.

This seemed especially true when he asked her to join him in the library to study the next night. *Well, that's that,* thought Celia, even though it took her over an hour to choose just the right outfit, one that would make it seem like she hadn't gone to any trouble at all. She wore her favorite pair of faded jeans, frayed at the bottom, with flats and a black camisole top with a low-but-not-too-low neckline that she hoped said sexy but friendly and approachable at the same time. She slipped on a couple of funky bracelets and added half-inch gold hoop earrings. She added just a little bit of lip gloss and tied her hair back in a sleek ponytail. She checked herself out from every angle numerous times in the small dorm room mirror before leaving, worrying that her ass might look huge or that the skin under her arms might jiggle if she moved the wrong way, or that she had something in her teeth.

They took a table in a corner of the library opposite each other. Todd spread out his books on macroeconomics, and Celia tried to forge her way through *Great Expectations* for English Lit 101. She kept sneaking glances up at him; when their eyes would meet, she'd look away or feel her cheeks

burn again. But Todd kept holding her gaze, grinning goofi-
ly, making her wonder if he might possibly be stoned.

Then their feet bumped together. He had kicked off his
loafers. One of his bare feet worked its way up her leg, tentatively at first, then bolder and more insistent when she didn't
put up much of a protest. When the feel of his skin on hers
reached a certain sensitive point, she had to stifle a giggle.

They'd wound up back in Todd's room, a frat house disaster zone really, complete with a curious odor of sweat
mixed with musk mingling with spilled beer, pot smoke, and
stale cigars. Celia could still conjure up the tingly bristle of
Todd's scruff as he nuzzled her neck and nibbled her ear,
could see the little kid-like grin on his face as he pulled off
her bra, and how she nearly passed out when his tongue
flicked against her...

"Anyway," Daisy Bernhart said, her voice jolting Celia
back from the memory to her mother's dining room table, "if
you want to talk about something else , shouldn't we be dis-
cussing the wedding?"

"Yeah," said Bernadette. "You told us you and Barry are
engaged—*finally,* I might add—but I still don't see any ring
on that finger."

"Plus, I will most definitely need a date and a venue if I'm
going to cater." This came from Kim, who was rejoining the
conversation, having finished nursing the twins and hand-
ing each little girl off to Rosalie in a deft, swift maneuver so
that Rosalie could burp them. It was Kim-Cuc who carried
these babies and gave birth to them, a fact that still sometimes astonished Celia because she was such a tiny little slip
of a woman. Kim-Cuc had actually come into the family over

thirty years earlier, part of the very last exodus of refugees from Vietnam who made their way first to Southern California and then to points east like Chicago and New York. She was an orphan, barely a newborn, and at the time Celia's parents were in the middle of their extended flirtation with the whole counterculture thing, which included food co-ops Celia always found a little unclean and 'Ban This!' or 'Protest That!' stickers on the back of the wagon.

Celia had distinct memories of Kim-Cuc's arrival. The family converged on JFK with a large group of others awaiting refugees, all of them in a nervous but eager huddle by the gate where the plane was scheduled to arrive. It was a thrill being up so late, Celia could remember, and vaguely exciting to watch passengers begin to disembark: first businessmen in rumpled suits, followed by a couple of blinking, dazed tourists, and a child about her age swinging a doll by one ragged arm. Then came a group of efficient looking women, each cradling a bundle to her chest, some swaddled in blue blankets, others in pink. One of these was thrust into Daisy's open arms, and Celia and her sisters strained to see but could make out nothing except a tiny tuft of spiky black hair poking up out of the top. Then Daisy unfolded the blanket to reveal the contents of her bundle, just a teeny-tiny squirming red thing with big eyes and a tiny button of a mouth. It felt like it was made of rubber when Celia poked it with a finger. "It's a baby!" Daisy had said, "A sweet, innocent little baby girl who was left to fend for herself and needs a home!"

"What's that got to do with us?" Bernadette had asked, crossing her arms and tapping a foot impatiently.

Frankly, that was a good question, as neither Celia nor her sisters were thrilled by this addition to the family, which instantly seemed to suck up their mother's attention like a sponge. But they didn't have a say, and the squishy loud little red thing was brought back to the Dutch Colonial on Riverview Road. It was supposed to be a temporary foster situation, but there were all sorts of delays and hold-ups with the family adopting Kim-Cuc, and she stayed with the Bernharts in Rockville Centre nearly three years until, suddenly, she was gone. And, of course, they all missed her horribly. It wasn't until years later that Rosalie and Kim-Cuc reconnected—at a lesbian speed-dating event of all places—and became a couple, like it was destiny, as Rosalie and Kim-Cuc liked to tell people as they shared a secret smile.

"I mean what's it going to be? Big wedding? Small? Have you given any thought to the menu?" Kim-Cuc asked. "Do you want to do a little plates kind of thing? You know, sort of Tapas-ish, although that's kind of out finally, thank goodness, because little plates are a huge pain. A buffet? Or a more traditional sit-down meal with a choice of chicken, fish, and of course something vegetarian and vegan?"

Dinner was over. Celia was still at the table, but her sisters and mother were now lined up, hip-to-hip. Rosalie washed dishes, Bernadette stacked them in the dishwasher, Kim dried various pots, and their mother carefully wrapped up the leftover chicken, still swearing it was not overly salted even though nobody was listening. They had all turned and were waiting for Celia's response, expectant faces lined up, each one like a question mark.

"First of all, before we discuss any other wedding plans," Celia said as she dug into her purse and pulled out the small blue velvet box, "the fact is, I do have a ring."

Popping open the box, she held it up for her sisters, mother, and Kim to see. Nestled inside more rich dark blue velvet was a real sparkler, a one and a half carat cushion-cut number from Tiffany she had admired one Sunday when they were just browsing, with little diamond chips all around a band of white gold.

Celia's mother let out a little whistle.

Rosalie bent in for a closer look. "Oh," she said, "that is nice. Of course, I hope you and Barry confirmed that it's from a reputable source. You know all about blood diamonds, I'm sure. It's horrible how people are exploited because of something so frivolous."

"It's from Tiffany's, Rosie," said Celia.

"When did he give it to you?" Bernadette wanted to know. "Did he get down on bended knee? Because when Kent proposed, he knelt. Not only that, he had Veuve Clicquot on ice, and he had covered the bedroom floor in rose petals. Did I ever mention that?"

"Only about a gazillion times," Rosalie said. Celia could tell she was calculating how much was spent on the champagne and roses and what better uses there were for the money, and at the same time wondering if they composted the rose petals when they were done with them.

"Well, did he get on his knees?" Bernadette asked again.

"Um," Celia said, "not exactly. No. He has this back thing that kicks in sometimes, and, well, who does that anymore, anyway, really?"

"Were you at least at a romantic dinner?" her mother asked.

"Yes," said Celia. "It was sort of romantic."

"Sort of?" asked Kim-Cuc. "It either is or it isn't romantic if you ask me. There's no in between."

"Well, it was our sort of anniversary, you know? I mean the anniversary of our first real date and..."

"Do you mean 'date' or the first time you slept with him?" This came from Bernadette, who was a stickler for these sorts of details.

"Does it really matter?" Celia asked.

Her mother said, "Of course it does. Unless it's both. Did you sleep with him on your first date, dear? Because you know how I've always felt about that. I've always advised against it. Not that anybody listens to me."

"Or was it your first orgasm?" Rosalie asked. "When Kim-Cuc and I..."

Celia held up a hand. "Really? Must you, Rosie? Because that's way too much information."

Indeed, she could feel her cheeks beginning to flush. Celia always liked to keep at least some aspects of her life private, in their own separate compartment, but this seemed impossible with her mother and sisters and Kim. Almost any topic was fair game, especially when they all got together for these Sunday Suppers, and especially if there was alcohol involved, as there generally was, with a couple of now-nearly empty bottles of Pinot Noir on the table.

"Anyway," Kim said, "why aren't you wearing it?"

"It needs to be resized."

"It's too big?" asked Bernadette.

"Um. No," Celia said. "Too small."

"Ah!" her mother practically shrieked. "You see, Celia dear, I was right after all. And you all think I'm such a ninny."

"About what, mother?"

"Your fingers looking pudgy! Like they gained weight. Are you watching what you're eating? Or is it just water retention?" She didn't wait for a response. "Well," Daisy continued, "what a shame that the poor man couldn't even properly slip on an engagement ring."

Her sisters nodded in agreement. All sorts of responses flew through Celia's brain. But all she could do was laugh. Finally, she said, "He swiped a ring out of my jewelry box to get a size, but he picked one I hadn't worn since I was in junior high. It had nothing to do with weight gain or water retention."

Her sisters, mother, and Kim all looked as if they believed her.

SHE HADN'T MARRIED Barry yet, Celia reasoned again, out loud to herself while driving the few miles home, still feeling the sting of her family's judgment, because she was just so busy with work. Of course, there was also the fact that Barry hadn't officially popped the question until recently. Not that she couldn't have brought it up herself and asked him. But with things so hectic over the last few years, she hadn't really noticed the time slipping by. And really, work had been crazy.

Celia sold pharmaceuticals. She was good at it, too (and people needed more and more drugs these days, it seemed, the hunger for them sometimes a little astounding, really, and slightly scary when she thought about it). She had been with the company since being hired for a part-time job when she was still in college. It was shortly after she had broken up with Todd – he needed some space, he said, one night after a movie, pizza, and a fast, furious round of screwing in his Jeep.

"Seriously, dude?" Celia had asked. "You couldn't have mentioned this *before* we had sex? You didn't notice the need for space then?"

"I like you, Celia. A whole lot. You know that," Todd had continued. "I just don't want to get too tied down, you understand? I mean, we're in college, right, so we don't want to get too serious."

"Jerk," Celia snarled as she jumped out of the car, determined he would not see her tears. She trudged all the way back to her room even though it was miles away and of course it was starting to rain, swearing off men altogether, wondering how she could possibly avoid Todd for the next years until they graduated.

Well, no more men until she stumbled into another relationship, this time with a pre-med student whose name she could barely remember but who always smelled of the antiseptic soap he scrubbed with furiously before and after lab classes, and, somewhat disturbingly, before and after meals. This new boyfriend had heard of easy part-time work for Ax-Celacron, the international pharmaceutical giant based nearby. Celia was making her way through college on student loans and occasional small checks from home, and she was always looking to earn extra cash. All she had to do was stand on the quad at lunch and hand out samples – a debut tooth-paste or some version of deodorant that was new and improved. It was not a taxing job if she ignored the often annoying or just downright mean comments and jeers her fellow students would throw her way. Not that most of them didn't also take the freebie, Celia was quick to note, an important early lesson in marketing: people love getting something for nothing.

When summer rolled around, the company offered her a real job at headquarters, a sprawling hushed campus of bland low-slung beige buildings filled with official-looking people, many in starched, stiff white uniforms, as if they were doctors or nurses. Some indeed were; others were not. Those were scientists of some kind or another, developing this new drug or that, in very secretive ways. Various labs and offices were either locked up tight or plastered with signs about showing I.D. or being under video surveillance AT ALL TIMES. There was another whole section of the campus that was completely off-limits where she suspected and later confirmed that they tested on animals, something that nagged at her as just not right.

Often, it was kind of creepy walking those hushed halls with just the sound of the squeak of her shoes against linoleum, which was polished daily to an almost blinding shine. Still, the pay was good, and the job easy, mostly keeping track of orders and some light filing. *"Making Lives Better!"* was the company slogan, and many of the employees seemed to repeat it like a mantra, including, in earlier years at least, Celia. Little did she know when she took that summer job she'd still be working for the company some twenty years later as one of its leading sales reps with the best drugs and prized territories up and down the northeast corridor, but sometimes it felt like the corporation had wrapped its arms around her, like tentacles, and that escape was impossible.

She met Barry through the job. This was early one morning, his building the first stop along her route, so she was freshly turned out in her day-to-day uniform: a navy blue pencil skirt she always prayed didn't make her look hippy, crisp white blouse and navy blazer, her hair neatly blow dried, pulled back and fastened with a conservative clip, her make-up and jewelry minimal, and sensible low-heeled nude pumps. Toting her wheeled sample case behind her after locking up the company sedan, Celia sometimes did feel like a flight attendant (and sometimes she fantasized that's exactly what she was. She was not Celia, headed to yet another suite of medical offices in the suburbs. She was Lisa, jetting off to some exotic destination, like Fiji to laze on a beach or Rome to gaze at antiquities).

That morning, she had a full schedule. She was running to catch the elevator when a hand appeared and prevented the doors from closing in her face or pinching her own fingers if she tried to stop them.

"Thanks," she managed, a little winded, when she first laid eyes on the man who had come to her rescue.

"Oh, I know how slow these things can be," said Barry.

"Tell me about it," Celia answered with a smile. She'd spent hours in medical buildings just like this, so there were numerous occasions when she was stuck as some doddering old geezer held up the elevator while trying to figure out where he was going or some old lady rummaged through her purse looking for that little slip of paper with the doctor's name written on it.

Barry smiled back, and then there was that awkward silence elevators seemed to breed.

Celia snuck a closer look as they headed up. He wasn't exactly handsome in the classic sense. But he was tall, with intriguing dark brown eyes, a slender nose, an easy smile, and sweet full lips. It was later that she'd sometimes notice the annoying slope of his shoulders or how his unruly hair was prematurely thinning at the crown. That morning, he wore chinos and a pressed polo shirt. Plus, he smelled good—squeaky clean. She pegged him as a patient, and they made a little more trivial small talk until Celia reached her floor.

It was only later, when she ran into him a second time, that she learned he was an Ear, Nose, and Throat, one of the best on Long Island apparently. Her sample case that day was chock full of AxCelacron's latest sinus drug, a breakthrough in inhaled decongestants, the company promised (although it was later recalled and the subject of numerous lawsuits after several unfortunate side effects cropped up that MAY POSSIBLY have led to one fatality. Or POSSIBLY two but that second one had yet to be proven). She was determined to write up some big orders because, as always, there were incentives, this time a trip to the Club Med in Cancun she was determined to win because she'd heard stories about how wild it could be. Barry, now in his white lab coat, was escorting a patient, a confused-looking lady in a velour track suit, from an examining room back to reception—*a nice touch*, Celia thought, because not enough doctors seemed to do it.

He was listening intently to the woman in a gentle, reassuring way, his hand on her back. Celia caught his eye and they traded smiles for the second time that morning.

A few minutes later, a nurse escorted her to Barry's office to wait. Celia always loved doctor's offices, even when she was a child. This was unlike Bernadette and Rosalie, and even Kim-Cuc when she was living with the family, all of whom were always terrified of them. They'd be screaming and hysterical the moment Daisy put them in the car, as if they knew exactly where they were going even if Daisy hadn't told them. No, Celia always felt safe in a doctor's office. Oh, she knew there was a bit of a hero or God complex at play. You felt sick, and the doctor made you feel better. Or at least she or he tried. Celia always found that comforting. At times, it even could be sexy, like the night she was on a blind date with a doctor before she met Barry when a diner at the next table went into full-on cardiac arrest in the middle of his soup course. This man was a surgeon, with the cleanest hands and most manicured nails she'd ever seen. He waved off the screams of the wife and other diners and calmly leapt into action. He saved the guy's life. It was like watching a good medical drama on TV, but here the drama was real, an adrenaline rush that carried over into sex later that night, which was more intense than Celia was accustomed to, another sort of rush to be sure.

In Barry's office that morning, she examined the diplomas on the wall and the medical books lined up on a shelf. There was paperwork and a laptop on the desk. It was all neat and tidy, the way Celia liked things, too: everything in its proper place. Also, there were lots of framed photographs.

These might have set off alarm bells had she been paying attention because they were mostly of Barry and his mother, Gloria, through the years: from Barry as the late-in-life baby he was, through his early toddler-hood as a doted-on only child, through awkward teen years with a floppy mop of hair, through high school, college, and on to adulthood. Gloria, with her complicated updo and her big jewelry, was in almost every picture. He asked Celia out to lunch that very day, within minutes, in fact, of Celia pulling out her research materials and her charts, and launching into her spiel about the inhalers, about how AxCelacron studies had shown that patients who suffered from acute sinusitis experienced easier breathing and fewer complaints of nasal pain or congestion than those in the focus group, or others on a placebo that had no steroids. When she began to list potential side effects, she could tell he wasn't really listening because he had a goofy grin on his face. This made it difficult to concentrate and, in turn, made Celia want to smile, too, as if they were in on some conspiracy.

He placed a big order and said, "What do you like to eat?" At first, she thought he might have been joking. She wasn't at her thinnest (hadn't her mother or one of her sisters commented on a recent gain the previous Sunday?) and maybe he noticed her smile suddenly vanish because he quickly added, "For lunch. I'm asking you to have lunch with me."

Which she did. And then dinner that Saturday night, at a fancy, romantic restaurant with linen tablecloths and candlelight. This was the date Celia counted as their anniversary because it felt like the time they really clicked as a couple, when they bonded and lingered over the meal, a shared dessert and an after-dinner drink. They found they had much in common: a love of old black and white film noir and screwball romantic comedies with wacky heiresses and dashing suitors. They loved beaches. And long walks on wooded country roads, provided they weren't *too* long—Barry turned out to be allergic to pollen. And pet hair of all kinds. And peanuts. And dust. Anyway, because she worked with and around doctors, there was common ground. Once when she was taking some much-needed vacation time and one of Barry's receptionists called in sick, Celia even filled in as a sub. She greeted patients and loved listening to their stories, even the problems.

They both loved sleeping in on Sundays. They figured this out after a second dinner date the following Saturday, which was the first time they slept together. Barry had brought her to his home, which, she would later learn, was the house where he grew up, a tidy one-story mid-century ranch, which had been recently vacated by Gloria, who had downsized from Mineola to a condominium in Florida. At first, Celia thought Barry living there was odd. "You never wanted to sell it and get your own place?" she asked. They had just arrived at the house and were standing just inside the front door, with all his mother's furniture and knick-knacks still in place, and the house still vaguely smelled of Gloria's favorite perfume, a heady floral scent from Charles of the Ritz that made Celia dizzy, a smell she could never fully eradicate from the house, no matter how hard she tried.

"Why go to all the trouble?"

"Well, to be honest, I couldn't get out of my parents' place soon enough. Not that I didn't adore them, of course, I just wanted a space to call my own."

"But I know everything about this house, everything that's been fixed or needs fixing. Every little quirk and exactly who to call to deal with it, which is a big deal. Plus, it's paid for. There's no mortgage to worry over. The taxes are pretty low. And it's a ten- minute commute to my office."

"Yes, but it's not yours. And it's filled with your all your mom's stuff."

"So I'll get somebody in to redecorate. Better yet, we'll get somebody in, and it could be ours."

Celia stared at him for a moment. In the few months they'd been together, they had fallen into the rhythm of a couple, but that next step? "Are you asking me to marry you?" she asked.

Barry froze. "Uh...Do you want to get married?"

She was silent a moment, the thought hitting Celia that this was quite different from 'Do you want to marry me?'.

She wasn't certain of the answer, either.

What she did know was that it suddenly seemed as if everyone she knew from high school and college was pairing off, getting engaged and married all at once, as if somebody had hit some invisible switch. Plus, it was around the time Bernadette married Kent (huge reception at the Plaza) and Rosalie and Kim-Cuc reconnected. Celia, feeling a little left out, was a bridesmaid more times than she wanted to count (with the frequently unflattering dresses she spent all that money on and would never wear again). Even her mother, for goodness sakes, had at the time what she called "a new man friend" (a little too soon after her father passed away, if you asked Celia, even if Daisy had been his caregiver for quite some time, and Celia knew how difficult that was).

So, yes, marriage seemed like the thing to do, but something held her back, and they decided she'd move in and they'd take their time because both of them wanted to plan a perfect wedding anyway. Celia insisted they pick a different bedroom than the one his mother had occupied as that would be just strange, as if when they made love, Gloria would be watching. They would take their time to fine-tune the details. And Barry was something of a perfectionist, Celia was to learn, and not just about the wedding, but about a lot of things. Like which flat screen TV to buy, or what sofa went with which end table. Or what set of tires tested best. Or which brand of laundry detergent was the greatest bargain. Celia could relate to this because she was this way too careful and methodical about important decisions, which really was something she had to train herself to be because her mother and sisters could be more flighty and slapdash about these things, her mother buying things based on how pretty they were, Bernadette picking the most expensive, and Rosalie always on the lookout for something second-hand or recycled, or handmade by indegenous women in Peru.

And somehow, while she wasn't paying close enough attention, a whole bunch of years passed, and here they were, still living together, unmarried, in Barry's mother's house. When she moved in, Celia had given up the small studio she had in the city – she barely used it anyway; it was basically a big closet. She stored shoes in the oven. They made changes to the house. Out went Gloria's shag carpets and stiff, formal furniture. They turned the living room into a study of creamy beiges, which Celia decided would be soothing after long days of office hours for Barry or when she returned from one of her sales trips, which were becoming more and more frequent.

Travel was one of the perks of the job in the early days, each excursion like an adventure. Celia loved it all, from the careful selection and packing of her outfits to the ride in a hired car to the airport with its smell of jet fuel offering the promise of someplace foreign, to the settling in on the plane, to the arrival in some new city she'd never been to and a hotel room with fresh sheets and towels, sparkling bathrooms, and thick just-vacuumed carpets, each new place seeming to call out for some daring exploration or discovery. Her imagination ran wild, concocting all sorts of mad affairs or even just hook-ups she'd have in these rooms with all the hot men she'd meet in the lounges downstairs. Lisa would have affairs like that, for sure. Of course, none of that really happened. Okay, well, she had one little fling in the early days of Barry when they weren't yet dating exclusively, but certainly nothing in the last few years, which might have been because she wasn't propositioned so much anymore in hotel lounges. Or if she was, it was only by the kind of men that made her want to run screaming back to her room, which Celia chalked up to the fact that she was no longer twenty-something but so close to forty she could taste it.

The travel ultimately became something of a routine, then a grind. There was practically no city Celia hadn't visited, and lately she was finding it harder to ignore ethical qualms about the safety of the drugs she was pushing, even though she mostly tried to keep these thoughts at the back of her brain, which sometimes worked and sometimes didn't.

Like now, she was using the planning of the wedding to occupy her mind when she pulled up at the house and grabbed the mail. She'd sit Barry down that very night, and finally they'd solidify some plans, maybe even look through some of those brochures stacked on the coffee table. At least settle on a venue. That would get everybody off her back, wouldn't it?

So she was preoccupied and barely noticed the frayed and tattered package mixed in with all the bills and catalogues.

Then she did take a closer look. It was a big yellow manila envelope, but the paper was worn, soft, and faded. It had heft, with something bulky inside. The name she didn't recognize, though the address was hers and Barry's. Then, upon closer inspection, Celia noticed the postmark was nearly forty years old, the origin now unreadable. She searched for a return address, but there wasn't one.

"Who in the world," Celia wondered out loud, "is Fionnula Gibbs?"

II.

"Do you suppose we should open it?" Celia asked.

The envelope sat on the table in the kitchen between them as they dug into the frozen dinners Celia had microwaved: turkey meatloaf for Barry and, for herself, glazed chicken with stir-fried vegetables.

"Um, well, I think that might be illegal or something," Barry said.

"You think postal inspectors will knock down the door and arrest us?"

"No, probably not."

"Besides, you're an Ear, Nose, and Throat."

Barry shot her a quizzical look.

"I mean," Celia continued, "it's not like you're an attorney and would get disbarred for breaking a law."

"Still," Barry said, "it isn't really any of our business."

He was right about that, of course. Through the rest of dinner, she silently tried to figure out why she was so curious about this strange and mysterious arrival. She couldn't pinpoint a reason. Barry's mother had bought the house shortly after the original postmark, so after dinner, Celia risked a call to Gloria to see if the name rang a bell. It didn't. She shouldn't have taken the risk—Gloria Kepler, in her deep gravelly rasp, the result of too many years of too many Virginia Slims, launched into a lengthy description of her latest pains, aches, and doctors' appointments, peppered, as always, with requests for free drug samples. The conversation veered into early bird dinner coupons and squabbles with other widows during daily card games. It was nearly an hour before Celia could get off the phone.

"I mean," she said to Barry later in the bedroom as she slipped into a nightgown, "what if she's still alive? Wouldn't that be a kick? To get some long-lost package from a friend?"

Barry nodded and went back to the game he was watching.

He wasn't really listening. She could tell from his faraway look and the sort of glassy vague smile he threw her way, that he had already lost interest.

She closed the bathroom door and continued her pre-bed ritual. She removed all traces of the mascara and eyeliner she had carefully applied that morning. She rinsed her face with warm water and patted it dry, the way her mother had taught her and her sisters: never rub – pat. Gently. She slathered on her night-time moisturizer, then scrutinized her face for any new creases or lines. She brushed her teeth. She flossed and rinsed her mouth with Scope. She flipped through a catalogue while peeing one last time, dog-earing a page when she spotted something she might like to order but would probably forget about until the next round of catalogues came, and there it would be again, like a rebuke, or it would be gone, and she'd feel a vague sense of annoyance, or even something like regret.

She climbed into bed, gave Barry a quick kiss, and let the sounds of the game lull her to sleep.

In the morning, the envelope was still on the dining room table, surprising her, as if she'd half-expected it to get up and leave. She considered tossing it. In fact, she walked to the trash bin under the kitchen sink and dropped it in, prompting Barry to say, "Probably for the best." Celia smiled and nodded in agreement. But then came a bizarre pang of guilt, as if she had abandoned a child. So, after Barry had gone upstairs to shower, she fished it out and parked the envelope in her briefcase.

A few hours later, she tore it open.

She tried to do the right thing first. Earlier in the morning, she had stopped at the post office in town, where she patiently waited her turn in an endless line of elderly people buying one stamp with painstakingly exact change. When it was finally her turn, the lady behind the counter gave Celia a blank look and said, "Well, it was delivered to the correct address, no?"

"Yes," Celia said. "The address on the envelope is ours. But this was mailed nearly forty years ago!"

The lady shrugged. When pressed, she muttered something about an investigation, but first Celia would have to fill out what appeared to be a giant ream of forms, and then the clerk pretty much admitted the envelope would wind up in the trash. Celia's curiosity about Fionnula Gibbs was only growing, and she felt oddly protective of whatever it was that had been sent, so she left the post office, the envelope tucked securely into her bag.

The envelope accompanied her in the car as she set out on the field calls she had scheduled for the day, first in Nassau and Rockland Counties, then into Manhattan, and then a lunch for a group of plastic surgeons and their staff. This association on the Upper East Side was a big deal – their orders for all the fillers and collagens and other injectables could fund an entire small nation—and required catering. Celia had arranged for platters from an upscale deli, along with loads of rich desserts nobody but the assistants, nurses, and assorted delivery people would touch.

After that exhausting day, she drove back out to her office and was finishing paperwork at her desk, the envelope forgotten until she noticed a corner of yellow poking out of her bag. Again, her interest in Mrs...Miss...Ms? Gibbs piqued. What did she look like? How old would she be now? Was she even alive? Was she married? A mother?

Celia turned to her computer. A Google search revealed in an instant over a hundred thousand references to Fionnula or Gibbs, but nothing about a person with that name who may have lived in their house at the time. She tried various social media sites and found nothing. She could have paid for a search that promised to unearth more, but that kind of prying somehow felt creepy. What if there was a clue inside the envelope that would help track her down? Wouldn't that make opening it okay, Celia reasoned?

The seal broke with little effort.

First came a dense puff of dust that made her sneeze.

When the air cleared, she peeked inside.

There was a book, a thick old volume, heavy in her hands when she slid it out. It carried a distinct musty aura that seemed to travel from a different era, or like an alien from some faraway planet. The cover was deep blue with an elaborate gold crest embossed in the middle. Celia looked at the spine. This was a cookbook: *Miss Ada's Definitive Receipts of Southern Cookery.* Published in 1895, a first edition. Celia wondered if it might be worth something as she flipped open the front cover.

Here was artwork, a fanciful sketch in blue and white, of a group of diners. Country folk, by the looks of the gingham dresses on the women and overalls on the men, passing platters of what looked like fried chicken. Scribbled in pencil, here and there, were dates and handwritten menus of unfamiliar dishes:

March 17, 1961

Frogmore Stew

Glazed Yams

Onions and parsley butter

Sweet Tea

Lady Baltimore Cake

(ask Mrs. D. which plates)

Who was Mrs. D., Celia wondered. At the bottom was written the name and address of a specialty foods shop, with an address on 27th Street in New York. Long gone too, Google revealed.

Celia flipped to the next page. At the top right corner, Fionnula had written her name, in neat script, in black ink. Now, why a book on Southern cooking? And why was she sending back her own book? The answer came a few pages later when she turned a page and found a sealed envelope. *Mom, Thanks for sending*, was scribbled across the front, and then, in parentheses, *Please read the enclosed when you're in a better mood. Love, Mary Rose.*

"Wow," Celia said aloud. "Better mood? What's that about?"

"What?"

Melanie, Celia's assistant, had just poked her head into the office.

Celia, feeling startled, slammed the book closed, feeling a stab of guilt as if she had been poking around a stranger's closet.

"Did you call for me?" Melanie asked. "I heard you say something."

"Oh, no. I'm good," Celia said.

Melanie lingered at the door, twirling a strand of her long blond hair. It was one of her habits that annoyed Celia, along with snapping gum and talking too loud on too many personal calls and generally being so much younger. The girl was barely twenty-two. The nerve. "Was there something else?"

"Don't you have a meeting...?"

"Holy crap!"

She should have been in the corporate auditorium ten minutes earlier for the new product roll-out. Danielle Chan, who headed global sales for AxCelacron, hated tardiness and would surely notice she wasn't there. Celia rushed to get her things together.

"You're a good internet sleuth, right?" she asked Melanie as she headed for the door.

"Oh, yeah. I uncovered a ton of dirt on my last jerk of a boyfriend. I could have had him put behind bars for years. Of course, it helps that my cousin is a cop."

Celia jotted the name from the package on a post-it and handed it to Melanie. "See if you can dig up anything on this lady."

"Okie-doke."

Celia raced down the hall. She could hear the fanfare – thumping bass she could feel in her chest and blaring classic rock and roll—coming from the auditorium even before she got there. She had been through these new product roll-outs before, of course, but this one was even more important: the long-anticipated debut of a new and improved line of female hormone replacements that would be worth billions.

She pulled open the doors just as lasers and klieg lights on the stage began a dazzling display, sure to make her eyeballs ache. She hurried down the aisle as the music reached a crescendo, finding a seat between her friend Sonya and her non-friend Bert Pitoniak. Both Sonya and Bert were longtimers at the company like Celia. Early on, a camaraderie had formed between Celia and Sonya, who was born in Ukraine, grew up in a tough section of Brooklyn, and had bigger balls than a lot of men Celia knew. But the slick, unctuous, and oily Bert only grated on her nerves. He was always creating some kind of bogus competition. As Celia settled in, Bert was already attempting to send her another lame message: "I am so going to slay you on this one."

Celia gave him a tight smile. Danielle Chan took to the stage to introduce the surprise guest, the new spokesperson for this new product, HeXaphyzone III. A chorus of oohs and aahs reverberated through the auditorium as the celebrity's face loomed on the large screen behind Danielle. Even Celia was impressed. The spokesperson was instantly recognizable: a movie star, a real one, famous practically since childhood. And now, of course, she was rather unnaturally youthful looking, with the hair, skin and body of a woman much younger. *How is it possible*, was the thought that first passed through Celia's brain. *How could this old lady look younger than me?* And be in better shape because there didn't seem to be an extra ounce on her as far as Celia could tell; she seemed to be made of nothing but muscle, sinew, and, well, a good amount of certain kinds of filler.

The CEO of the company made the introductions and guided the star to a seat while Danielle took to the podium.

"Picture your mother before the HX III patch," she began, as the PowerPoint image changed from the company logo and the *"Making Lives Better!"* slogan to a photograph of a decrepit old woman with a walker. "She looks old. Her skin is dry as paper. Her hair is brittle. She can't sleep. Then there are the mood swings: one minute she's happy, the next she's in tears. She never has sex. Doesn't have the desire. Or the energy. And now imagine her after only three weeks of treatment."

Click. The image morphed into a lithe, youthful version of the same woman, who seemed to have shed about forty years. Also, she was in a romantic clinch with a sexy well-muscled gray-haired man on a beach at sunset. "Quite the difference, huh?" Danielle said.

Click. The next image was a sales rep like Celia, but it was a professional model in AxCelacron blue shaking hands with a white-coated doctor, also surely an actor. *I look nothing like that,* was all Celia could think. "You reps have a mission..." Danielle said, urgency in her voice as...

Click. A close-up of the new product in its attractive package.

"HX III," Danielle continued, "has the potential to revolutionize the female synthetic hormone replacement game while contributing significantly to this company's bottom line. And all of you can help make this debut one of the corporation's best ever!"

Here, the CEO jumped to his feet. The auditorium erupted in thunderous applause. In fact, all of them were primed to be excited, had already been through what Danielle called HX University, seminars and classes where they were schooled in all the changes that take place in a woman's body during menopause (of course, Celia had witnessed most of these first hand in her mother, who had all of the above symptoms, along with severe hot flashes and occasional urinary incontinence).

They were then given a quick appraisal of possible side effects, which included bloating, blood clots, various forms of cancer, and, well, death. Celia tried to block that part out of her mind, as usual, along with thoughts of where the drugs actually came from (some from plant life, others from animals that were never clearly identified) and how exactly they were tested.

Later, they all moved from the auditorium to an outdoor atrium for the cocktail party where all the sales reps who had flown in from regional offices were regaled with copious amounts of free alcohol and food. It was here that Celia got a closer look at the new celebrity spokesperson. Up close, the icon looked more like the wax version you'd see at a museum. This was reassuring – maybe Celia didn't look so bad after all – and somewhat scary, as the woman was just too eerily well-preserved, and so frightfully skinny it looked like she might shatter altogether if you bumped her too hard and she toppled over, a face-plant not out of the question as she was wearing spiked heels that would intimidate women far younger, and that cocktail glass she was clutching a little too tightly reeked of pure gin.

By the time Celia got back to her office after the festivities, it was dark and quiet. Melanie had left for the day. Celia gathered what she'd need as she was hitting the road in the morning to begin the HX III push.

She was about to shut off the lights when she noticed the yellow post-it attached to the screen of her laptop. Melanie had found an address for Fionnula Gibbs.

III.

"I'll show you my sales projections if you show me yours."

Celia rolled her eyes.

"Bet mine are bigger."

"Seriously, Bert? Really? At this hour?"

Somehow, Bert Pitoniak had wound up as her seatmate on the next morning's early flight to Atlanta. Yes, Celia had prized territories up and down the east coast, but Bert had early on taken control of every lucrative doctor's office and medical group south of the Florida border. After getting bumped off his direct flight to Miami, he snagged a spot on her plane. She had just settled into her business class seat, had everything – her iPad, her make-up kit, her energy drink, and her healthy, low-calorie snacks just so – when Bert came loping up the aisle, his black sample case wheeling behind, a dopey grin on his face. Now, they were barely airborne, and he was already getting on her nerves. "Bert, why does everything out of your mouth have to be sexual innuendo?"

"Who said anything sexual?"

"I don't know. Maybe it's the way you say it. You understand that these days, that sort of behavior will get you in a whole world of trouble."

Now Bert gave her one of his annoying winks.

"And why are you always winking at me?"

"It happens to be a tic, Celia. I can't control it."

Celia opened her mouth, but nothing came out.

"Maybe," Bert said, "if you had once bothered to ask me about it over all these years, you'd know that already."

"Oh, my God, Bert. I didn't, uh..."

"Gotcha! Ha! Man, are you gullible, Celia. Sometimes I do wonder how you get such high sales figures when sometimes you seem like such a pushover."

"You're a jerk, Bert."

"No, you know what I think your problem is?"

She didn't think Bert could possibly have any insight about her problems, but she decided to humor him.. "Okay," she said. "What is my problem?"

"Your problem, Celia, is that you're not a good enough actor."

"What is that supposed to mean?"

"You don't truly love this business. You don't believe you're really helping people. But you need that belief—you must have it deep in your core—in order to be truly successful. Oh, sure, you follow the script, but is your heart really in it?"

Celia said, "I have consistently been a top producer for this company. I have devoted years to being a success at this job."

"But something's missing, isn't it?"

There was no way she was going to admit it. But lately, that's exactly how she felt, like she was going through the motions. Instead, she said, "You know what, Bert? Maybe if you stop worrying about what's going on in my head, you'd produce figures as good as mine."

"Okay. Fine. Just trying to be a help. I'm just...hey, what's this...?"

Poking out of her briefcase was the cookbook. Celia made a move to stop him, but the plane hit a big air pocket, dipped suddenly, and she fell back into her seat in a messy and somewhat embarrassing way. Before she knew it, Bert had the book in his hands and was inspecting it. "I didn't know you cooked."

"I don't really. I can do scrambled eggs. And, well, Barry likes my turkey burgers as long as I don't put in too much seasoning."

Bert started to flip through the pages, nearly tearing one. She grabbed the book back and safely tucked it away again.

"Jeez, Celia, what's the big deal? It's just some old book."

"It's not mine, okay?"

"Well, whose is it?"

Celia decided not to answer. She smiled, jammed in her ear buds, and tuned Bert out for the rest of the flight. Part of her was enjoying keeping this little mission to return the book a secret. But another part of her knew if she told Bert the truth, it might sound a little crazy, as if she were coming unglued, and he could use that as an excuse to take over her territory.

When they landed in Atlanta, they went their separate ways with Bert again challenging Celia on how he would produce the best results in the shortest amount of time, and Celia giving him a brisk 'Yeah, whatever,' while silently swearing to herself there was no way she'd let him win. Because while what he said may have struck a chord, one thing Bert seemed to miss in her was a deep sense of competition. She didn't like to lose.

A SHORT WHILE LATER, she was sitting in her rented car – another in what seemed like an endless string of white four-door sedans with beige interiors reeking of air freshener – but it wasn't her normal route of sales calls she began to plot. Instead, she programmed the address Melanie had found into the GPS. It was near a town called Blairsville, north of Atlanta and close to the Tennessee border, about an hour's drive out of her way. Celia figured she'd drop off the book, spend a few quiet minutes chatting with what was sure to be a delighted and enchanted Fionnula—who would surely serve her sweet tea and cookies—and then head off to plug hormones.

Her mother called just as the Atlanta metropolitan area vanished in her rearview mirror. "Please understand, dear," Daisy Bernhart said in a fluttery, tremulous voice that sounded like it might lapse into hysterics at any moment, "that it wasn't my fault."

"What wasn't your fault, mother?"

"The hospital people want to talk to a family member, and I couldn't reach Bernadette or Rosalie."

"You're in the hospital?"

"Well, I'm *at* the hospital. I'm in the waiting room."

"Okay. Then who's in it?"

"Lois. But like I said, it's not my fault."

Lois Hudson lived across the street in a two-story Dutch Colonial; her house and the Bernharts' were practically mirror images, inside and out. The families – there were three Hudson boys about the same age as Celia and her sisters—had been close for nearly fifty years now, Daisy and Lois bonding through all the car pools and afternoon sports practices for their children, through all the cocktail parties, through the mid-life crises of their husbands and near-divorces, through the holiday open houses and political fundraisers. They were practically inseparable now that both were widows.

Celia, sensing this might be complicated, pulled over to the side of the road. "Mother, what happened to Lois?"

"Well, we had planned on having lunch in town at the diner because we have those coupons, you know two-for-one on Monday, which means meatloaf is the special, and you know how I feel about their meatloaf. Anyway, first I had to stop at the market because this week for sure I was going to do Oriental casserole for Sunday Supper, and while, yes, I have the water chestnuts, I needed the fried noodles they carry at Gristedes and..."

"Mother, Gristedes closed twenty years ago."

"Oh, for heaven's sake, Celia. You know what I mean. The supermarket. I don't particularly care for that newfangled place that took over – never have if you must know—with all those fancy foods and the organic this and the non-GMO that and gluten-free whatever they charge you an arm and a leg for just because, and those snooty clerks and..."

Celia's phone beeped. Bernadette. She told her mother to hold and switched over. "I'm in a meeting," Bernadette practically barked. "Why is a hospital calling about Mom?"

"I'm on with her now. I don't have the full story yet, but..."

"Hold on," Bernadette ordered, as if she was issuing a demand to one of her underlings. "I'm conferencing in Rosalie."

Celia put her phone on speaker and rubbed her temples.

Rosalie, most likely in her office in the County Services building, sounded rushed and harried. "What did Mom do now?"

"Let's find out," Bernadette said, "Conference her back in, Celia."

Celia transferred back over to her mother, who was still mid-conversation. Daisy continued to prattle away: "...which were three for a dollar last week without any coupon at all, and so Lois and I made the date right then and there to have lunch – she likes that pot pie they do so well except only the chicken, she finds the beef too gristly—and do some shopping, and maybe if we were feeling up to it even take in a movie because down at the quad the picture that won all those..."

"Mother, this is Bernadette. Please try to focus now, and tell us what is happening!"

"Oh, Celia," Daisy said, "stop trying to impersonate your sister because you think she'll intimidate me. I know it's you I called. I'm not some old ninny."

Celia rubbed harder at her temples and glanced at her watch. *How long is this going to take*, she wondered. "It's all of us, Mom. Bernadette. Me. Rosalie. Now, please just tell us what happened to Lois."

"Well, I backed into her and broke her femur, if you must know."

There was a gasp of breath somewhere, probably in Rosalie's office. Then silence as the three sisters took in the news. Just recently, Celia and her sisters had been trying to figure out a way to get Daisy to give up the keys to her gigantic, ancient, wheezy Jeep Wagoneer, the car she drove when they were kids, now missing all its hubcaps, spewing out funny smells, and so rusty it had actual holes in the floor where you could see road rushing by underneath. But Daisy was having none of it. She insisted the car was perfectly fine, saying exactly that to Celia one time as she was also reattaching one of the sideview mirrors with duct tape.

"I'm just going to assume you backed into her car, right Mom?" Rosalie asked, trying to sound upbeat.

"Well...," Daisy began, and then her voice sort of trailed off.

Bernadette interrupted. "My God, Mother, you did not run over your best friend, did you?"

"Who said anything about running Lois over? I barely tapped her with the bumper. She was in my blind spot as I was backing out. And one of those horrible Shopper Moms in some giant SUV..."

"Soccer Moms," said Bernadette.

"One of those idiot SOCCER moms," Daisy continued, "was blocking the view on my side, so I was concentrating on trying to see past it, and I forgot Lois was out there waiting because the nitwit on the other side had parked so close she couldn't get the passenger door open more than an inch. So really, it was the fault of those two cars."

"Still, Mother," Celia said, "you injured your best friend."

"I was barely moving, Celia. If you want to blame somebody, how about Lois and her brittle bones? I've been telling her for years she needs to eat more calcium and cut back on the wine at night, but does she listen to me? Oh, no, she does not. If you'd peek into her garbage bins and count the wine bottles she goes through by the week, you'd get quite the surprise. And I'm not being nosy. I'm concerned."

They finally broke through Daisy's inane conversation and decided on a plan. Lois would need some help upon being discharged, and her sons were scattered across the country with spouses and children of their own. Rosalie, with her office closest to the hospital, would pick up both ladies and bring them to her house for the next few days. "Are you absolutely sure?" Celia asked. "Because with the babies and Kim-Cuc and all..."

"We'll be fine," Rosalie said, and Bernadette, pressed to get to her next meeting, rushed them all off the phone. Celia was more than a little relieved to be so far away as she piloted her rental back on the road.

HER RIDE SOON TURNED scenic, with lush, green mountains in the near-distance, then a picturesque blue lake, followed by what appeared to be acres and acres of farmland, then small houses widely spaced on large wooded plots, and finally, a shopping center with a nice home-spun look. The address she sought was a medium-sized, one-story structure on the outskirts of town with faded pale yellow clapboard and peeling blue paint around the windows. A ramp sloped gently up to a front door decorated with Halloween decorations – Jack O'Lanterns and peaky witch hats but also skulls and skeletons and ghosts—even though the holiday had long passed and should have at least been replaced by ones for the next—Thanksgiving or even Christmas. Celia immediately, and rightly, pegged it as an assisted living facility, a nursing home really, and it looked the way these places always did: determined to put up a cheery front, but ultimately forlorn.

She pushed open the door. Inside, it smelled of rubbing alcohol, talcum powder, and cafeteria gravy. Celia's heels seemed to click extra loud against the shiny linoleum as she crossed to the reception desk. A Muzak version of "Imagine" wafted softly through hidden speakers. She waited as a large-boned girl, barely out of her teens and wearing too much eye makeup, wrapped up a call. "I wouldn't go there," the girl said in a voice tinted by a slight Southern drawl. "You have no right to bring that up. No, you don't. No way. I gotta go. How can I help you, ma'am?" she said brightly as she set down her phone. Celia tried to cling to the sense of mystery she was chasing, ignoring the fact that she had just been referred to as ma'am.

"I'm looking for a Fionnula Gibbs?"

"Are you a member of the immediate family?"

"Well, um, no I'm not. But I have something that belongs to her. Something that had gone lost. I'd like to return it."

"Why don't you take a seat. Somebody will be out in a jiffy."

Celia turned and moved toward a sofa, side-stepping an elderly gentleman in a motorized wheelchair who asked her if Peggy was here yet, and when she said she wasn't sure, he whizzed off rather sprightly. She settled into the sofa. There on the coffee table were issues of magazines she'd already read. She gazed at pictures on the wall, pastoral landscapes mostly, and one featuring an oddly eerie clown. She pulled her phone from her purse and tried Barry but ended the call when she got voicemail.

A door opposite her opened, and Celia heard, "Oh, nuts." An ancient-looking lady with a cotton candy-like puff of pure white frizz framing a fine-boned face, in a robe that was falling open in a dangerous way, was trying to come through, but her walker was wedged in the frame.

Celia jumped up from the sofa. "Can I help you with that?" she asked as she gently slipped the robe back into place.

"Aren't you sweet, darlin'?"

"Are you Mrs. Gibbs?"

"Good Lord, no, I'm *Ms.* Norris. I missed the Mrs. Boat, as they used to say. Not that I have any regrets about that, mind you, from what I've heard about marriage. Are you new here, dear?"

"Well, no, I..."

"Because I've been waiting nearly an hour for that ice cold cup of Sarsaparilla."

"Um..."

"Oh, you kids these days don't know a thing. Just dumb as wood! Root beer!" she said as the walker freed, and she toddled across the reception area headed for what looked like a dining room where Celia caught a glimpse of several other residents, most of them staring blankly into space or fast asleep in wheelchairs.

Celia sat back down. Everybody seemed to be waiting for something in this place, she mused as the sound system began softly piping in a Muzak version of "Mrs. Robinson." Before she knew it, she was silently humming along to it, and, although she tried hard to block it out, something else kept repeating in her head: missed the Mrs. Boat? She'd never heard that one before. Now, because she couldn't seem to help it, she had a vision of herself in a place like this. How many years down the line would it be? Thirty? Forty if she was lucky and avoided all the things that could get you if you weren't paying close enough attention. In this brief flash, she seemed completely and utterly alone. Bereft, she might even say. So she had married Barry and he had died? She was a widow? Her mother and sisters were gone? No children to look after her...

"You asked after Mrs. Gibbs?"

"Oh!"

The voice jolted Celia out of an image that was growing more disturbing because it had suddenly dawned on her what all these people were waiting for. When she regained her bearings, a man was standing before her. He had a neat comb-over, wore Dockers, shiny loafers, and sported a crisply pressed, striped, button down shirt.

"Yes," Celia said. "Mrs. Gibbs. Fionnula Gibbs. I found something that belongs to her. I thought I might return it."

The man took a seat next to her. "I'm Greg Owens, director of client services. I'm sorry to have to report some sad news." He smoothed some stray hairs at the top of his head. He looked down at his shoes. "Gosh, this is always hard," he continued. "but Mrs. Gibbs passed. About two months ago."

Celia had never laid eyes on the woman, but for some reason, she nearly burst into tears. To cover it, she started blathering. "Well, it's just a book. A cookbook. A very old one. But there were some notes in it I thought she might find amusing. Plus a sealed envelope from what I understand is her daughter. What'll I do with it now?"

"Dante might want it."

This had come from the large girl with the make-up and drawl behind the reception desk. Celia and Greg swiveled their heads in her direction.

"Dante's her grandson," she added. "He used to come once a week. Like clockwork. He'd bring her flowers and this salt-water taffy he had to special order from some place all the way the heck near Atlantic City. Said Mrs. Gibbs just loved it. Well, I tried the taffy once. Dang near lost a filling trying to get it down, but I wanted to be polite, so I couldn't spit it out, now could I? Anyway, he was her only visitor as far as I could ever tell."

"Teena, do we know where Dante lives?"

"Up the road a piece. Hodges Creek. I think we have an address on file."

"Of course, we could forward the book for you if you'd like," Greg said.

Once again, Celia felt she was on a mission she had to complete on her own. "This Hodges Creek?" she asked. "Is it far?"

HODGES CREEK MAY HAVE been just up the road a piece, but neither Teena nor Greg mentioned that 'up' was meant in a literal sense, that the road first narrowed until it was practically one lane, and then it rose at a precipitous angle into a series of spine-tingling hairpin curves that cut into a southern section of the Blue Ridge Mountains, which Celia had always admired from a distance but had never really seen this close. After the first turn, with her brakes squealing, her transmission grinding, and visions in her head of careening into the rocky ravine below, Celia realized retreat might be a good idea. But the road was too narrow for a u-turn, and reversing in the rental car was an even more terrifying prospect.

Then, in the middle of another frightening curve, her phone chirped. Celia pulled to a full stop before unclenching her hands from the wheel and glancing at the screen. There was Barry, Face-timing her, in a somewhat eerie close-up. "Hi, sweetie," he said. "I'm about to go in and explore Mrs. Goldstein's right sinus cavity, but I saw you called."

"I did. I was going to see if you could check in on my mom. She's at Rosalie's because..." Celia started. Almost an instant later, Barry's face began to dissolve into a mess of morphing pixels with brief flashes of identifiable body parts. So, she thought with a chuckle, he was turning into an ear, nose, and throat for real. "Hello? Barry?" Something akin to static came squawking back, along with snippets of what he was saying. She caught 'What happened to..' and '...in a minute, Mrs. Goldst..' before the call dropped completely.

Suddenly, she had no bars. Then the GPS screen went blank. She figured it was the mountains. This made her stomach flutter with something like fear, but she nudged the little rental sedan forward. It bucked and shimmied up one more steep incline, in protest it seemed, and Celia understood. This road was unlike most along her sales routes, those being mostly six lane interstates or straight city boulevards with familiar outposts everywhere: fast food chains and gas stations and convenience stores. Here, dense green pines on either side formed a sort of canopy overhead, and she heard the sound of what she thought were crickets but might also be some other kind of dangerous insect or animal she didn't know about. She pushed the car through one final sharp curve, and then the road widened and straightened out again.

Opening before her was what she figured was Hodges Creek. Here was what appeared to be the Main Street, lined on both sides with small shops, a couple of which were boarded up and sad-looking. One that was open seemed to be a sort of general store and gas station with a couple of rusty pumps out front. She spotted a coffee shop and a bar that looked somewhat suspect, with a small group of men hanging around the front door, their heads together in a shady way, she thought. She reached the far end of the main drag where a bedraggled church stood sentry, its steeple leaning precariously to the left. She put down her window when she saw a woman dressed in some odd get-up pushing a baby carriage.

"Hi!" Celia called out. "Am I in Hodges Creek?"

"Well," the woman answered, "sorta."

Celia noticed the occupant of the baby carriage was not a baby at all, but an aging, overweight dachshund—it had a grizzled gray muzzle and dim watery eyes and was panting slightly. The woman didn't seem to register Celia's surprise and continued in a matter-of-fact tone, "I call it Farnham's Hollow. But some folks insist on calling it Hodges Creek because they did officially change the name many years ago as the result of some financial troubles that Mr. Farnham found himself in."

"Right," said Celia. "Okay. Well, do you know a Dante Zebulon?"

"Don't you crazy city folks have restaurants back home?"

This conversation was growing even more confusing. "Well, yes we do, but I'm not..."

"Keep going straight out of town. First fork you come to, stay right. When the road dead-ends, you'll find what you're looking for."

She turned and wheeled the dachshund in the baby carriage away.

Celia hit the gas. She passed a few crumbling antebellum mansions, some newer ranch-style houses, the spooky hollowed-out remains of what must have at one time been a factory of some sort, and a few rusty double-wide trailers before the road ahead narrowed again. After a few more turns, all of them blind and harrowing, she came upon a small wooden bridge that crossed over babbling water (this must be Hodges Creek, she thought), and there was the fork. She wondered what was to the left but took the right fork, as directed. Now she was going downhill fast, the rental picking up speed and gaining momentum, brakes squealing again as she rounded a curve, and she came into a clearing where the road ended in a little circle. Beyond it sat a tumbledown shack with a wide covered front porch. A battered old pick-up truck sat next to it, along with a couple of other sedans that looked like rentals, and one large motorcycle. Celia parked next to them and pushed open her door.

The first thing to hit her was the smell. Something was on fire. But in a good way. The sweet aroma of hickory mingled with something porky, and Celia was surprised to find her stomach gurgling and her mouth watering. It was way past lunch; she realized she hadn't eaten since a power bar on the plane, which had tasted like cardboard. She made her way to the shack, now noticing a couple of long wooden tables on the front porch where people were eating something off brown butcher paper. Celia spotted a rack of ribs on one plate, what looked like a sandwich of some kind on another, and was that cornbread? This looked like serious business. The eaters focused and intensely concentrated on their food. One man tore into a rib, his fingers greasy. A lady licked sauce out of a tiny cup. Another lady, with a severe haircut and rectangular trendy glasses, was painstakingly photographing a bowl of coleslaw from multiple angles. Without as much as a glance in Celia's direction while reversing her cam and snapping off a selfie, she said, "You're too late. He sold out an hour ago."

"Sold out of what?"

Now all eyes looked over at Celia as if she had committed some dire sin.

"Hello? The barbecue," said the man with the greasy fingers. "That's what everyone comes to Hodges Creek for these days. Which blog have you been reading, and which pod have you been listening to?"

"I'm just looking for Dante Zebulon."

The lady licking the last bits of sauce out of the cup managed to pause long enough in making notes on her phone to indicate Celia might find him inside.

The screen door let out a squeaky protest, and it shut behind her with a loud BANG! Inside the shack were more wooden tables and more people scarfing down food off brown butcher paper. At the far end was a long counter in front of a small kitchen area. There was also an old-time cash register with loud clacking keys, giant numbers, and a chimy clang to note each sale. Behind it stood a short, muscular young woman with pale freckled skin, narrow wary eyes, tattoos up and down both arms, piercings in strange areas of her face, and bright neon orange hair in a buzzed Mohawk. "Come back tomorrow," she said as Celia approached. "We're sold out!"

"So I gather," Celia answered. "But I didn't come for the food." This earned her a suspicious look from the girl. "I'm looking for a Mr. Zebulon."

"Try out back," she said, indicating with a thumb over her shoulder that it was through another door. Celia began to think of those little Russian nesting dolls she once loved, where you keep opening one, and one smaller one, and then one more until you finally get to the smallest and one tiny little doll.

She stepped outside again. To her left there was what looked like a barn. Beyond that was a fenced area. Inside were some pigs, lolling in the mud. *How adorable*, Celia thought until it hit her: people were eating barbecue in there. She forged ahead, ducking around an old tire that hung from a large tree. Next to it was a rather new-looking jungle-gym type deal, all yellow and red and orange plastic and complicated, with one of those slides that seemed so enormous to her when she was a kid and now appeared almost comically puny.

She turned to her right. Here was a small, squat building with weathered gray shingles. A prominent chimney belched out thick white fragrant smoke. Just as she stepped closer, the door swung open on squeaky hinges. First came more clouds of smoke. Then came a man.

She pegged him at late twenties or early thirties. He was tall, well over six feet, Celia figured, with a mess of black shaggy hair falling across his face, dark olive skin, shiny with a layer of sweat, and more than a few days' stubble, really the beginnings of a beard. He was solidly built, his ash-smudged gray sleeveless T-shirt revealing clearly defined biceps and triceps. His faded jeans were ripped at the knees, Celia noted, as he walked right on by and bent to swipe an ax off the ground. This he flung sideways. It landed with a *thunk* in the trunk of a tree. He started gathering up logs from a giant pile. *Well, this is all a little rude,* Celia thought. *I'm standing right here, and he's ignoring me.*

"Excuse me?" she finally said, "Are you Dante?"

Something like a grunt came back. He continued to pick up more wood than she figured one man could possibly carry. Certainly not Barry, with his sciatica always acting up and his bug phobia because of that one time he told her he moved a rock in the back yard, only to find he had uncovered a massive pile of worms. "Anyway," she continued, "you don't know me, but..."

"Listen. I don't talk to reporters or bloggers or whatever you want to call yourself. To me, that's all a bunch of noise." His voice was a little gruff with the hint of a drawl, too, she noticed. His arms now loaded with wood, he started back to the smoke house.

This annoyed Celia. "Just a minute there, mister!"

Well, she didn't mean to sound like a schoolmarm. The words just popped out of her mouth. But Dante stopped and turned to look at her. She realized she might resemble a schoolmarm in her regulation sales rep blue skirt and crisp blue jacket, her sensible heels, and her hair secured in a neat clip. She noticed now that his eyes were a deep blue-green that reminded her of the sea. Why did she suddenly wish she had changed before coming here? "I have something that belonged to your grandmother."

Celia could swear he flinched when he heard that, as if she had pinched him. "My grandma died two months ago," Dante said, turning to grab even more logs.

"But she was Fionnula Gibbs, right?"

He looked back at Celia, and she reached into her bag. "Long story short: a few days ago, we got this package at our house up in Rockville Centre. That's in New York? Well, it was postmarked nearly forty years ago and addressed to your grandmother." She held out the book.

Dante set down the logs. He regarded her for a moment, absently stroking his scruffy chin. Celia couldn't help wondering what he'd look like if he'd shave and get a haircut. Or maybe just a shower. He was standing closer now, and she could detect a smell coming off of him, something a little funky, but also that sweet, heady aroma of hickory smoke and pork fat, which brought to mind laying in bed under warm covers when she was a kid, her mother down in the kitchen frying bacon on Sunday mornings, and the intoxicating aroma that would permeate the house. He took the book and started to leaf through it.

"She was a housekeeper and cook. For a family up north," Dante said. "From what I gathered, they weren't very nice to her. But she stuck with the job because she needed the money, didn't have the choice. Her husband abandoned her. She was a single mother in a time when that wasn't very easy."

"To Mary Rose, right? That was her daughter?"

"Lady, who are you?" he finally asked.

"Celia. I'm Celia Bernhart. Senior VP of Sales with Ax-Celacron."

This earned her a blank stare.

"I'm sure you've seen the commercials...*Making Lives Better!*'"

"I don't watch much TV, ma'am," said Dante. "Mostly just some Netflix and Hulu and stuff on my iPad, but who has the time?"

Celia nodded, but she was stuck on the ma'am. Second time in one day. This was truly getting annoying. When did she turn into a ma'am? She didn't expect that until way after her thirty-ninth birthday, which was still days away. "Okay," Celia pressed on, "anyway, also there was a letter addressed to your grandmother tucked in the book. It's from Mary Rose.

Your mom. How cool is that?" She held out the sealed envelope.

For a second, Dante just stared at it. Something was troubling him, Celia could tell, but before she could ask what it was, he said, "I got things to do."

He turned and trudged toward the barn.

Celia was suddenly struck with the idea that she had made a mistake, coming and prying into a stranger's past like this. *I'll apologize, leave him the letter, and go,* she thought as she followed.

She stepped into the barn. First, she was confronted with what seemed like a hundred years' worth of junk, piled haphazardly. In a corner under an old dusty tarp, there appeared to be some sort of vehicle. She skirted it. She didn't spot Dante, but noticed a set of stairs leading up to a second floor. "Mr. Zebulon? Dante?" she called out from the bottom of the stairs. "I'm sorry. I didn't mean to upset you. I just want to leave you the letter, and I'll go."

"You can come up."

She climbed the stairs. At the top was a total surprise after the chaos of the first floor. A loft-like space opened before her, uncluttered and almost minimalist, with a few simple pieces of furniture and bare wood floors deeply scuffed with age. Dante was perched on a low-slung weathered brown leather sofa, a bottle of bourbon and a shot glass on the coffee table in front of him. He poured a shot and held it up toward Celia. "Oh. Um. I don't think so because I have to..." But he downed it before she could get the sentence out.

"Give me the letter," Dante said.

She handed it over. He inspected the words written on the outside. "'Read this when you're in a better mood?' What do you suppose that means?"

"You got me," Celia said.

"You want to read it to me?"

"No, I think you should."

"They didn't get along so good, my mother and grandmother. From what I can remember anyway. Always fighting about something."

"Well, I have two sisters. Daughters and their mothers. I could tell you stories."

This earned her a hint of a smile. "Then there was a car wreck," Dante said, "Killed her and injured my dad so bad they used to call him soft in the head. I was about five, so my grandmother took me in. I get emotional about it sometimes."

"Totally understandable," said Celia.

"That's her over there," he said, pointing to a framed picture on the wall. It was a black and white portrait of a stern-looking, scowling woman.

"She looks nice," Celia said.

Dante didn't respond to that. He tore open the envelope and pulled out the folded piece of paper inside. It was white fading to yellow, with an ornate flowery border, Celia could see. Like the book, it smelled as musty as a neglected attic. She fought the urge to sneeze.

"'Dear Mom,'" he began to read aloud, "'Thanks for loaning me the cookbook. Was very helpful. I used recipes for boiled dressing, sweet potato pie, ham biscuits, deviled crab and slow braised collards.'"

Celia's stomach gurgled loud enough to hear on the other side of the room. Dante looked over at her, again with the hint of a smile and the addition of a raised eyebrow. She blanched and wished she could disappear. "I haven't eaten all day, and it sure does smell good around here," she explained.

"I could fix you something."

"Probably the last thing you want to do. I mean, you own a restaurant, right?" Celia asked.

"Yep. Lunch only for now. We do barbecue. Ribs. Pulled pork, which you can have as a plate or on a bun. Might add brisket, but maybe not. That's really a Texas thing, and I don't want to ruffle no feathers or step on any toes because Texas Barbecue is very serious business. Couple of sides. I'm still figuring out dessert."

"So you're the chef, too?"

"That's too fancy a word for what I do. Pitmaster is the more accurate term. Although I still have a lot to learn about smoking meat if you want the truth. But this was once my granddaddy's place, back in the day. My mom wanted nothing to do with it. My grandmother let it go to shit. I'm trying to bring it back. The right way. The slow, old-fashioned way. So if you see a pickle on the plate, it means we made it in-house. What do you like to eat?"

"Finish the letter first."

He looked startled, as if he had forgotten all about it. He glanced down and started to read again. "'All recipes great. Bought my own copy. Love and xxxxx's, Mary Rose.'"

He stopped reading and looked up at Celia. "You'd think there'd be something bad if she wanted her to read it when she was in a better mood. I will say my grandma did have a temper, and some pretty strong opinions about certain things."

"There's more on the back," Celia pointed out.

Dante turned over the piece of paper and started reading again. "'As to that other matter we began to discuss until things got ugly and you called me a no-account dirty...'"

He suddenly stopped reading out loud. His expression seemed to darken as if a shadow had crossed his face. "Oh, man...what?"

Celia, caught up in the drama, couldn't help herself. "What? What is it?"

"That no-good son of a bitch!"

"What? Who's a no-good..." Before Celia knew it, the man was on his feet and scrambling down the stairs. "Hey! Where are you going? Wait!"

She followed him down but crashed into a huge pile of boxes, sending them all toppling to the floor. She got up, oriented herself, and headed for the door, arriving outside just in time to see Dante peel out in that old pickup truck. She watched it roar fast down the same road she had come up so gingerly, kicking up big whirligigs of dust in its wake.

"Well, that's that," she said to herself and started to head for her car.

Until she heard a voice: "Where's my dad going?"

She turned. There, at the top of the slide on that complicated jungle gym, was a little girl. Celia pegged her at about five or six, maybe a bit older. She had dark olive skin, curious twinkly eyes, and a tumble of jet-black curls. She wore blue jeans and a caramel-colored cardigan sweater with pinwheels knitted into the design. "Oh!" Celia said.

"Where did my dad go?" she repeated, slowly, now looking at Celia as if she was just hard of hearing or something.

"Um..."

Flummoxed, Celia went into her routine client introduction. "Hello!" she chirped brightly, extending her hand for a firm shake. "I'm Celia Bernhart, Senior VP of..."

She trailed off, realizing her position in the world of pharmaceuticals wasn't going to score points here. "What's your name?" she tried, gamely.

"Penelope. But I'm not supposed to tell strangers my name."

"You're absolutely right. That's bad. You shouldn't do that."

"What did you do to my Dad? He didn't even say good-bye."

"Dante's your father?"

"Uh-huh," said Penelope.

"Well, where's your mom?"

She shrugged and clammed up.

"But you live here? Is that right?"

Penelope gave her a small nod. Then, with barely a warning, she swooped down. Celia instinctively held her breath because from somewhere deep in the folds of her brain came the memory of toppling off a slide like this and skinning her knee, how much it stung when her mother applied iodine, and how her sisters had blithely gone on playing on a nearby teeter-totter, laughing at her dorkiness. But Penelope negotiated the slide with ease, leapt up adroitly at the bottom, and brushed off her hands. "I'm hungry," she said brightly. "Are you making my snack?"

"Oh. Well..."

Celia looked up at the barbecue shack. It seemed suddenly deserted, all the customers gone since they had run out of food. That girl with the Mohawk and all the tattoos and piercings came banging through the screen door, a helmet tucked under an arm. Celia now could see she wore camouflage-patterned pants tucked into black lace-up boots with thick soles. "What'd you do to Dante?" she asked Celia as she passed, clomping in a sort of bow-legged way toward the Harley parked near Celia's rental.

She was starting to feel a little defensive. "Nothing," she insisted, with emphasis. "I gave him a letter that belonged to his grandmother is all."

"Well, he sure seemed pissed off about something. Bye, Penelope."

"Bye, Roberta," Penelope replied.

"Wait," said Celia. "Is anybody else here?"

"Nope." She put the helmet on and buckled a strap under her chin.

"But we can't just leave this child..."

Roberta leapt aboard the Harley, and it growled to life with a roar. She gave Celia a thumbs up, revved the throaty engine, and took off down the road.

"What about my snack?"

Penelope looked up at Celia. She had very large eyes that did, indeed, seem hungry at that moment. Celia silently considered her options. She could leave and be done with this. What business was it of hers, anyway? But abandon a child? Really? Then, to Celia's consternation, Penelope grabbed her hand. It felt soft and warm, but also slightly clammy, though not in a bad way. "C'mon, we could have cookies," Penelope said as she led Celia back to the barn.

"Well," Celia said, fishing her phone from her purse because it was definitely looking like she'd be checking in to her hotel late, and her afternoon schedule of appointments was quickly getting shot to Hell, "I'm sure your daddy will be back very soon. So yes, indeed, I will fix you a snack. I can so do that." She snuck a peek at her phone. Still no bars. This was irritating. "I'm just wondering, does your daddy have a telephone?"

"Yeah."

"I mean, like, a land line?"

"What's that?"

"A telephone attached to a wall."

Penelope stopped to ponder that. She appeared to give the idea serious consideration. Meanwhile, as they stood there, Celia noticed that the points of her heels, though sensible in height, were beginning to sink into the soft brown earth. She extricated them with a 'thawcky' sound that made Penelope laugh. Then the little girl said, "I don't think his phone is attached to the wall, but I have a telephone."

"Oh, could I borrow it?"

"Sure!"

Penelope began to skip toward the barn. Celia couldn't remember the last time she'd seen a little girl skip, and the sight brought a goofy grin to her face. She considered skipping after her, but it wouldn't work in the heels. So she trotted after Penelope, noting with a little consternation how out of shape she felt, already winded after just a few feet. She made a mental note to get back to the gym when this trip was over, not just for the cardio, but she needed to fit into a wedding dress, didn't she? She followed Penelope, passing again through the dim chaos of the ground floor of the barn and up the stairs. She suddenly feared she'd run out of things to say—*how do you talk to a child?* She figured she'd make it up as she went.

"My phone's in here," Penelope said, disappearing down a short hallway and into what must have been her room.

Celia headed that way, pausing at the open door across from Penelope's. Dante's room? There were items of clothing scattered about: jeans here, boxers and sweatpants crumbled in a corner, a T-shirt draped over a lamp shade. There was a low platform bed with fluffy pillows and mussed-up sheets. Peeking out from under one pillow were the head and whiskers of a slumbering cat.

"Here, you can use this." Penelope had stepped up next to Celia again. She held a small old rotary style phone. It was plastic and a neon shade of orange.

"Um..."

"It's not attached to the wall now, but I could get some scotch tape, or we could paste it," she offered.

"You know what? Forget about the phone," Celia said.

"When's my daddy coming back?"

"I don't know, sweetie. But I guess you're stuck with me until he does."

"What's your name again?"

"Celia."

Penelope seemed to turn the name over in her head, really concentrating, or at least puzzling, over whether or not she should put her trust in Celia. Celia did her best to be reassuring. "You said something about cookies?"

"Yeah," Penelope said.

"Why don't we get you that snack, then."

"Yay," said Penelope, her face widening into an infectious grin.

Together, they walked back down the hall. The kitchen took up a corner of the loft-like space and was dominated by a hulking, ancient six-burner range. Open shelves held a variety of dishes and bowls, all in white. Cast iron skillets and banged up sauté pans dangled from a rack attached to the ceiling. Celia poked around in search of cookies, peeking into cabinets, cupboards, the refrigerator, and a blue and white jar on the counter. She came up empty. "Well, where would these cookies be?" she asked Penelope.

"Oh, we don't buy cookies," she answered. "We make them."

"You mean, like, from a mix?"

Penelope shook her head no.

"What? You mean from scratch?"

Penelope nodded and began pulling ingredients from various places: large containers of flour and sugar, butter from the refrigerator, and chocolate chips. She piled them on the counter as the cat, awake now, leapt up onto the counter, hunched its back, and shot Celia a suspicious glare. Penelope scratched the cat's ears as she handed Celia a bowl. "I'll need two eggs, please."

Celia started to open the refrigerator. "No," said Penelope, "From the coop."

"From the what?"

"The chicken coop. Where the chickens live. Out back. Just watch out for Darleen. She'll try to peck your hand if you're not real gentle."

Celia was starting to feel woozy and disoriented as if she had tripped and slipped through a crack into some alternate universe. "I have an idea," she said. "That little town down the road? Do they have, like, a candy store? Or an ice cream shop?"

"Yes."

"How about an ice cream cone, then. My treat!"

This earned Celia an even bigger grin, one that revealed a set of tiny white teeth. It made her smile back almost reflexively.

So first, Celia wrote a note and pinned it to the fridge in case Dante came back and wondered where his child had gotten off to, not that he had thought about that before he left, it occurred to her. She got Penelope strapped tightly as she could into the middle of the back seat, which she read in a magazine in some doctor's office was the safest spot for a child. Then came the terrifying drive back down the curvy mountain road, which she took even slower now that there was another person—a small one—in the car. No sooner had Celia parked and was letting Penelope lead her toward the small pharmacy where she said they sold ice cream when that woman wheeling the dachshund in the baby carriage approached. "Well," she began almost breathlessly, "you missed all the excitement. Hello there, Penelope."

"Hello, Ms. Nedra," Penelope answered, suddenly adopting a more serious tone.

"Excitement?" Celia asked, "About?"

Here, the lady leaned in closer and practically whispered. "Her father. Carted off to jail just a few minutes ago for attacking Lester Brenneman right outside the Short Stop Inn. I, myself, had to rush Lester to the hospital in my cab. He had a head wound, which can be very dangerous, what with concussions and such. He actually bled. I suppose I'll have to clean up that mess now. Anyway, the police are charging Dante with assault is what I gather."

Celia's mouth opened, but her brain was having difficulty forming a response. Penelope reached for her hand again. "C'mon," she said.

Celia dug into her purse and pulled out some singles. "Why don't you go and get yourself an ice cream, honey, and I'll be there in one minute."

"Okay. What about you?"

"Um..."

"Cone or cup?"

"Oh! Well, whatever you're having."

She nodded, took the money, and headed inside the pharmacy. Celia turned to the lady with the dachshund. "Okay, Ms. Nedra? Would you happen to know if there's anybody I can call to watch Penelope?"

"Well, there's her father, of course."

"Yes, but you just said he was taken to jail. I don't really know these people. And I kind of have to be on my way."

Now she eyed Celia with suspicion. "If you don't know these people, what are you doing buying Penelope ice cream?"

"She wanted a snack!"

"Well, I know there was a great-grandmother. But I do believe Mrs. Gibbs passed."

Celia was about to say that she knew all about Mrs. Gibbs when her phone started chirping. She glanced at the screen, surprised there was suddenly service; it was Danielle Chan calling from the office. "I have to take this. Do you mind?"

"Indeed I do," said Ms. Nedra, huffily. She pivoted and steered the baby carriage away, muttering something about the disappearance of manners, the wheels of the carriage squawking in protest.

Celia suddenly felt exhausted. She sank onto a weathered wooden bench outside the pharmacy and for a second or two just enjoyed the feel of the afternoon sun beating down and warming her face. "I don't see any numbers coming in, Celia," came rapid-fire from Danielle the instant Celia hit answer. "Are you running into resistance on HX III? Because none of those potential side effects in the insert have really been proven. And Bert Pitoniak's numbers are off the charts already, I must say."

"I'm sorry, Danielle. No, no resistance. I got slightly sidetracked, but you'll start seeing numbers tomorrow, okay?"

"Promise?"

"Yep! Gotta run. Bye!" Celia said as brightly as she could, ending the call as Penelope slowly approached, carefully balancing a teetering ice cream cone in each hand.

"I didn't know if you wanted chocolate or vanilla."

"Which one do you like better?"

"Chocolate."

"I'll take vanilla."

Penelope handed Celia hers, along with some change she dug from a pocket. Then she sat next to her on the bench. They licked at their cones in silence at first, Penelope taking dainty little bites, being extra careful, Celia could tell, not to knock the scoop off the cone. Celia, by now famished, attacked hers with relish. The cone was delicious, with little flecks of real vanilla bean, tasting so fresh it was almost as if it had been churned just for her. She finished every last bit of ice cream and cone. "It's good, huh?" she asked Penelope.

"Uh huh," said Penelope. "Why is my father in jail?"

"Oh. So you heard that?"

"Uh huh."

"If you know where the police station is, I guess we should go find out."

"I know where it is."

"Are you sure there's not a friend's house you want to go to?"

"Out of everybody in the entire world, I only like Tabitha."

"Okay. Boy, that's something, isn't it? Well then maybe I could drop you at Tabitha's house?"

"She has Chicken Spots. She's been out of school a whole week. Maybe more. I lost count."

"Chicken pox, you mean?"

"Oh, yeah. Pox! Dad says it's contaganonious, and we can't play for like ever."

Celia thought for a moment. "Contagious, I think you mean."

"Okay! And dad says they're dopes because Tabitha didn't get her shots."

Penelope took the last bites of her cone. She turned to Celia. There were chocolate smudges all around her mouth and on her hands, almost comically big, making Celia wonder how on earth she got so dirty so fast. Celia's own hands were sticky too, so she fished in her purse for Kleenex and hand sanitizer, cleaning herself and then wiping down Penelope's face, and her small hands and fingers. She had a sudden memory of her own mother doing the same thing when she was a child, and it gave her a small pang of something like regret, which Celia tried to put out of her mind as she followed Penelope down the street to the small red brick building with a squad car out front.

Inside, she parked Penelope on a hard plastic bench in a waiting area that smelled sharply of disinfectant while she headed over to talk to the uniformed man behind a desk. He was young and rail-thin with a large beak-ish nose, prominent sideburns and heavy-lidded eyes. "Hi," Celia began, "I was wondering if..."

"You here about Dante?" he interrupted, and then said, "Hi, Penelope."

"Hi, Deputy Hayes," the girl answered.

Of course. This was a small town, Celia thought, so they all must know each other. "May I speak to Mr. Zebulon?"

"You his lawyer, ma'am?"

Ma'am? Again? Third time in one day? "I'm not his lawyer," Celia said.

He eyed her up and down, then seemed to decide she was harmless.

"Well, he's back in lock-up. Sheriff didn't say he couldn't have visitors, so I don't see why not. No children under the age of eighteen allowed, though. You ain't eighteen yet are ya, Penny?" he said with a grin.

"Nope," Penelope said, laughing.

"Sorry then. You'll have to stay out here."

"That's okay." She was swinging her legs back and forth and closely studying the 'wanted' posters on the wall.

Deputy Hayes led Celia through a locked door and down a short hallway. He left her after a warning about no funny business, which she puzzled over for a moment. Then she was standing before the bars of a cell, which was sort of fascinating, actually, because she'd never seen a real one before, only ones in movies and on television. She noted a toilet with no seat and a tiny white sink with rust stains, a steady drip dropping from the faucet. Dante was sprawled on a bare mattress that looked awfully uncomfortable. He was holding a wadded-up towel over a bloody gash on his forehead.

"Oh my God," Celia blurted out.

Dante sat up. He glared at her. His shirt was torn, and his jeans looked even more scuffed and muddy than they'd been up at the barn.

"Are you okay?"

She got one of those grunts again, as if it might make her disappear. Then, when she still stood there, he said, "Now what do you want?"

Celia was about to tell him not to take that tone with her when, for the second time that day, she was feeling like a schoolmarm or somebody's batty spinster aunt, which technically, it annoyed her to realize, because of Rosalie and Kim-Cuc's twins, she was. "Now just a minute," she began. "I have somebody with me. A little girl who happens to be your daughter? She's waiting out there – in a police station, which is no place for a child, I might add—because somebody just up and left her all alone to fend for herself."

"Oh, shit," said Dante. "Roberta left?"

"Yeah," said Celia, "She did. So, yeah...Shit."

She had him on the defensive now. This felt satisfying.

He paced back and forth for a moment. He ran his hands through his shaggy black hair. He looked like he might want to punch something. Then he said, "Okay, you're going to have to watch her until I can get out of here."

"Me? Why me?"

"Because there's nobody else right now I can trust."

"How do you know you can trust me?"

"I don't. But I haven't got a choice, do I? She eats dinner at six. Make sure she gets a vegetable in her. And I want her in bed by eight. Oh, and Mrs. Whiskerson will need her shot."

"Mrs. what...?"

"Penny's cat. She's diabetic."

It took Celia a moment to wrap her head around that one. Then she said, "Listen, I can't watch your daughter. Or her cat."

"Yes, you can."

"I happen to have a job. An important one, for your information. I had meetings and appointments in Atlanta lined up today, back to back, and then there are more in Charleston the day after that, and now they all have to be rescheduled."

"Yeah, well, that's too bad. But actually, this whole mess is your fault."

"My fault?!"

Here Dante sat up. He tossed aside the towel and approached the bars. She could see the cut was no longer bleeding but was just starting to scab over. She thought briefly about the possibility of infection and the antibiotics her company manufactured she'd recommend to treat it. He stopped in front of her, staring through the bars.

She was expecting an apology for putting her in this predicament. Instead, what Celia got was, "Yes, your fault. Who asked you to come and bring me that damn letter? You know what's wrong with people these days? Always got to be poking their noses in everybody else's business. Nothing is private anymore. Everything has to be shared, every minute of the day. Nothing is sacred. Well, you know what I think? Stop looking at your God damn phone. Look at yourself or the people around you."

"Oh, for crying out loud! I thought I was doing something nice!" she shouted.

Celia had reached the end of her rope, physically and emotionally. It had been a long and increasingly confusing day. For a person who always liked things neat and orderly—her meetings scheduled to the minute, her routes precisely mapped—the day had descended into disorder and was threatening, with the introduction of a child, to spill over into chaos. And so her rant steadily grew in volume. "I certainly didn't have to go out of my way to do what was meant to be a good deed, did I?"

Dante looked slightly remorseful. "Okay, Listen, I..."

She cut him off. "No, I could have just done what most people would have done. Do you know what that might be?"

"Well, my guess is..."

"Most people would have taken that envelope and that dusty old book and tossed them in the trash without a second thought!"

Again, Dante tried to interrupt, but this time, he started to smile.

This pissed Celia off more. "You want to know something else? Do you? Well, I'll tell you anyway. I could have saved myself a heap of..."

This time, she didn't finish because suddenly Dante leaned in. She felt his hand on the nape of her neck, pulling her close. Suddenly, it was like she was outside her body and watching the scene unfold. She could step back or push him away, but she was frozen to the spot, unable to make that decision. Then came the warmth of his lips on hers. In that instant, it was as if every nerve in her body snapped to attention. A tingling ran from the top of her scalp to her toes. She didn't want it to stop.

Until she came to her senses. She shoved him. He reeled back, stumbled, and almost fell.

"What? Are you out of your mind? What are you doing?"

"Well, I kissed you, I guess." There was a wicked glint in his eyes, Celia noted, even though he was making an attempt to look serious.

"Who even remotely gave you permission to do that? This is the twenty-first century! It's not some stupid medieval fantasy show! You don't just get to grab whatever you want. You understand that, right? It is not acceptable!"

"I couldn't get a word in edgewise. It shut you up, didn't it?"

He was grinning now.

"Oh, my God. You must be insane!"

"I've been called worse."

"And by the way, are you just assuming I don't have a husband, or even a boyfriend? Is that what you think? That I'm some lonely and pathetic old thing you can just take if you want, and I'll just fall at your feet?"

"No, you're kind of hot, actually," he said. "Any man would be lucky to have you."

Celia ignored that. "Well," she added, "for your information, I happen to be engaged. To a very prominent ear, nose, and throat."

"Really?" Dante said, "And, one would assume, a penis?"

"You're an idiot."

"And besides, if you're so engaged, where's your ring?"

"IT NEEDS TO BE RESIZED!"

Dante was looking at her as if she were some sort of crazy person. It did sort of feel that some other entity had taken over her body and was now making decisions. This new person did something Celia might never have done. She'd had enough of this man and his attitude. So she whirled on her heels and strode out of there without another word, leaving behind, she hoped, a sense of awe and mystery.

IV.

Of course, things only grew stranger as day turned to night. Before ferrying Penelope back up the mountain road, Celia stumbled on a spot where bars appeared on her phone, so she stopped right then and there to take care of business. Never mind that this had her perched on the arm of a statue (Otis T. Hodges, 1797-1863, founder of this place) in the small, somewhat derelict square in the center of town; people passing by eyed her curiously even if Penelope seemed amused, especially when she found she had to hold the phone out in front of her, just above her head, at just a slight angle. Yes, Celia felt silly, but she simply couldn't pass on such good reception. And besides, hadn't she twice seen a lady who apparently drove a cab pushing a dachshund in a stroller? And they found Celia strange?

Anyway, she rescheduled all the appointments she'd missed. She returned increasingly urgent texts from Danielle Chan. She ignored an obnoxious one from Bert Pitoniak, already boasting about sales figures. She checked in on her mother and Lois at Rosalie and Kim's (things were not going well, it seemed) and called Barry.

"You're spending the night where? With whose child?" he kept asking, apparently unable to comprehend what she had done even though she had explained clearly how it all started with that errant envelope, and her decision to deliver it. When Barry launched into what sounded like it might be a lengthy "I told you so," Celia pretended her phone was cutting out and promised to call first thing in the morning.

Back on the second floor of the barn, she settled Penelope on the sofa with a coloring book. Then, because it was clear there was no escape from being stuck here until morning, she figured it was time to change out of her blue suit, which she'd had on since leaving for the airport at dawn. It was starting to get that limp, bedraggled feel of work clothes worn way too long. Although her flight had been only hours earlier, it seemed as if months had gone by. She dragged her bag from the trunk of the rental and hauled it upstairs to the one bathroom in the place, a small white square with vintage tile in a mosaic design on the floor, white-tiled walls, and a large claw-foot tub in front of a window that framed a view of the sun setting over the mountains. The tub looked so inviting, and Celia felt so grubby. She ran steaming hot water, and because the big pink bottle was just sitting there – surely it was Penelope's – she added some bubbles.

While waiting for the tub to fill, she called out to Penelope to see if she was good, and when she responded that she was, Celia stripped down and wrapped herself in a towel. She stood before the mirror and removed her make-up. Then, because she couldn't help it – it was research really—she nosed through the medicine chest. On the top shelf was a razor, a bar of shaving soap and a brush. She smelled the soap, which was spicy and musky all at once. There were the requisite bottles of aspirin and antiseptic, but there wasn't an AxCelecron product in sight, she noted. There was an open bottle of a woman's perfume she'd never heard of. She took a sniff. It was so flowery that she got a little dizzy. She spotted tweezers and boxes of band-aids. Behind the band-aids stood an open box of condoms. This made Celia flush and slam the door closed.

She took a good long soak. Refreshed, she put on sweats that still smelled of the dryer sheets she loved and an oversized T-shirt. She rejoined Penelope, who quickly flummoxed her all over again.

"When's dinner?"

"Um..."

This simple question threw her. She realized this must be what it is like all the time when you actually had children around. She'd devoted an uncountable number of hours thinking about this exact situation, especially lately, with forty approaching like a rumbling roll of thunder after a flash of lightning. Oh, there was still time, but she knew the longer they waited, the more problems she'd encounter. She knew too much about the hormones and drugs they'd pump into her, knew each and every side effect—because although she generally avoided reading those inserts, this time the side effects might apply directly to her, and so she had them sort of memorized—she was well aware of the possibility of blood clots, the potential for an embolism, and the raised chances of certain cancers years down the line.

But Celia always saw herself as a mom, always imagined what it must feel like to have life growing inside of her, sometimes even fantasized about giving birth, and was admittedly a little envious of Rosalie and Kim-Cuc and how lucky they were to have twins. Of course, in her musings, she envisioned an unrealistic, pain-free, and glowing version of childbirth. Kim had had a terrible, awful labor that went on endlessly – certainly because she was so tiny—as Rosalie stroked her cheek and spoke softly to her. Celia, Bernadette, and their mother escaped to the waiting room at the first possible chance even though they could have been in the delivery room with Rosalie the whole time if they chose. None of them were interested in all the sweating and screaming and potential for witnessing the emission of embarrassing bodily fluids. Daisy had been through it, she kept telling them. She knew.

Also, Celia had always pictured herself as a young-ish mom, not one already feeling some new aches and pains in certain joints or getting winded from not-all-that-much exertion. But that time was long past. Was she more like Bernadette, who didn't seem to care one way or another about babies? She couldn't be sure Bernadette and Kent wouldn't surprise them with news of pregnancy one of these days. They must, at some point, get tired of shopping and traveling, mustn't they?

Would Celia and Barry too be one of those childless couples? Would they wind up with pets they'd dote on, sending out holiday cards with dogs or cats they'd dress as Santa? She certainly didn't want to be one of those moms she'd heard about who got late starts and were confused with the child's grandmother. That was a horrifying sort of...

"Or, instead of dinner, we could have more ice cream," Penelope said hopefully, tugging on Celia's shirt and snapping her back to the issue at hand.

"Really? Is that so?" Celia asked, amused.

"Uh huh."

"Well. I think dinner's a better idea," Celia said.

She marched over to the kitchen. She quickly discovered that, as with the cookies, prepared or frozen or store-bought dinners were nowhere to be found. Nothing could be popped into the microwave, even if there was one. Ordering pizza or Chinese or Thai seemed out of the question, too, in a little town like this. "I make a mean plate of scrambled eggs. Would you like that?" Celia asked.

"Yes," said Penelope. "And toast with butter."

"Okay, then. Now, you mentioned something about chickens?"

"Uh-huh."

"And that's where you get the eggs?"

"Yup."

"How about you show me where they live?"

Celia followed Penelope outside, past the fenced-in area where pigs were splayed out, grunting softly and rolling around in mud, to a small wooden structure that was surrounded by more fencing. Several chickens were on the other side of the fence, milling about, moving in odd jerks and starts, poking their beaks into the ground and squawking as Penelope unlatched a gate and walked in. Celia hesitated. It all looked a little unsanitary, and she had just taken that nice bath. "C'mon, it's okay," Penelope said as she picked up one of the chickens and held it to her chest. "Hello, Maude," she said. Maude squawked a response but seemed to settle in a contented way.

Celia tentatively stepped in and closed the gate behind her. "Where are the eggs?"

"Inside. In the nests!"

She pointed toward the little wooden structure.

"Ah."

Celia felt like a dolt, completely out of her element. "Can you show me?"

Penelope set Maude back down and headed for the hen house. Celia followed. She had to stoop to pass through the low little front door. Inside, it was long and narrow with a steep peaked roof that had that new lumber smell. It was dark, too, with an earthiness that was somehow not unpleasant. On either side of a center aisle, shelves were built into the walls. There, some of the hens were nestled into little bales of hay, softly cooing. They eyed Celia warily. Others appeared to be asleep. Penelope gently reached her hand under one cooing hen. When she pulled her hand back out, there was an egg, which she turned over to Celia. It was a perfect oval in the exact shade of brown Celia had searched high and low for when she and Barry were painting their den and never found. It was warm to the touch, alive in a way, nothing like picking up an egg out of a carton from the fridge. "Wow," she said.

"Now you try," Penelope said.

Celia hesitated. "Will I get bitten?"

"Just go real slow."

She eased her hand under another warm hen and pulled out an egg of her own. For a moment, she just marveled at it, how utterly different it was from grabbing a carton off a shelf. Together, they plucked several more from the nests and placed them in a small wire basket hanging on a wall, Celia coming away with only a peck or two on the wrist, like the sharp little nips you'd get from a puppy, none even drawing a drop of blood.

Back in the kitchen, Celia cracked open the eggs to find yolks a deep shade of yellow she'd never seen. She made another potential error by nearly throwing out the shells – "The pigs get them!" Penelope pointed out – and when the eggs were scrambled into fluffy soft curds, and the toast slathered with butter (did they churn this, too, Celia wondered?) they sat down to eat. After a brief, awkward silence, Celia asked Penelope to tell her about her day, and Penelope chattered about her teachers and school and some girl she didn't like and some boy she once kicked, either in the shin or the butt; Celia couldn't be sure because the story was told with food in Penelope's mouth. There was no dishwasher in this kitchen, so after dinner, Celia stood at the sink and hand washed the plates while Penelope wiped them dry with a crisp white towel. Then, because Penelope said Mrs. Whiskerson might lapse into a coma if they skipped giving her a shot, they corralled the cat. This was the hard part, the cat suddenly morphing into an unwieldy fast-moving ball of claws, shrieks, and squirming limbs. But Celia, with her quasi-medical background, wasn't squeamish about loading the syringe with insulin and injecting the cat, as Penelope showed her, first scruffing her neck to create the divot between her shoulder blades, then a quick plunge with the needle, adding a mumbled apology as the cat fled. Still, they were so focused on the task at hand, neither noticed the arrival of Roberta, the girl with the orange Mohawk and all the tattoos. Celia was wondering if she lived here, too, but

Roberta said, "Dante called. I'm supposed to help you prep for tomorrow."

"Prep what?"

"Well, for starters, butts, ribs and shanks need a good rub."

Celia looked at her blankly.

Roberta said, "The meat. For the barbecue?"

"Oh!" Celia said, confused. Was this suddenly on her shoulders, too?

"Plus," Roberta continued, "we have to get the ones that have been marinating into the smoker. Oh, and the pigs need feeding, but Penelope can take care of that, right, Penny?"

"Right," said Penelope.

"So c'mon, and we'll get started. I don't want to be here all night. I have a life of my own, you know."

She headed down the stairs. Celia considered refusing to chip in. Okay, she'd watch the child for the night, but keeping this place running was certainly not her responsibility unless she decided to accept the idea that Dante being in jail was indeed somehow her fault. So she headed downstairs and followed Roberta to the barbecue shack where, in the kitchen, she was already gathering items from shelves and slapping a big battered stainless steel bowl on the counter. "Now," Roberta said, "because this rub recipe is secret, you'll have to turn around until I get it all together."

"Are you joking?' Celia asked.

"No. We take these things very seriously down here. For all we know, you could be some kind of spy."

"A spy for who?"

"I don't know. Some rival barbecue joint out to steal our recipes, to sabotage us just when we're gaining some traction?"

"People do that?"

"Of course. But Dante is dead-set on sabotaging himself. He just does not care about getting the word out in the right way and how it could make this business grow. I mean, we don't even have a proper website up. I keep talking to him about the importance of branding and social media, not to mention the importance of great merch."

"Merch?" Celia asked.

"You know, T-shirts for sure, but also hats and mugs and shot glasses and decals and whatnot. But does he listen? No, he does not. Or there's that big barbecue fest down near Macon coming up. I've suggested he enter. But he doesn't seem interested in that either. Now turn around, and then we can continue our little chit-chat."

Celia decided to just go with it. She faced the wall, where pots and pans hung from hooks attached to a peg board. She could hear the opening of various jars, the clickety-clack of measuring spoons, and the soft whoosh of spices being dumped into the bowl. She could identify at least some familiar smells, like garlic powder and one that was a pungent onion-y.

"Can I ask you a question about something else?" Celia said after a moment.

"I guess."

"Who is Lester Brenneman, and why did Dante get into a fight with him?"

"Well, I don't know all the details," Roberta said, "And I'm not one to gossip, but what I heard is that he got some letter that proved what folks have been whispering about for years."

"Whispering about what?"

"That Lester Brenneman is his real father, not Brooks Zebulon."

If Celia had regretted delivering the cookbook and letter before, now she was even more regretful. But how was she supposed to know there was going to be life-altering information in it? "So I take it Dante doesn't like this Lester guy?"

"No, they've always been good buddies. They hang out and knock back beers at the Short Stop in town all the time. Go fishing sometimes down by the creek. Tinker together with this or that when something breaks down."

"Then what's the problem?"

"Some people might have an issue – not me, mind you – but, well, Lester's Black. Oh, believe me, those folks would never admit it, but that's their problem."

"Oh," said Celia. "Huh."

"Like I said, not an issue in my book, but I do know for a fact that Dante's grandmother Mrs. Gibbs was a raging bigot. Blacks? Mexicans? Asians? She hated them all, pretty much equally. I heard that's what caused the rift between her and Dante's mother all those years ago. The idea that Mary Rose might have had an affair with a Black man while married to Brooks, who was white as the day is long. Is, I should say, because he's still around somewhere too. I'm sure that didn't go over well in these parts, and I should know—It's hard enough being gay in this town, and that's today, not thirty or forty years ago when it could have been lethal."

Celia heard the whisk clacking against the metal bowl. The blend of spices seemed to grow even more fragrant. "So you're saying he beat up Lester because he's Black?" she asked.

"Of course not!"

"Well then, why?"

"What I heard is Dante was pissed that Lester never told him the truth. Here they've been buddies all these years. Going on fishing trips like I said. Or hunting. Called Lester a coward, and Lester didn't appreciate that, so he took a swing at him, and Dante swung back and knocked his lights out. Okay, you don't have to look away anymore."

Celia turned to find the bowl now nearly full with a fragrant red-orange mixture. Roberta now pulled open the doors to a large walk-in refrigerator. Celia screamed. Before her was a pig hanging upside down by its hind legs, its eyes still intact, its mouth a rictus.

"Jesus!" Roberta said.

"I'm sorry. It looks like a body." Celia caught her breath.

"Well, it is a body."

"I meant a person," Celia said, then lowered her voice. "Did he kill it?"

"Who, Dante?"

"Yes."

"Oh, no. Local slaughterhouse does that dirty deed although he told me once he might have to do it. Out of respect for the animal, he meant, I think. He butchers them, though. He's pretty handy with a knife."

Celia nodded. Roberta disappeared into the walk-in and came back out carrying a large tray. On it were more recognizable cuts of meat, racks of ribs and large roasts of some kind, the pink meat heavily marbled with creamy white fat. "We're always planning three days ahead. So this meat gets the rub today but doesn't go into the smoker until three days from now. The ones going into the smoker got the rub three days ago. Understand?"

"Um. Yes," Celia said.

Roberta set a rack of ribs in front of Celia. "Now watch. Like this." She pulled a large handful of the mixture from the bowl and began massaging it into the meat. "Think you can handle the ribs while I do the rest?"

"I can do that."

"Massage it in there real nice, okay? Make sure you get it in all the nooks and crannies."

"Yeah, yeah. On it."

So they worked side-by-side. Celia grabbed fistfuls of the spice blend and methodically rubbed it into the racks. She found something soothing about the task because she could do it without thinking. "Can I ask another question?" she said, after a few minutes of silence.

"Shoot."

"Who is Penelope's mother?"

"Oh, a real piece of work. Luanne Grimes."

"Does she live around here?"

"Nope. Last I heard? She was in Daytona Beach. Working as a cocktail waitress is what people say, but I think she's stripping."

"So they're divorced?"

"No, Luanne and Dante never did get married. He don't like to talk about it much. I guess he fell hard for her, but it wasn't exactly reciprocated."

Roberta stopped what she was doing and looked around to make sure Penelope hadn't rejoined them. She lowered her voice and continued, "Don't think she ever really wanted that baby, either, although she sends up presents all the time, half of them useless to a little girl like that. Anyway, Dante was working at some restaurant down in Florida. Line cook, I think is what he was doing. That's where they hooked up originally. But when his grandma took ill, and when he said he was moving back up here, Luanne told him to take Penny, too. Claimed she didn't need a kid cluttering up her life, or some such thing."

"Oh, that's awful," Celia said.

"Right? Penny seems to have adjusted okay, though. She's a real daddy's girl. Actually, he spoils her. Don't you think so?"

"Well, I barely know them really."

Here, Roberta stopped massaging those larger cuts of meat. She took a closer, more appraising look at Celia, who suddenly felt uncomfortable, like she was being judged, and not in a good way. "Who exactly are you again?"

"I'm Celia Bernhart. I sell pharmaceuticals."

"You're a drug dealer? You don't look like a drug dealer."

"No, I mean legal drugs. Prescribed by a doctor."

"Oh. Uh huh," said Roberta.

Celia detected a little eye-roll and a touch of hostility in the air. "Do you have a problem with what I do?"

"Nothing. I know your type. That's all."

"Really? What type is that?"

"You're one of those people I see in the elevator when I go to the doctor's office over in Atlanta. All buttoned down and official. Toting a suitcase full of samples. Bringing those fancy-ass cupcakes to the receptionists. I seen you types doing stuff like that. Bribery is what it looks like to me. Always look like you're in some hurry to get to the next office and talking all loud on your phone or frantically texting. Everybody else is invisible because you're just focused on selling more shit for people to take to counteract the side effects of the crap they took before. You one of those folks?"

"Actually, um...well, I prefer to think about it this way: we're making lives better," Celia said brightly.

Roberta made a sound like a balloon deflating. "Really? That's so. Tell that to my brother T.J. You want to know what happened to T.J?"

"Um..."

"Well, I'll tell you. Turned the big four-zero, T.J. did, and started getting all achy in the joints, which is sort of to be expected if you want my opinion. Gout, the doctor said it was, and so he wrote out a prescription for these pills to take. Of course, T.J. was also on pills to control his blood pressure, and he was on some blood thinner, too. So one morning he gets up, takes a shower, puts on his clothes, starts mixing up a batter for waffles and then, while waiting for the waffle iron to heat up, drops dead of a heart attack. Right there on his kitchen floor."

It wasn't the cardiac arrest that caught Celia's attention. Or the cocktail of drugs. It was the idea that this brother of Roberta's dropped dead at forty. This clanged like a gong in Celia's head until she forced the thought out. "Well," she asked, "Was he overweight? Out of shape? Did he exercise regularly, or was he sedentary?"

"T.J. wasn't exactly skinny. I'll give you that. In fact, probably the doctor should have just told him to lose a good fifty pounds. And eat better. T.J. loved his junk food."

Celia, in her mind, made him obese, one of those enormous, pear-shaped people who had trouble walking just a few steps without getting all out of breath. *I mean,* she thought, *waffles for breakfast? Doesn't that tell you something?* Obviously why he died so young. She knew there was the possibility Roberta was right, that it was a bad combination of the meds, but she wouldn't say that. "Okay, I'm done here," was what she said as she finished the last of the racks of ribs. She noticed her hands were bright orange and found a towel to wipe them on, but she couldn't seem to get the orange out. She rinsed them, but they stayed orange. "Hey," she said. "How do I get this off my hands?"

"Oh, well you should have put on gloves. Did I forget to mention that?" Roberta held up her gloved hands and wiggled them.

"Yeah. You did forget to mention gloves."

"Well, it'll come off after a couple of days. Just don't touch your eyes. Or, you know, your privates. Chili powder and cayenne can cause all sorts of, well, discomfort in those areas."

"Great!"

Roberta was done, too. Celia helped her load the trays back into the walk-in. Then they grabbed trays of cuts that had been rubbed days earlier and carried them down to the smokehouse in back. Fragrant smoke still chugged out of the chimney as Roberta unlatched and opened the door. Celia, at first almost overwhelmed by the smell of hickory mingling with long, slow-smoked pork, took her first peek inside. She noted a small space, a hulking black box made of steel taking up one side. Roberta opened the door of the black box, and there on one rack were the cuts that were fully smoked, large fatty shoulders just beginning to shred apart on their own, ribs lined up on another rack above, and dangling from hooks at the top, links of sausage practically bursting at the seams. A few chickens were on a final rack, a concession, Roberta noted, to non-pork eaters. As she removed the meat, she handed Celia a shred of pork from the shoulder. Celia bit into something so meltingly tender she figured she wouldn't even need teeth to eat it.

Roberta finished loading the next round with Celia's somewhat inept help, and then led her out to the back of the little shack. Wood was stacked near the firebox. Celia watched as Roberta stoked the fire and added hickory chips that were soaking in a small vat of what she thought was water but later learned was apple juice (okay, she snuck a peek at the label when Roberta wasn't looking) which, she was told, added one more level of flavor.

"Now," Roberta began, "if we're doing this right, somebody needs to be out here in about six hours to check on the smoke and rotate the meat."

"So I have to get up at, like, two in the morning?"

"Yep! Fun, huh? And I'll be back at eight sharp tomorrow morning to pull them out and start on making sides. You good with that?"

"Okay. Sure," Celia said.

"One more thing." Roberta pointed at a small round thermometer built into the firebox door. "Check the temperature. It should never go above two hundred and twenty five degrees. Low and slow is the way to go. Got that?"

Celia surveyed the primitive set-up. "Well," she said, "Where's the knob?"

"What knob?"

"If I need to turn the fire up or down."

"Oh, honey, there is no knob."

"So how do I adjust the temperature then?"

If it goes too low, add another log from that pile. If it's too hot, leave the vents open a bit until she cools down. Understand?"

She didn't really, but she was too tired to argue. "Uh huh," Celia said. "Yes."

Roberta rattled off more instructions about ash sweeping and log size. She told Celia to call if she had any questions, then spat out her number too fast and was out of there, roaring off on her motorcycle.

Celia headed back toward the barn. She found Penelope sitting on the fence, watching the pigs finish their dinner. "I bet it's past your bedtime," she said.

"It is," said Penelope. She had a big smile on her face as if she had gotten away with something. Celia recognized that smile from times with her own mother. But she figured she better get Penelope off to bed.

Back inside, Celia helped the little girl change into a nightgown, watched while she brushed her teeth, and then tucked her in. It startled Celia that they had become so comfortable together as if they'd known each other forever instead of a few hours. She was about to leave the room when Penelope said, "What about my story?"

"Oh. Okay. Well, then. Which book do you want me to read from?"

"My dad makes up a story for me at night."

"Good Lord, what is it with you people?!" Celia couldn't help it—this popped out of her mouth. She knew it sounded a bit extreme, but really–no convenience foods? Eggs from a hen house? No microwave? What century were these people living in?

Penelope frowned. "Don't you make up stories?"

"Well, not since I was.... No."

"I guess that's okay . I'll just lie here. Stare at the ceiling. Maybe I might fall asleep. In an hour or two. And you have to stay with me until I do. Sometimes I have nightmares if there's no good story, though. It's true. Ask my dad if you don't believe me."

Celia sensed that she was being played—where do small children learn to manipulate like this, she briefly wondered—but she decided to go along for the ride. "I could try, I suppose."

"Okay."

Penelope scooted over on the bed, patting the space comically and fluffing the pillow next to her, making room for Celia to sit. Celia settled in next to her. Of course, at that instant, her mind went blank. Try as she might, she couldn't think of a single thing, which was distressing, but just as she was about to throw up her hands and concede defeat, an image popped into her head; it was a night long ago, just after the infant Kim-Cuc had arrived and joined the family. She had taken one of the bedrooms, forcing Celia, Rosalie and Bernadette to share the second in the three-bedroom house. They weren't used to sleeping like this, all bunched together like puppies or kittens. Bernadette, as the oldest, had her own room, and Celia and Rosalie shared. So they were acting fussy and distracted, clearly exasperating their mother, who also had the new baby to contend with. Their father had come into the room, determined to get the girls to sleep. He told them a story he seemed to spin out of thin air about three little princesses and their mother, the queen. There was the haughty oldest Princess, Celia suddenly recalled, the wise and caring youngest, and, oh, then there was the middle one.

The middle one!?

Celia couldn't remember much else about the story, but she'd never forget how her father had referred to her, so bland and generic.

"The middle one!" she said out loud.

"What?" Penelope looked at her, confused.

"Sorry, sweetie," Celia said. "You wanted a story? Okay."

She did the best she could. She made up a tale about a little girl, a pony – no, a brave white steed - and how together they fought in a battle against an evil witch and some horrid garden gnomes that came to life. This girl was no pushover. She was a fierce warrior, Celia made sure. Okay, Celia soon realized, the story was scattered and unfocused—she was making it up as she went along, after all—but it seemed to do the trick. Within minutes, Penelope was asleep.

Celia watched her for a minute or so.

She started to rise, but laid back down. Where should she spend the night? The sofa in the living room? The floor? Dante's bed, with its pleasantly rumpled sheets? She considered finding a spot with bars so she could text Barry. She wondered if he was missing her, but why would he? Wasn't he used to her being on the road so much of the time? Still, she couldn't shake the sensation that she had been gone for months. She was so tired she could barely move even when the cat silently leapt up onto the bed, eyed her warily for a moment, and, apparently not bearing a grudge about the shot she gave her, climbed right onto Celia's stomach, pawing at her softly and purring dramatically, like a motor was hidden somewhere beneath all that fur. It was a lulling sound, like the white noise machine Celia sometimes used at home when Barry snored. Before long, Celia, too, dropped into a deep slumber.

V.

"Picture your mother," Celia began as the PowerPoint presentation on her laptop displayed the image of the old lady, "before the HX III Patch. Her skin is dried up. Her hair is brittle. Her sex drive is..."

"Wait, what's wrong with your hands?"

This was the second time already that day a doctor had interrupted her in the middle of her pitch with the same comment.

It was true. Her hands were still orange. No matter how much she scrubbed, it seemed that the spice blend she had massaged into the racks of ribs and the pork butts (which weren't actual butts but shoulders, Roberta had explained, to Celia's relief) had marked her indelibly.

"Are you taking too much beta-carotene? Drinking too much carrot juice?" this doctor asked. "Because you know too much beta-carotene can turn your skin orange. Or turmeric, which everybody's nuts for these days. Although that's more a yellow than an orange. But suddenly you can't throw a stone without hitting turmeric."

"It's not carrot juice or beta carotene or turmeric," Celia said. "It's paprika and cayenne and some other things that are top secret."

She didn't bother to explain why a spice rub was embedded in her skin; it was just too long and complicated, and she had sales to make if she was going to catch up to Bert Pitoniak, who now had a whole day's head start.

"You should have worn gloves," Dante had said when Celia showed him her hands earlier that morning just before his court appearance. "There's a whole box of them right there on the counter. That's what they're for, actually," he added while licking chocolate glaze from the donut she had brought off his fingers.

"Well, Roberta told me about the gloves when we were done. Which I think she did on purpose, to teach me a lesson or something."

"Roberta has her own way of doing things," Dante said.

"I sort of picked up on that."

Her idea was never to see Dante again after his night in the slammer, which was, oddly, how she kept referring to it, as if she were some moll from an old gangster film. What did she need his attitude for, anyway? She had a simple plan. She'd get up, shower, slip into her blue skirt, a fresh cream blouse, and button up her blue jacket. Like the cool, organized, and efficient person she was, she'd fix Penelope a fast, nutritious breakfast. She'd get her safely off to school, say her goodbyes, and that would be that.

But after waking up in a strange bed, Celia felt disoriented and foggy. When she went to rouse Penelope, she found her to be cranky and slow-moving. With much coaxing, Celia got her out of bed and scrubbed clean. Then it was time to get her dressed for school. This fast grew into a battle of wills of the kind Celia had only heard about from friends who had children the same age; Penelope decided she would wear her nightgown to school. Celia took the tack of insisting she put on real clothes. For a few minutes, there was a stand-off, each side refusing to budge until finally Celia pulled open Penelope's closet, determined to find something a young girl would want to wear, but when she racked her brain to try and remember what that might be, she came up blank, and nothing looked the same as she remembered, anyway. Also, opening the closet had been a mistake. Boxes wrapped in bright gift paper and ribbons that had been stacked willy-nilly came tumbling out. One box came apart as it fell. There was a crashing sound as what was inside hit the floor. It was a digital camera, a complicated, expensive-looking one.

"You broke it!" Penelope said.

Celia had picked it up. The lens had separated from the camera's base, but Celia realized it simply needed to be screwed back into its mount. She did so, then held it up for Penelope. "No," she said. "See? Not broken. It's supposed to do that. That's the way it works. So you can change the lens if you want."

Penelope was having none of it. Or maybe she was just still feeling fussy. Celia couldn't be sure. But she said, "My mother sent me that for my birthday, and now it's ruined."

Maybe it was. Celia hit the power button just to check. The camera came to life with a high-pitched squeal that made the still slumbering cat leap off the bed and scrabble under it. Celia pointed the camera at Penelope and snapped a picture. She turned the little screen to show her. "It's good. See?"

It was a decent picture. Celia had caught Penelope midway between pout and smile. Now Penelope smiled wider. "Take another," she said, this time grinning so wide it almost made Celia laugh.

They made a deal. Celia would take a few more pictures if Penelope would agree to put on the pair of blue jeans and the sweet little top Celia plucked out of her closet. She suddenly recalled her mother once complaining that raising children was an endless, exhausting series of deals to make and that it helped, as a parent, to develop a poker face. Was her mother right about more things than she gave her credit for?

A little later, they headed into town. The coffee shop was just across from the square with the statue where Celia had found cell reception. It was a small store front, with 'Belle's' written diagonally across the window in fancy gold script that was now faded and scratched. Celia could smell bacon sizzling when she parked the car out front. For the second time in a matter of days, she found her mouth watering, and though she usually skipped breakfast or made do with a Power Bar, her stomach started to churn.

Inside, the coffee shop was like something from a bygone era. The floors were linoleum, big black and white squares, scuffed and worn almost completely away in spots. Booths outfitted in snappy red vinyl lined one side. Opposite was a long counter with swiveling stools, also covered in red. Somebody was way into rabbits because small rabbit figurines were everywhere, in various sizes and shapes on shelves that lined the walls and on the counter as salt and pepper shakers. Stuffed versions dangled from the ceiling. A somewhat motley collection of locals tucked into platters of eggs and bacon or big stacks of fluffy pancakes and sausage, the small discs deeply browned and crisp on the edges.

Celia nodded at the one person she recognized, Miss Nedra, who sat with her dachshund, who was lapping at a bowl of what appeared to be oatmeal; she gave Celia a grudging nod back. Behind the counter was Belle herself, ancient looking, a little rabbity with her slim, narrow face and tiny nose, also bone thin and shrunken, with almost-translucent papery skin. She wore way too much rouge, and her full head of honey-colored hair was spun up and lacquered into a low beehive. She moved in a sprightly way around the space as if she was half, or even a quarter, her age, darting this way, then zig-zagging another, again rabbitlike. "Well hey there, Penny," she chirped as Penelope hoisted herself onto a stool at the counter, "Who's your new friend?"

"That's Celia," Penelope said.

Celia waited for yet another suspicious glare but instead was met with a warm smile and a "What can I get you, hon?"

"Donuts for my dad, please, Belle."

They left with a bag of donuts fresh from the fryer and barely made it to the car before Celia dug into a hot cruller that had been rolled in sugar and cinnamon. Penelope ate a jelly donut. They split a banana fritter before Celia insisted they save the last two – glazed, one chocolate, one caramel and studded with toasted pecans—for Dante. These he inhaled the second Celia got them out of the bag while Celia recounted the night, leaving out the part about how she slept right through a two AM wake up to check on the smoke house, and then assured him that she had left Penelope safely at school. Somehow, before she knew it, though, Dante was due at the courthouse, and when he asked that she come and wait until he was released, there was something in his eyes that...

"Now, Miss Bernhart, I know you done told me to sit tight in the waiting room, but my programs are coming on, and I got nowhere to watch."

Celia was jolted back to her meeting with the doctor when they were abruptly interrupted, as here was Lester Brenneman trying to barge his way past a nurse into the office, poking at the door with his weathered walking stick. Celia could see questions forming on the doctor's face: *'Who is this wrinkled old gray-haired Black man? Why is there a large bandage on his forehead? And just what is he doing here?'*

Celia said, "Excuse me, Doctor Woodman, could you give me a second?"

"Well, I have a facial peel to give in..." He glanced at a shiny gold Rolex the size of a small grapefruit. "...six and one half minutes."

"Great. Be right back."

She hustled Lester out of the office and down the hall to the waiting area, which was filled with Atlanta women of a certain age, all with smooth, frightfully unlined faces and complicated hair. Each one pretended not to notice as Celia settled Lester into a chair. "Mr. Brenneman, please, I promise I'm almost done."

"Now sweetie, didn't I tell you to call me Lester?"

"Lester. Just a few more minutes, okay?"

"Well, but I always watch my programs and..."

Celia pulled her iPad from her briefcase. "Which program do you want?"

"Well, there's the cooking show with the lady with large boobs."

This got the attention of the women in the waiting room. Celia stifled the urge to laugh and then, clueless as to who he might be referring to, pulled up the Food Network. She handed Lester the iPad, gave a quick tutorial she knew from his look of pure bafflement was flying right over his head, and returned to close her deal.

She still was trying to figure out how exactly she got saddled with this man—it was a strange growing entourage, starting with Penelope and her cat and now Lester. It began with a courtroom drama, yet another new experience for Celia, who had never even served on a jury and was suddenly beginning to feel like her life had been, to this point, completely sheltered. She had agreed to accompany Dante to court for his arraignment, which, it turned out, was back in the neighboring town of Blairsville. While she had some free time, she called Barry and got his voice mail. Then came a call from her mother. "You have to get us out of here," Daisy began. "They are being just downright mean to Lois and me. And Lois with her bum leg and all."

"Oh, I am so sure Kim and Rosalie are not being mean, mother."

"They are. All I did yesterday was ask for a hot cup of tea and do you know what Rosalie said? She said 'help yourself,' and so I did. Now I'm not even going to start on the fact that they can't keep one box of just regular old plain tea bags. No, they have to have all these strange sounding herbal varieties –

just the leaves, so you have to go through this whole tiresome brewing process so that by the time you're done making one little cup, you don't even want the damn tea anymore—and God only knows what kind of havoc these herbs do to your insides. I read somewhere once that while it's true peppermint can be..."

"Mom, I don't have all day here."

Daisy continued, "Well, later she accused me of leaving Kim-Cuc's favorite kettle on the stove and letting all the water boil out and just about ruining it, but I did not do that."

"Didn't you mention you did exactly that a couple of weeks ago when you were steaming broccoli? Burned the bottom of the pot and you had to throw it out?"

"That wasn't my fault. Your father's crazy sister Judith called and kept me on the phone forever. You know how she can be. Always about her and her little problems. You know what she was complaining about? Her neighbor hadn't moved the bins from the curb in a timely fashion after the trash men had been by. So I said, 'Judith, you have to...'"

"Well," Celia interrupted, trying to move things along, "they might have just been concerned that you'd set the kitchen on fire."

"Oh, please, Celia, everybody acts like I'm some batty old lady."

Celia held her tongue. What had happened to the capable woman who knew how to do everything and had all the answers? Or at least pretended she did? Celia had distinct memories of a mom who juggled not just three small girls but also the toddler emigre Kim and whatever pet they had at the time all while running a house and dealing with a typical husband and all his varying and sometimes baffling or inexplicable needs. Rather suddenly, it seemed, that super-woman was replaced by a dithering elderly person. Now, her mother insisted Bernadette be conferenced into the call and expressed the desire that she and Lois drive into New York and move into Bernadette and Kent's very large apartment on the Upper East Side. They could maybe take in a Broadway show or an exhibit. When Bernadette nixed the idea of their mother driving anywhere and mentioned the fact that Lois was in a cast, Daisy said, "Oh, well that. But Lois doesn't want to stay in bed all day, either, do you, Lois?" There was some sort of high-pitched, squeaky but muffled response. Celia couldn't make out whether Lois was agreeing or putting up a protest. She was growing impatient with this whole business of her mother's and decided to leave them with something dramatic: "I have to run. Court is almost in session."

There was a chorus of 'whats?' and 'waits!!' as Celia ended the call because indeed things seemed to be stirring in the courtroom, where she had found a seat in the spectator section. Even though she'd never served on a jury, she'd been called for jury duty once and questioned by lawyers and prosecutors. She recalled expressing the thought that a person might not find himself in a courtroom if he didn't commit a crime. Was that why she'd been dismissed? Had she been a little harsh and judgmental—not open-minded enough? What she did remember was feeling annoyed because the jury summons was getting in the way of her day.

Now a door opened to the right of where the judge sat—the bench?—and the sheriff's deputy led Dante, in handcuffs, to a table where an overworked-looking bald man in an ill-fitting beige suit, a lawyer Dante hired Celia assumed, was seated. When Dante saw her, he flashed her a little smile. He was still in his ripped jeans and T-shirt, his shaggy hair a mess, and Celia suddenly realized she might have brought him a change of clothes or a shaving kit because he was never more beardy. At a second table on the opposite side sat a woman Celia pegged as the prosecutor. The only other person in the room was the man with the walking stick and the bandage on his head she now knew as Lester Brenneman, who sat behind Celia in the very last row. It was hushed in the room, and it smelled funny – a nervous smell was how it struck Celia, the sharp sour odor of sadness and defeat.

Soon, a second door toward the front of the room opened. A uniformed bailiff emerged and asked them all to rise. Out marched the judge in a crisply ironed black robe. She was short with a severe bowl cut of closely cropped gray hair, and she moved with stiff precision, like she'd been in the military. This, oddly, made Celia nervous for Dante. Then came a bunch of legal mumbo-jumbo Celia couldn't understand before the judge rapped her gavel and called the court to order. Even Celia sat up straighter as charges of assault were read against one Dante Frederick Zebulon of Hodges Creek. Something about the Frederick struck Celia as funny. She tried to stifle a laugh by loudly clearing her throat, but she inhaled something that went down the wrong pipe. This started a coughing fit, so everybody turned to look at her anyway. "I'm sorry. Excuse me," Celia said. She felt herself flushing again.

Once Celia regained control, Dante's representative asked that the charges be dismissed. He claimed Dante acted in the heat of the moment due to some upsetting news he had just received. Here, Celia wanted to confirm having delivered the long-lost letter to Mary Rose, but she kept quiet. The judge put on little reading glasses, then glanced down her nose at Dante. "Well, Mr. Zebulon," she began, "This isn't your first time at the rodeo, is it now?"

Dante stood. His hands were clasped behind his back. He looked down at his shoes. Celia thought of a little boy who had been caught doing something bad.

"No, ma'am, Your Honor," he said. "And I'd sure like to apologize to Lester. I didn't mean to hurt him."

He did look remorseful, Celia thought, as he faced Lester and said, "I wasn't thinking clearly. I'm sorry, man."

"Apology accepted!"

Everybody turned to look at Lester, who gave the judge a nod as if he knew her, too.

Celia was expecting that to be the end of it. The judge would accept apologies all around. Dante would be set free. He could go home, shower, and put on fresh clothes. Suddenly, there was an image in her head of Dante in that big claw foot tub, wet and sleek like a seal, reaching for a bottle of shampoo. She quickly banished the image. Anyway, she'd be on her way, be done with these people, and she could get back to business. Yet again, complications arose out of nowhere. It wasn't Dante's first time at the rodeo. This was his second charge of assault within the past year, according to the prosecutor. This caught Celia's attention. What kind of deranged, violent person was he? It turned out he had been set upon by the ex-boyfriend of some woman he'd been dating, and they'd gotten into a nasty scuffle. Both had wound up behind bars. The judge said, "Regardless of who started what, Mr. Zebulon, you need to be taught a lesson about how to solve problems without using your fists." She paused to consult her calendar. "I'm setting trial one week from today but bail is denied. Maybe a week in county lock-up will give you time to sort out your issues."

She rapped her gavel and was about to stand, but Dante said, "I can't spend a week in county, Your Honor. Who's going to watch my kid?"

"And I got a concussion," said Lester Brenneman. "The doctor says somebody's gotta look after me for at least forty-eight hours. Otherwise, I could go into a coma. I figure it should be Dante."

"Really?" the Judge said, "And why is that?"

"Because he's my..."

Lester, about to say something, stopped mid-sentence. He seemed to struggle with a thought before continuing along a different track. "Well, because he's the one who knocked me senseless in the first place."

"And who's watching your child now?" the judge asked Dante.

"She is."

He turned and pointed right at Celia.

The Judge peered down her nose at Celia. "And who are you?"

Oddly, what struck Celia is that people the past couple of days kept asking her that very same question. "I'm Celia Bernhart. I sell pharmaceuticals."

Maybe because she had been caught by surprise once again, it came out kind of high-pitched and shrieky. Also, in this big, echoing courtroom, she sounded empty and hollow. But there was no time to process that because before Celia knew it – despite numerous objections that the idea was impossible – Dante had been led away, and she had been saddled with Penelope and Lester for the week.

She'd been trying to explain to Barry on the phone outside the courtroom, with Lester hovering nearby, when it suddenly occurred to her that she'd be here on her birthday. Her thirty-ninth, last year of the decade, which was still troubling to her and scary because there was so much she was supposed to do in that year, and where would she ever find the time? Now she'd be with strange people in a strange place. This suddenly made Celia – usually so in control of her emotions – begin to cry, big heaving sobs that wracked her body and made her nose run, so that even Lester Brenneman edged closer and put a reassuring hand on her shoulder.

"It's all right, sweetie," Barry said, "I'll just come down to you. We'll celebrate there instead of here."

"You will? Really?"

"I'll book a ticket right now."

"That would be good."

She ended the call and pulled herself together. She thanked Lester for not thinking she was insane. Lester shuffled a little, gingerly patted the band-aid on his head, and said, "Oh, now, don't you worry, Miss. I know you girls and your hormones."

She could have taken offense at the comment. It was old-fashioned, entire decades out of touch really, and not just the hormones. Girls? Really? It had been nearly thirty years, she figured, since she could be referred to as a girl. Thirty years? This almost made her start sobbing again. And then there was this: considering the fact that Celia was indeed carrying a briefcase full of hormones and, some would say, foisting them on women like they were candy, she had to smile, and she started to laugh, which naturally lifted her mood. She fished wadded up balls of Kleenex from the bottom of her bag, dabbed at her eyes, plopped herself down on the stairs outside the court house, and called Danielle Chan.

She asked for the week off. Danielle balked—they were at the height of a product launch, after all – but Celia promised to do her best while inwardly cursing Danielle. She had barely taken a day off in years. How much of herself was she supposed to devote to this company? Still, she pulled a map up on her phone and studied which appointments she could make that were within driving distance so she could take care of business while Penelope was in school. If Lester needed to be monitored, she'd bring him along. What better place for him than a doctor's office if he had a concussion?

And so the next few days unfolded in something of a blur. A grumbly Roberta showed up at the crack of dawn on her noisy Harley and kept things running at the barbecue shack, tending to the meat and starting on sides, stirring big pots of the special secret sauces and waiting on hungry customers through lunch. Celia would drop Penelope at school and, with Lester Brenneman riding shotgun, head to the next doctor's office. Okay, she had to admit she looked a bit odd, crisply turned out in her suit, toting her official- looking black case full of samples, an elderly man with a walking stick and a bandage on his head by her side. Her fellow drug reps, some she knew by name, others newbies, threw curious looks their way or tried too hard to be polite to Lester when they realized he was with Celia and not some random person going to his own appointment. In fact, once she got past some of his old-fashioned opinions, Celia found Lester easy to talk to, a congenial companion, free with advice although some of it was admittedly wacky, like he had all sorts of crazy ideas about cure-alls and tons of superstitions, too. In the car between appointments, instead of shouting back to some silly talk radio program or listening to yet another book-on-tape or another pod or just staring vacantly at the road ahead, she had actual conversations with him, which brought to mind car trips with her own father when they would banter back and forth about one topic or another, or he would explain why he loved some jazz riff on the radio.

She missed her father terribly, as did Bernadette and Rosalie, Celia knew. For as long as she could remember, she and her sisters were competing for their father's attention, each of them eager to win praise for this or that or avoid punishment or a lecture if they did something bad or committed what he considered some mortal sin. Dave Bernhart was a quiet man, soft-spoken, tall and wiry, almost shy, some would say, and often dominated by their mother, who could be far more free-spirited and certainly had some dizzy schemes. He worked on Wall Street, but this was before the real go-go years; he was employed by a buttoned-down old-line firm in the research department, quietly going about the business of digging through a company's books, or analyzing a line of products, and then writing long, detailed reports about whether or not the brokers should recommend buying or selling the stock. So every morning, he put on a suit and took a train—the same train—from Rockville Centre into the city, which Celia and her sisters always thought seemed so glamorous and exciting but, their mother told them much later, was a job he found dull and stifled by. "Who ever read those reports?" he'd complain. He liked being outdoors. He liked hiking to the top of mountains and pitching tents and swimming in the sea. He talked of one day moving them all to a farm; they'd have a lake, and he'd buy a canoe. Or better yet, he'd build his own boat. This never happened. Dave Bernhart kept working until retirement and then he got sick and died. Celia always wondered about disappointment simmering beneath the surface, something she frequently noticed in men. But she didn't sense it in Lester, and this made her curious. On one long stretch of interstate between sales calls, Celia said, "You're retired. And you seem happy. What's your secret?"

"Oh, well, that's easy," Lester said. "Every morning, after my shower and shave, I take a nice big slug of a good single-malt scotch."

"You drink in the morning?!"

"I don't get drunk, honey. Just loosens things up a bit. Gets the joints in gear if you know what I mean."

"But," Celia asked, "were you happy when you worked? What did you do, anyway? Did you love your job?"

"Do you love yours?"

"We're not talking about me," Celia said.

"As a matter of fact, I did love it. Still do. I never stopped. I mean, I retired from the garage I worked for on a regular basis, but I still do jobs here and there. I fix cars. I'm a mechanic. Fix everything, pretty much. Refrigerators. Washing machines. You got something broke, I can probably get it up and running again for you."

"That's a good talent to have," Celia said. "We're hopeless about that stuff in my house. We either call in a repairman who quotes some crazy-ass price or we toss whatever broke and replace it. I guess that's not a good thing."

"Nope. People treat everything as disposable these days. Anyway, some in town used to call me Mr. Fix-it."

Celia smiled. "That's a good name to have."

Lester nodded. "They still do, I guess, because I'm still tinkering with things all the time. You don't forget if you know how to fix things that are broken. And you don't like to stop trying to make things work. So people bring me things, and I fix them."

"Is that how you met Mary Rose?"

Lester gave her a long sideways glance. The question had popped out of her mouth somewhat unexpectedly, and now it hung there in the air between them.

"Why is it suddenly everybody's business what happened between me and Mary Rose almost forty years ago?"

Celia almost said, "Because I dragged the issue out of the past by delivering that letter." What came out instead was, "Don't you just think it's better that people know the truth?"

"Truth is overrated," Lester grumbled. "But if you must know, her car broke down. She was a nurse. Well, she wasn't officially a nurse. She was in school studying to be one. She had bought herself a car to get back and forth to school—this old Triumph. A TR-6, to be exact. Now, anybody with even the least amount of sense in his or her brain would warn you away from buying some persnickety, fragile piece of machinery from all the way over in England, but I suppose nobody told Mary Rose that the TR-6 was going to cause nothing but frustration and, well, sorrow. And also a shit-ton of money. Or maybe they warned her, and she just went ahead and did what she wanted anyways. That was sort of part of her personality if you ask me. Headstrong. Got that from her mother Mrs. Gibbs is what I figure."

"So you fixed her car? Then what happened?"

"Actually, I didn't fix it. Was one of the few things I could not get a handle on. That old Triumph was a head scratcher. Although I did order this manual all the way from Great Britain. Never did crack it open. Bet I still got it somewhere."

"Really? After all this time?"

He chuckled. "People call me a hoarder," he said, "but I save stuff because you never know, do you, when you might need something? Anyway, I towed the car back to her place, and we got to talking during the drive. And she invited me in to her house for a bite to eat, and then things just..."

His voice trailed off. He looked out the window. Celia realized Lester was in tears although he was doing everything he could to hide it from her. Once again, this strange crack in the universe she seemed to have slipped into provided a new surprising twist. "You know what?" Celia said, "This is none of my business. I didn't mean to upset you, Mr. Brenneman."

"Lester..."

"Lester," she corrected herself.

"It's not like I didn't want to tell Dante. It's not like I didn't want to live up to my responsibilities. I stood by Mary

Rose all through the time she was in a family way. It was one of those difficult pregnancies, too, with all the gas and the heartburn all the time. Fire in her belly is what Mary Rose called it. That's why she called him Dante, get it?"

"Um..."

"For the inferno! Dante's Inferno. It was some book she read, I reckon, but don't worry. I'd never heard of it either until she told me, and then I went and got a copy, but honestly I couldn't make head nor tail of it. Funny thing is, he turned out to be a whiz with fire. Building them. Maintaining them. It's why he's such a good pitmaster, I suppose. Knows how to get a fire not too hot, not too cool. But just right. This is a talent that very few people have, you ask me."

He was named after flames. That did sort of make sense to Celia, the more she considered it. Then it occurred to her that fire was dangerous, and that if you moved too close, you'd burn.

She had been named after a distant cousin on her mother's side who had the unfortunate luck of dropping dead from an aneurysm just before Celia was born. Now that she thought about it, long-dead Cousin Celia – Cecelia, actually, but Daisy dropped the first letters when she learned the meaning behind the name was 'dim-sighted' or even 'blind'!—Celia knew this cousin had been unmarried, too, a clerk at some office in Manhattan. She had died at her desk, apparently in the middle of filing something—just keeled over, according to the stories Celia had heard, her office-mates looking on in helpless horror as they waited for an ambulance to thread its way through gridlocked mid-town traffic. Her namesake's sudden and sad demise had always bothered Celia as if this would portend something in her own life.

Lester, meanwhile, was talking about Dante and Mary Rose. "Anyway," he was saying, "I wanted to do the right thing by her. And the child."

"You must have tried to, well, fix things," Celia added helpfully, hoping to smooth things over and calm him down.

But Lester was on a roll, the words now tumbling out of his mouth. "Mary Rose made me promise to keep my mouth shut. She said that when she told her mother, it got real ugly real fast. Said she was terrified of what her husband would do to her if he found out. And then of course the child took more after her side of the family. He didn't look Black much at all, 'cept for that curl his hair gets. So we kept it secret. And then Mary Rose died and Mrs. Gibbs took the kid. I should have stood up to her, I suppose. But I was always a little afraid of Mrs. Gibbs."

He snuffled a few times, fished a handkerchief—a surprisingly neat and expertly pressed, precisely-folded white square—from his pocket and blew his nose.

Celia changed the subject. She wouldn't mention Mary Rose or Fionnula Gibbs again.

SOMEHOW, SHE GOT THEM all through the next few days – juggling her work appointments with shuttling Penelope back and forth to school, through feeding chickens and collecting eggs, through nightly calls from Dante to check in, through Roberta's perpetual sour mood about running the smoke house and barbecue shack singlehandedly—and then it came, the event she was vaguely awaiting, anticipating she might even say, but part of her was trying to put out of her mind altogether. Her mother would do it with all her daughters, place a call to each on her birthday at the precise time of their birth. This wasn't so bad for Rosalie (one-fifteen PM) or Bernadette (ten AM on the button!), but Celia, after a particularly long and difficult labor, didn't show up until four-twelve in the morning. "Well," her mother began when Celia picked up the call – at four-twelve exactly – "at least I have one daughter who still has a few good years left."

"Excuse me? What?!"

"Of her thirties, I mean," Daisy added hastily.

Celia considered cutting off the call or at least pulling the pillow over her head and screaming into it. Instead, she said, "I have two years left, actually."

"But you just turned thirty-nine. Didn't you?" Daisy said, suddenly sounding unsure.

"Yeah," said Celia. "But I consider forty the last year of the thirties."

"How on earth do you figure that?"

"The '0' year is the last year of the previous decade. It's a fact. Google it, Mother, if you don't believe me."

"Well," Daisy said, "You've always been good at not seeing what's right under your nose."

"What's that supposed to mean?"

"Nothing, dear. Anyway, I'd say today is the first day of the rest of your life. Just think, next year you will be fabulous at forty." Daisy paused. "But quite honestly, it's not fabulous at all. That's all something made up by the advertising people. Forty's when it all starts to go to hell. Not at first, mind you, but slowly, decrepitude will creep up when you're not paying attention."

"Mom!"

"Take your father, for instance. With the peeing. Or the not peeing and complaining about it . All the time with the complaints. And not just about bathroom issues. Here's a hard truth about getting older—the list of things to complain about gets longer. It just does. Why, with your father, he..."

"Please stop, Mother. Please."

"Well, okay," Daisy said. "But will you come and get me and Lois out of here already?"

"Why? What's wrong with where you are?"

"I told you already—Rosalie and Kim are being quite unpleasant."

"Somehow I doubt that."

"No, they are really getting on our last nerve. I'm not sure how much more I can take it. So you'll come, right, dear?"

As if Celia didn't have enough on her hands. "I'm losing you, Mom. I really must run!"

She made that fake static sound and cut the call off.

She glanced at the time. It was so early. She still could sleep if she wanted, or at least laze in bed and daydream. But that would be impossible now, with her mother's words about aging ringing in her ears. She checked her emails. Barry had sent an e-card, one with dancing dogs meant to make her laugh – and he signed off with how much he couldn't wait to see her later. Her sisters had sent texts. There were some work emails to fire off and a snide birthday message from Bert Pitoniak she deleted.

She pushed a purring Mrs. Whiskerson off her stomach and rose from the sofa, which, days earlier, she had decided would be a more appropriate place to sleep than with Penelope in her bed. In the shower, she took a little extra care, shaving her legs because she'd been meaning to for days, and under her arms.

After her shower, she stood before the mirror and took a long, critical look at the face that stared back. She still could pass for vaguely young-ish, she thought, even more so when she stepped a foot or two away from the mirror, dimmed the light, and squinted. Upon closer inspection, things were not quite so encouraging. She plucked out a strand of gray hair, wrapped it in a piece of toilet paper, and buried it in the trash. She examined lines on her neck and the small creases on her forehead she knew she could erase with a couple of quick injections. She squinted again because it helped to blur and somewhat erase the few extra pounds she still had done nothing about, especially in the last few crazy days when she was too preoccupied to watch calories or even think about what she was putting in her mouth even though she knew that soon she was supposed to be shopping for a wedding dress. She examined her breasts, which seemed to be defying gravity for now, then turned around to assess the status of her ass. There was a plumpness and what seemed to be troubling new dimpling there.

She faced the mirror again. She was, it suddenly dawned on her, older than she'd ever pictured her imaginary alter-ego Lisa. Lisa never got beyond her mid-30's, tops, in Celia's mind.

She didn't expect anything from Penelope or Roberta or Lester Brenneman even though she secretly did – they did know her birthday was approaching because, well, she had mentioned it several times, just in passing of course – so she felt a small sting of disappointment when nobody said a word. Until later, when they got to Belle's Coffee Shop for breakfast. Although it had only been a matter of days, Celia was feeling like a regular, with a favorite seat in a booth at the back and a naughty, irresistible breakfast of flaky biscuits smothered in a rich, creamy sausage gravy (okay, she knew where those extra pounds were coming from). This day, there was a candle in the biscuit, and Belle, in a croaky drawl, led them all in a rendition of the birthday song.

Afterwards, Penelope said goodbye to Lester, who had been cleared by the doctor of any threat of a concussion and was finally allowed to return to his own house. Celia drove him a few miles outside town to what turned out to be a tumble-down shack off the main road. "Can I help you in with your stuff?" she offered because he still had the cane and his small suitcase seemed awfully heavy.

"Well, that'd be nice. 'Course, I have to warn you that I didn't have a chance to tidy up before I left the day that Dante knocked my lights out."

"Oh, well....I'm sure it's just fine."

It wasn't.

She had heard about the types of people who hoard, had seen shows about them on television, but she'd never seen actual evidence (if you discounted her mother's habit of saving old coupons past their expiration date and clothespins – she had jar after jar of them tucked away in strange places for some reason Celia could never fathom—and also enough supermarket twist-ties to last a century). Inside Lester's little house, yellowed newspapers and musty-smelling magazines were piled floor to ceiling in the living room. A narrow pathway led to a recliner, which sat in front of a giant old console TV with an antenna fashioned out of wire hangers and crinkled tin foil. There were more of the same piles of clutter, she could see, in the kitchen and in the bedroom beyond.

"Now, you will not believe this, but I think I just may know where that manual for the Triumph might be."

"Um..."

Lester started to root through one towering pile. He was down near the bottom of it when the upper levels began to teeter and sway in a dangerous way. It looked to Celia like it might just topple over and bury him altogether. Or her.

"Oh, please, you don't have to..."

"Now, honey, it's no trouble at all. Fact is, you never quite know what's gonna turn up that might be useful. Just a few weeks ago, I had a pressing need for an Alligator wrench—not a Monkey wrench, I specifically needed the Alligator—and lo and behold, one turned up under the floorboards of the toilet!"

She couldn't talk him out of his search. She made him at least promise to be careful and keep his phone in his pocket, turned on, just in case. Still, Celia worried about leaving, but Lester insisted he was fine and continued to root through one of the stacks.

So she hit the road again. Earlier that morning, Celia had carefully plotted a route that took her from suburban Alpharetta to Douglasville. She rushed through her appointments, eschewing her usual chit-chat with the nurses and doctors and techs and getting right down to business. Later, with Roberta having promised to fetch Penelope from school and watch her for the early part of the night, Celia headed to Hartsfield International. On the way, she detoured to Phipps Plaza in Buckhead. She didn't want to show up to meet Barry, on this special day, in her drab blue work suit. So she took her time window shopping, although most of the boutiques seemed to carry only the kind of glitzy outfits she'd look ridiculous in: blouses in garish colors way too low cut—these required the kind of cleavage she just did not have no matter the push-up bra—and jeans that would only fit a model, that only looked right if you had very long, skinny legs, a tiny waist, and wore spike stiletto heels, something Celia could never pull off.

Luckily, there was a Nordstrom. She tried on and discarded several pairs of slacks before settling on a pair in black that flattered her hips and flared at the bottom in a sort of daring, carefree way. After further deliberation, she chose a creamy peach pullover cotton sweater that smoothed out the bumps and gave her a streamlined look. She bought new lingerie, too, because she felt like treating herself. Finally, she selected mid-heel slingback pumps in a racy faux snakeskin. After paying for everything, she pulled off the tags and wore her new purchases out of the store, stopping first at a perfume counter, where she spritzed herself with something that had hints of jasmine, and stopping one more time because a cosmetics rep said "I could really make those eyes pop."

"I don't want that raccoon look," Celia said.

"You won't. Promise."

She let the rep have at it. When she was done, Celia, who usually made do with a little mascara and liner, was happy with the results: a little smoky-eyed but not too sultry, and somehow the lady had found a way to practically erase her freckles. In the car, she touched up her lipstick, unclasped her hair, brushed it out, and decided to leave it loose.

At Hartsfield, Celia left the rental in short-term parking. She trotted to the baggage claim where she looked forward to her rendezvous with Barry, wondering what he might have brought as a gift and hoping he hadn't spent too much, but wouldn't it be nice if he had? Maybe he'd handled something to do with the wedding or the honeymoon, another subject they had yet to tackle. His flight had arrived early, she knew, because she had been periodically tracking its progress. Luggage from the flight was already tumbling down the ramp and turning on the carousel, being plucked up by passengers, all of them with that tired, wan, worn-out, half-confused look, eager to get on their way. She recognized Barry's suitcase because he'd taken a tip from some travel magazine years ago and put his initials in red enamel paint on the silver clasp. For years, Celia had been trying to convince Barry never to check bags unless absolutely necessary. But he hated toting his bag around while waiting for a flight and the scramble to shove it in an overhead bin.

She retrieved the bag and set it on the floor, then scanned the area, feeling disoriented. Usually, it was the other way around – passenger present, bag missing. This was something new. Where was Barry? He wasn't over by the concessions stand or the queue for Uber and Lyft pick-ups, with its gaggle of arrivals stabbing at their phones. He wasn't at the information desk. He wasn't at lost luggage, where a group of angry people were yelling back and forth in some foreign language she couldn't identify as a stressed-looking airline rep kept throwing up her hands in frustration.

She looked toward the men's room. Any number of guys going in and out could have been Barry, but it turned out none were. She tried to call. It went straight to voicemail. She sent a text and got nothing back. Was he buying some last-minute gift? Flowers? A card? Was that him outside at the curb, standing next to a long black limousine under a giant mass of red balloons? From this distance, it could have been him. She smiled and started to hustle toward the door, on-ly to stop short when the man was joined by another man in what was clearly a romantic embrace.

The last bag left the carousel. The claim area quickly cleared out in that short, quiet lull between arrivals. Celia began to worry. Had he suddenly become ill? Experienced some kind of attack? Thrown out his back again? Had he been mugged? Then her phone started to chirp, and she saw it was him.

"I'm in baggage. Where are you?" Celia said.

"Now, don't get mad," Barry answered.

"Why would I be mad?"

"Well, because I'm in Florida."

It took her a moment to process this. "What...?"

"I was at JFK. I got there really early. I had already checked my bag and was waiting for the flight. Then Bernice called."

"Bernice? Who's Bernice?"

"Mother's home health aide?"

"I thought her name was Coral."

"Coral quit. There was some kerfuffle about a missing bottle of Galliano. My mother insists she's had it since 1973 or something. Suddenly, she wanted a sip, and it was gone. She's certain Coral boosted it. Bernice is new. I think she's Jamaican. Or is she from Trinidad? Anyway, she thought Mother was having a coronary."

"Oh, God."

"Apparently, she was in terrible pain. She was clutching her chest. She was literally screaming, 'Get Barry, where's my son?' This was in the ambulance on the way to the E.R. I could hear it because that's where Bernice was calling from. The ambulance! I mean, I could hear the siren, too, and the EMTs and all their back and forth. And I guess I sort of panicked. There was a flight leaving for Ft. Lauderdale right at the next gate. They had a bunch of open seats. I jumped on it."

Here she thought she detected a little catch in his voice as if he might just burst into tears.

"Oh, Barry. She didn't...I mean, is she...?"

"She's fine! Turns out it wasn't a heart attack."

"It wasn't....?"

"Nope. It was indigestion. Do you know what she had for lunch?"

"Um, well..."

"She and her girlfriends played cards all morning and then, apparently throwing caution to the wind, decided to have Cuban food. And I don't have to tell you what garlic does to Mother's colon."

In fact, he didn't. Celia knew all about Gloria's colon because nine times out of ten when Gloria would call, she'd get a full report, whether she wanted it or not, about what Gloria had eaten that day and how it affected her tummy, or, worse, specifics about bowel movements, or how Gloria suspected some restaurant might have slipped raw onion or some exotic spice she'd never heard of into her food.

Barry promised he'd get there as soon as he could. Tomorrow maybe? Then he rushed off the phone because Gloria's doctor wanted a word.

Celia felt shell-shocked.

Here it was—her birthday – not the MAJOR one she figured she'd soon be OBSESSING about, but an important one nonetheless because it signaled the end of something—and she was standing in the now-empty baggage claim with nothing but Barry's suitcase. She thought she might cry, just dissolve into a big, noisy mess of tears and blubbering. She had frequently seen people like that in airports and was always put off by them, though, so she held herself together. Numbly, she picked up Barry's suitcase and headed outside. Overhead, gray clouds were rolling in from somewhere south—dark, angry looking clouds—and she thought she detected the distant rumble of thunder. "Oh great," Celia said to nobody in particular. "Rain too? What's next?"

The storm held off until she got back to Hodges Creek and parked the car. Then came a flash of lightning and a crashing rumble of thunder, apparently so close it shook the car. Rain started coming down in sheets. The barbecue shack had already closed, but as always, its aroma lingered, and Celia could smell hickory through her closed windows as she waited for a break in the storm. She was hungry.

It turned out to be one of those strangely unpredictable storms, a drenching deluge one second, the sun poking through a sliver of clouds the next. The instant the break she was hoping for came, she yanked off her new shoes and dashed toward shelter, her feet squishing through a fast-growing river of mud.

Inside, she raced up the stairs. Penelope was at Roberta's. The cat was nowhere in sight, cowering somewhere, no doubt.

Celia was alone.

She thought about calling her mother back to finish the abruptly ended call from the morning. She could try Rosalie or Bernadette. She could already hear the pity in their voices—poor Celia, all by herself on her birthday. That sort of thing would never happen with either of them. Oh, they most likely wouldn't come out and say how sad they thought it was, but she knew they'd hint at it. Who needed that?

She opened the refrigerator. Nothing looked appealing. In the freezer there was ice cream from the drug store in town. She grabbed a spoon and dug in. Butter Pecan, freshly churned. It tasted rich and delicious, the pecans, she knew, grown locally, and the butter and milk from some nearby farm, too. She fought the urge to finish off the entire container, and to ensure she wouldn't after two – all right three or, well, four because it was her birthday – very large spoonfuls, she squeezed in big globs of dish soap, flooded the container with warm soapy water, added the morning's coffee grounds, and buried the container under all the smelly trash in the bin.

She spotted a bottle of bourbon on the kitchen counter. She poured herself a shot and knocked it back. At first, it burned, but then the alcohol sent a pleasant warmth all through her. The storm had passed, but the air felt heavy and thick with humidity. She pulled off her sweater. She poured a second shot. Normally, she wasn't much of a drinker – a glass or two of a nice dry Chardonnay or a Pinot with dinner was the norm, maybe a Margarita or two with Mexican food. She took a third shot—or was it the fourth? – (funny how they didn't burn going down any more)—and plugged in her ear buds, cranking tunes to full blast and dancing to some of her favorites. *Okay, some might call them oldies now, but...well let's not go there*, she thought. She gazed out the window. More clouds gathered overhead, and a dark mist encircled the nearby mountains. Then rain came down again, clacking against the roof in noisy waves. After another slug from the bottle of bourbon itself, she found herself on the kitchen floor. The ceiling moved in undulating circles.

This was alarming.

Celia said, "Uh-oh."

She squeezed her eyes closed. There, that was better. Room no longer spinning. She suddenly felt very tired. Also, the sound of the rain and the occasional rumble of thunder were hypnotic, lulling her into something like sleep.

She wasn't sure how long she was out. At some point, she became aware that she was no longer alone in the house. She heard movement somewhere in another room. Was it the cat? She had one arm on either side, palm down, as if holding the floor in place. Everything felt stable, but she was afraid to open her eyes in case the ceiling started again to swirl and eddy. She heard water, but this sounded like the shower running in the bathroom. That wouldn't be the cat, would it?

Then it was quiet. Until she felt something sharp suddenly stub into her ribs and heard, "Ow! Fuck!"

She became aware of something hovering over her, something that smelled of shampoo, soap and, well, man.

Celia opened her eyes.

Dante, fresh from the shower, a towel around his waist, was on his knees next to her.

"Hi," said Celia, then "Whoa...!"

He hoisted her up into his arms and stood, all in one swift motion that reminded her of being on a roller coaster. She didn't have control of her muscles. She felt like a rag doll, her arms dangling back toward the floor until, with nowhere else to put them, she wrapped them around his neck. His skin felt warm. She got a dizzying, lopsided view of her sweater in the corner of the kitchen where she'd tossed it when she pulled it off. It suddenly occurred to her she was wearing just the new slacks and bra. All she could feel was relief the bra wasn't one of her old ones that was frayed around the edges or, worse, ripped.

"Why are you here?" Celia asked. "You're supposed to be behind bars for two more days."

"I got out on good behavior," Dante said. He started to move with her in his arms.

Somehow, that struck her as funny, that she was so close to an actual criminal. Also, it felt wicked and dangerous. Then she said, "Wait! Where are we going?"

"I can't just leave you passed out on the kitchen floor, can I?"

"Dude, I was so not passed out."

"Uh huh."

"Nope. I was um...you know, resting. Resting my eyes. I am now, and always was, perfectly in control of all my faculties."

Faculties? She started to giggle a little. *Such a strange word.*

"Okay. And where's my kid?"

"She's fine. She's with Roberta. They were giving me some time alone because it's my birthday. She'll bring her back later."

"You know the last time I let Roberta look after her, she let Penny get her nose pierced."

"What? Oh, my God!!"

Dante grinned. "That was a joke. I mean, there was a nose ring, but it was a fake one. It popped right off. In fact, I think it was candy, and she wound up eating it. Or it might have been plastic and she ate it. It's hard to keep track of these things. But they happen and you wind up in the Emergency Room. Which is always fun! So it's your birthday?"

"Uh huh."

"Well, happy birthday then."

"Can you guess how old I am?"

"I'm not good at that. Must be a big one, though, if you felt the need to get hammered."

"I am not hammered!" Unfortunately, these words came out slightly slurred.

"Uh huh. The cat drank all my bourbon?"

"Okay. I had a sip. Or, okay, maybe two."

"Right."

He continued carrying her through the living room and into the bedroom. He carefully set her on the bed. Celia still had her arms clasped around his neck. His skin felt damp from the shower. He smelled of soap, something with eucalyptus and mint. She noticed he had tattoos, two of them. One, on his chest, was what appeared to be flames encircled by small, intricately inked-in boulders. A second, on the inside of a bicep, was a strange symbol she couldn't quite identify even if it seemed familiar. She suddenly realized he was looking at her, puzzled.

"What?" she said.

"Where'd them freckles go?"

"There was a make-up salesperson at the mall. She packed on the concealer and..."

Celia went silent because he had placed an index finger on her cheek. He moved it in a slow gentle circle.

"There they are," he said. "Found 'em!"

His face was inches from hers. Clearly, they didn't provide razors in jail because his scruff had definitely crossed into the territory of beard. He was smiling. Celia smiled back.

Okay, maybe she was still a little drunk – or more than a little—and emboldened, and clearly not thinking straight, because the next thing she knew, she was moving her hands up and down his muscled back. She grabbed the towel and ripped it from his waist. She flung it to the floor. Dante went crimson. He stammered something, but she couldn't quite make out what he was trying to say. He tried to back away. Celia pulled him closer. She mashed her lips into his. He didn't try to stop her now. In fact, they couldn't stop, she knew, as he yanked off her slacks, slid off the brand-new panties, and unhooked her bra. This sort of reckless abandon had only happened once or twice in her life – she assumed it had to do with hormones in both parties, a phenomenon of nature or chemistry, impossible to resist, she figured, and Celia knew all about hormones, didn't she? She was an expert, really, had been to actual hormone school. Soon, they were moving as one, his lips on hers. He softly nibbled on her ear. Then he was at her neck, his beard grazing it, and she held him tighter until something exploded within her, coming in waves, a force that both took her breath away and made her scream.

VI.

Later, Celia would find it remarkable how soundly she slept—a deep, almost coma-like slumber that lasted all the way until she heard a neighbor's rooster crowing at the crack of dawn. As she started to come out of the thick fog, it struck her was that she was naked, and just as she was starting to puzzle that out, she realized there was a body next to her—a warm, hairy one, also unclothed, she determined, when she snuck a peek.

"Oh, my God!"

It all came back in a flood of quick carnal images, and heat rose in her face.

She threw off the covers and leapt out of the bed, for a moment surprising even herself with her agility at such an early hour.

This made Dante stir. He rolled over, a sleepy grin starting to form, and Celia realized she was standing there before him, still stark naked. She grabbed the comforter and wrapped it around her torso.

"Well, hey there," he murmured groggily.

"Shut up! Do not say another word. This did not happen," Celia snapped.

She felt disoriented, unmoored. She scanned the room and tried to figure out simple basics, like where exactly she'd left her clothes. "In fact, now that you're out of jail, I can leave, and you can forget I was ever here."

"Don't think that's likely to happen," Dante said. "In fact, I think I've got a sort of thing for you."

"Ha! You don't even know me!!"

Here, he arched an eyebrow. He grinned again. "I know a little. More than a little, I'd say. I know how you liked it when I put my..."

She cut him off. "Well, you're going to have to forget about that, bub."

She caught a glimpse of her bra lying on the floor near the kitchen. She turned and strode out of the room, attempting a semblance of dignity but realizing that was probably not happening. Nearby were her panties, the new slacks she had bought, now all rumpled and wrinkled, and the sweater. She snatched them all up and dashed into the bathroom, averting her eyes along the way from the sight of Barry's baggage standing in the corner. She sat down on the edge of the tub and rubbed at her temples.

She began to stand and spotted her reflection in the mirror over the sink. Her hair was all disheveled, her make-up streaked. Not a good look. She sank back down. "Oh my God," she said, and then "Oh. My. God!" as another thought flew through her brain: *here I am, this is me—Celia at 39—hungover, naked, and in some strange man's bathroom at dawn. What has happened to my life?!*

Suddenly, the door opened. Dante lumbered right by her and stood before the toilet.

"Excuse me," Celia sputtered, jarred back to the reality of the situation, "but just what do you think you're doing?"

"I gotta pee. Like a friggen horse."

"Oh, my God. You are an animal! A big, hairy, smelly animal!"

She grabbed the first thing she could find—a roll of toilet paper—and hurled it at him. It bounced off his head, then ricocheted into the waste basket.

"Nice shot," Dante said. "Anyway, it's not like you haven't already seen it all." He added a sly wink.

There came a strong steady stream that did, indeed, make Celia think of a horse. She bolted out of the bathroom and slammed the door behind her. Feeling a sort of panic, she started swiping up her things. It was shocking—she'd only been here a few days, and already her stuff seemed to have comfortably nestled into permanent homes as if it all had lived here forever—her phone in its charger on the kitchen counter, her purse and make-up kit on the coffee table next to the sofa, which had been her bed, her suitcase open and on the floor, now mostly unpacked. She started throwing things back into the suitcase, not in that precise and organized way as she usually did, but willy-nilly, like some crazy person, as Dante came out of the bathroom in clean boxers. "I could make coffee," he offered.

"Did I say not to talk? I don't need you talking to me right now. I really, really don't. So just, you know, zip it."

"Or how about some breakfast? I'm pretty damn hungry, now that I think about it. All I got in the pokey was crap they'd microwave from the freezer."

"And yet still he's talking!"

"I could whip up some biscuits. I hear you like Belle's—a whole lot—but mine are better. I use leaf lard, and she uses shortening. Plus, I make my own baking powder, which most people don't do nowadays. Okay, which almost nobody does ever, or hasn't since the advent of packaged baking powder, which came in 1843, in case you were wondering. But home-made baking powder makes a huge difference. And it's so simple. If you want to know how to..."

Celia stopped what she was doing and held up a hand. "Wait," she interrupted, "First of all, who told you I like Belle's biscuits?"

He had to think about it, apparently, because it took a moment for him to answer. "Um. Well, I believe it might have been the sheriff. Although it could have been the deputy. He's a gabby fellow, that one. Every time I'd try to grab a quick snooze, he'd launch into one of his stories, and then, oh boy, I'd be in for a long one."

"Okay," Celia said, "Great. The sheriff or the deputy. And whoever it was had to add, 'a lot?' What did he mean by that, you think? Was it something about my weight? Because, you understand, I was trying to do my business while watching after your child, Lester Brenneman, and his freaking possible concussion. It's not like I had a lot of free time to get to a gym or find a Pilates class in this place, did I?"

"Well..."

"And, seriously? Make your own baking powder? Are you just insane?"

"Actually, the truth..."

"Also, just what is it with this town where everybody has to know everybody's business and then has to comment on it?"

"This from the person who blabbed to the world that my father isn't really my father?"

"Blabbed to the world?!"

"You know what I mean. You added fuel to the fire is all I'm saying."

Celia felt like letting out a scream of frustration. So she did. She screamed. Loud. It felt good. Of course, it also woke up and frightened Penelope, who Roberta had brought back sometime during the night and now cried out from her room.

Dante said, "Be right back."

He trotted down the hall. First, Celia heard Penelope's fear turn to delight at seeing her dad. Then she took advantage of Dante's absence. Celia slipped into her clothes. She grabbed the rest of her things – more scattered clothes. Her phone. Its charger. Her laptop. Its charger. Her makeup kit. Her brush and hair dryer from the bathroom. She shoved it all in her suitcase, scribbled a hasty goodbye note to Penelope, grabbed Barry's bag, and ran.

She was safely inside her rental and in motion when, in the rearview, she caught a glimpse of Dante dashing out of the barn waving his arms. Also, he seemed to be yelling something, but she couldn't make it out. She jammed on the gas and pointed the car toward the road. She wove down the precipitous mountain curves at a speed that made her almost dizzy. It was near where the road flattened out when she noticed Dante was following in his pick-up.

"A chase!" Celia thought, incredulous, but also, she had to admit, somewhat exhilarated because here too was another first.

She pushed the rental harder, screeching around a turn onto the town's main drag, Dante's truck now right on her tail. She raced past the old church, roared by the town square, zoomed past the coffee shop until something out of the corner of her eye standing outside the local bar caught her attention, an unmistakably familiar silhouette – like an image imprinted deep in her brain.

Instinctively, Celia slammed on the brakes. In that same instant, she knew she'd made a mistake, as this was followed by the harsh, grating sound of metal on metal. A powerful jolt propelled her forward.

And then everything went black.

CELIA'S MOTHER SAID, "And they nag at me, my daughters – all three of them, like clucking hens with the nag-nag-nagging—about how *I* drive?"

Celia had her eyes shut tight, but she could hear a whole lot of familiar noises—a doctor being summoned to ICU, stat, the squeaky shuffle of rubber-soled shoes against polished linoleum, a reedy old-lady voice calling 'Nurse! Where is the nurse?' and a cacophony of different beeps and alarms. Also, that overwhelming smell of disinfectant was everywhere.

There was a man's voice close by. It was Dante who said, "Well, ma'am, I'd peg you as a real good driver. A real fine one."

Daisy Bernhart said, "The fact of the matter is, I haven't had an accident in forty years. I have a perfectly clean record. Which is more than I can say for all three of my daughters, I can tell you that."

"I'll just bet you're super careful."

"Indeed. I always signal when I change lanes. I come to a complete stop at intersections. No just rolling through like most people. Do not get me started with those back-up camera thingies. You still have to check your mirrors, I say, and turn your head and look. Back-up camera be damned!"

"Plus all the distractions in new cars these days," Dante added. "Your bluetooth and your Apple Car Play and whatnot. How's all that tech helping anybody, really?"

"Oh," Daisy burbled, "I could not agree more."

With her eyes still closed, Celia said, "What she's leaving out is she ran over her neighbor Lois from across the street and busted her leg. That would count as an accident. Unless you did it on purpose?"

"Oh, pish-tosh," said Daisy. "You'll make your friend think I'm some sort of absolute ditz. I barely tapped Lois. I did not run her over, for goodness sakes. And she is perfectly fine. Or, well, she will be once the cast comes off and she gets done with what her son insists will be a very short stint – barely a few days—in a rehab facility. Although frankly, just between us, people rarely come out of those places unscathed." She lowered her voice to a whisper. "If they come out at all."

Celia pondered whether or not she should open her eyes. Oh, she knew all these sounds and smells from her years visiting doctors, knew exactly where she was. She was in a hospital. Usually, she was just briskly passing through, her sleek black-wheeled case full of samples and swag rolling swiftly behind her, unconcerned with all the actual drama unfolding at every turn—the muffled sob here, the anguished outburst there, the glazed look of utter boredom of the unlucky sitting in waiting areas, anxious for any news—or maybe she was diligently tuning it all out. But here she was on an examining table in the emergency room in Blairsville.

She was terrified.

She could feel some sort of brace around her neck that limited her ability to turn her head to the left or right. She wiggled her toes and moved her hands, just to make sure everything was working the way it should. It seemed to be. Her neck throbbed, and she had a headache. Still with her eyes closed, Celia said, "Okay. Can somebody please tell me what happened?"

"Well," Daisy began, "I had just arrived in town. I was asking directions to try and find you when you came tearing around that corner going way over the speed limit. You know you've always had that sort of lead-foot tendency. Anyway, I do believe you saw me and slammed on the brakes without a thought as to what might be following. Didn't I teach you to ALWAYS be aware of not just what's in front of you, but what's behind you as well because you just never know?"

"I don't recall that," Celia said.

"Well, so much for listening to your mother! Anyway, this nice gentleman rear-ended you. Consider yourself lucky because he says he's not going to sue."

Celia opened her eyes.

There indeed was her mother, perched on a stool next to the bed in a favored old sweater set Celia recognized from her youth, a simple skirt, and a strand of faux pearls around her neck. She was working a Kleenex between her fingers so that it was mostly shreds. Celia suddenly noticed how old her mother's hands looked, bonier, and with age spots. Oh, and Daisy's sweater was on inside out, Celia realized, but didn't mention because she thought it might embarrass her. But she could plainly see the tag sticking up.

On the other side of the bed sat Dante. He seemed to be all in one piece, except for a small scratch on the bridge of his nose that was already scabbing over. "You hit me? Really?" she asked.

"Yep," he answered.

"But you're okay?"

"I'm good," Dante said. "My old tank of a truck is a total wreck. But no worries. It's insured."

Celia tried to sit up just as a doctor stepped into the room and up to the bed. She was a seriously stressed-looking woman, with unruly dark curls, in rumpled green scrubs. "Whoa there, Ms. Bernhart," she said, gently pushing her back. "We want to limit movements as much as we can."

"But I..."

"Now, now...I'm the doctor. And you are one very lucky woman."

"Lucky?!" Celia exclaimed, pointing at Dante as the dangerous aspect of it all was sinking in. "This man could have killed me!"

"Not from what I hear," said the doctor. "I hear he pulled you from the car before it caught fire."

This was news to Celia. "Fire?"

Daisy said, "Oh, it was so exciting, dear. Although very frightening at first, I must say. Just like watching some program on TV. He pulled open that door like it was nothing even though the door itself was a bit mangled, and he dragged you to safety. And then...BOOM! Your car exploded."

Something like a snort came from Celia, and she rolled her eyes at Dante because, for some reason, this just annoyed her. "Seriously, dude? Are you for real? Pulling people from burning wreckage?"

He gave her a little shrug and stared down at his mud-caked boots, but she could detect, through all the scruff, a small smile.

"Please," Celia continued. "That just doesn't happen in real life. So, here's the thing: I'm dreaming, right? This is all some bizarre dream."

Daisy said, "And they all think I'm a bird-brain."

"Or wait," Celia said, "I've got it: I'm having a hallucination? Is that it?" Here she turned back to what *appeared* to be her mother. "I mean, the idea that my mom is sitting here makes no sense. What would you be doing in rural Georgia?"

What appeared to be her mom opened her mouth, and more words came out. "I've been telling you for days," Daisy said, "that Lois and I wanted out from Rosalie and Kim's because they weren't being very nice or hospitable, I might add, but nobody listened to us. When Lois' son – you remember Marvin with the cow-lick? – well, when he came to take her to rehab back near where he lives outside Houston, I packed a few things in a carry-on, and I left. So, no, this is not a dream, sweetheart."

"You what?"

"I bolted. Flew the coop."

"You ran away?"

"You could say that. Although, well, I didn't physically run. I took a car service to LaGuardia, and I bought a ticket and rode on a plane. Next to a very nice young woman who's running for Congress. Against a man who's been accused of doing some very nasty things. Well, no surprise, there is my opinion, and I told her exactly that. So more power to her. Hashtag something or other, right?"

"But...that's nuts, mother. Running off and catching a plane? Who does that? Bernadette and Rosalie must be sick with worry."

"Well, I left notes for both of your sisters. If they care enough, they'll figure out how to find me."

"Notes? Who reads notes anymore? You have to text. We've told you that."

"Oh, pooh."

Her mother folded her arms, smiled, and that was that. Celia knew better than to argue.

Meanwhile, Dante, while absently stroking his beard, put in, "And what was I supposed to do? Leave you in that car to roast like a slab of pig on a spit?"

Celia ignored him. She wasn't convinced she still wasn't stuck in some strange dream. She reached out and pinched her mother's arm. Daisy flinched and let out a yelp. This was, indeed, real flesh and bone.

"Meanwhile," Celia said, "did somebody call Barry? And where is my phone? I have to check in with the office."

"I tried Barry," Daisy answered. "I left a message. But, as to all the things in your car..." She went quiet, like there was bad news she was reluctant to disclose.

"What? You're not going to tell me it all burned up?"

"Well..." Her voice trailed off vaguely. She looked at Dante.

"There really wasn't a whole lot of time before all that leaking gasoline ignited," Dante said.

"Oh my God!"

Her phone? Her laptop? iPad? The loss of everything all at once was almost too much to process. Celia laid her head back on the pillow, closed her eyes tight, and asked for pain meds from the nurse who was just trudging into the room.

SHE LEFT THE EMERGENCY room after only a few more hours, most of it taken up with a dizzying array of insurance paperwork that had to be signed or initialed or needed both initials and signatures. Because the doctor's strict orders were to restrict movements to her neck for at least seventy-two hours, a debate ensued about where to go. Dante offered his house. Daisy accepted. Celia piped in with absolutely not, she and her mother would stay in a hotel. But the only hotel near Hodges Creek, Dante told them, was a motel, and not a nice one at that, what with all the rumors about bedbug infestations and rampant drug activity and prostitution. Plus, Dante added, Penelope had heard about the accident and wanted to see Celia to make sure she was in one piece; she wasn't going to disappoint a child, was she? Plus, all her stuff had burned up, and he could at least furnish basic supplies. When Daisy threatened to get Bernadette and Rosalie on the phone so they could all put in their two cents, Celia, knowing she'd lose the battle, finally gave in.

So she was ferried back to Dante's. This was done in Lester Brenneman's giant old Lincoln Continental, which was a shiny silver, looked jarringly brand new, and was neat as a pin on the inside, nothing like the chaos of his house. Apparently, Dante and Lester had smoothed over their differences, because as soon as they made it back up the long winding mountain road (Lester, chattering with Daisy up front, was being especially slow and careful on the turns to spare Celia), he and Dante disappeared into the barn, their heads together about something, while Celia was put back into Dante's bed (she thought all the pain meds might help her erase all those images of what had happened in this very spot, but Celia, oddly, considering her profession, hardly ever took pharmaceuticals, just didn't have the need for them, and the drug seemed to have the strange opposite effect of making her horny). Anyway, the doctor's orders were for rest. So she was waited on hand and foot by her mother and Penelope, who treated this all like a game, and even Roberta, when she wasn't working at the barbecue shack, seemed anxious to make sure Celia was okay.

The first priority, of course, when she wasn't nodding off because the drugs did indeed make her sleepy, was getting Barry on the phone. Except she hadn't figured out exactly what she was going to say, or how she truly felt about what she'd done, or what she should do about their future.

She had been unfaithful.

She had cheated.

No argument there. Or, well...

Okay, they still weren't married although some might argue it was a common-law marriage, but she had broken an unspoken vow. She had drunk a good bit of that bourbon, she reasoned, so maybe she wasn't entirely to blame, or at least wasn't in control of her emotions, or, well, her senses. Okay, she knew it wasn't fair to blame alcohol. Generally, she was always such a good girl. Well, almost always, and the truth was she usually meant well, and that should count for something, shouldn't it?

But she had been bad.

Then there was this nagging thought: *At my age?* Well, actually, she insisted to herself, she was still in the last two – *yes, TWO, especially if you count the year you're in and why shouldn't you, and I don't care what anybody says*—years of her thirties, and this was something a woman in her thirties might do, wasn't it? Okay, she had to admit, early thirties—very early—would be more likely, when the crazy twenties still hadn't completely worn off, not that her twenties were all that crazy. In fact, they couldn't be described as crazy at all, and suddenly she wondered where all that time had gone, how those years slipped by so fast. Was that what this was all about? A delayed reaction of some kind because she hadn't done enough crazy stuff when she could have gotten away with it, when people would have laughed it off or forgiven her or said 'Well, that's normal' or 'You should hear the crazy stuff I did'?

And then another frightening thought crowded its way into her brain. Were they safe? Did he even use a condom? She had never been one for the pill; she'd feel bloated or suffer wild mood swings, and she'd get so irritable that the smallest annoyance could make her snap. Or just about any food would cause nausea. Or her breasts would feel tender.

Or she'd have to worry about whether or not she might, at some point, have a stroke. She had experimented with the copper IUD but wasn't currently using one. Now, she wondered if she had to consider bigger issues than disloyalty. She'd always been so careful about pregnancy, could recall the day Daisy sat her and her sisters down for a very important, life-altering discussion about what she called female issues. This was directly after Bernadette—ever the trailblazer among the three girls—had gotten her period while on a sleepover at a friend's and was rushed home, sobbing hysterically, certain she was at death's door. Daisy shooed their father out of the house and seated her daughters on the sofa in the living room, Celia, as always, plunked in the middle between Rosalie and Bernadette. Bernadette insisted she knew how babies were made, but Daisy soldiered on for Celia and Rosalie, even consulting a book that featured sketches in black and white that made them all—their mother too—blush. After racing through the basics, Daisy took them all into town for soft-serve, and that was that.

So Celia was always careful, all through high school (as if there were any chance of pregnancy) and college, and then with Barry. She'd only been late once—this was years ago, early in the relationship—and she'd swear she could pinpoint the instant that something had sparked deep down inside. She didn't mention it to anybody, relishing the idea of having a secret, which added spice to an ordinary day. Still, there was a hint of doubt, so Celia, mid-sales route, detoured into the nearest pharmacy. Because for some reason she wanted it all to seem casual and nonchalant—that something potentially momentous, a life altering moment, might not be happening—she tucked an EPT in a basket along with the stuff of ordinary life: toilet paper, dishwashing soap, breath mints. She headed straight into the first restroom she could find, raced into a stall, and after ripping it open with trembling hands, followed the directions on the box.

A second test the following morning confirmed the positive result. Barry had already left the house; she'd tell him over dinner, she figured. Maybe they'd go somewhere special. And then, later that day, she was jolted by cramps, an unfamiliar but severe pain, and somehow, without consulting her OB-GYN or even doing another test, she knew that the baby was gone. In the days that followed, Barry—her mother and sisters too—kept asking why she seemed down, so sad and lethargic. But Celia never said a word, not about the loss, or the sense of utter failure. Now it dawned on her that getting pregnant at her age likely wouldn't be so easy, anyway.

She cut off that thought.

But what about STDs? Had it even occurred to her in her drunken stupor to ask? He was a criminal, after all.

She tried to push these thoughts out of her head as she dealt with the frustrations of waiting for a replacement phone (the absence of her phone made her feel as if she had lost a section of her brain, or a limb, or at least some body part, certainly a form of withdrawal, she thought, and this was before even considering all the information she had stored that might be lost, and oh, the agony of putting it all back together, and why wasn't she better at backing up things when she knew she should be, and what about all those passwords?). In the meantime, she borrowed her mother's. Of course, this one was a basic model, years and years out of date, with no bells and whistles, and between its lousy power and the spotty reception, she was having trouble getting Barry. She did manage, after several tries, to reach Danielle Chan.

Danielle proceeded to lay her off.

This was a first, and like everything about the last few days, it was disorienting. Okay, well, she wasn't technically laid off. But she was told – no, Danielle Chan ordered her was more the way it seemed – to take the time off she had earlier requested but had been denied.

"You seem to be going through – I don't know—a thing," Danielle had said.

"A thing?"

"You seem distracted, Celia, and quite frankly, the company and, more importantly, the HX III patch can't wait for you to sort these issues out. Women of a certain age in desperate need of hormone therapy can't wait, now can they, with their dry, itchy skin, their sluggishness, and their awful, erratic mood swings?"

"Well, no," Celia agreed. "But I'm not going through a thing. I'm good. Great," she added, even if she knew, deep down, she wasn't.

"Take a week. Take two," Danielle insisted. "Because, come to think of it, you do deserve it."

"What about my appointments?"

"Bert Pitoniak can cover your territories," Danielle said.

"But he..."

Before Celia could protest any more, the line went dead. This time, she thought Danielle might have actually hung up on her. She couldn't be sure.

What stuck in Celia's head were the words about Bert covering for her. Part of her hated the idea of him winning because that was sort of how it felt. Another part of her wasn't sure she cared. She was stewing over this still when the phone rang. There was Barry's number on the caller ID. Celia froze, feeling pangs of guilt. Of course, there was no voice mail set on her mother's old phone, so it kept ringing and ringing.

"Hi!" Celia chirped. It was way too bright and perky.

"Hey! Finally!" Barry said. "My God, I've been crazy with worry since I got your mother's message."

More pangs of guilt. He was worried about her. She was a cheat. She almost groaned. Instead, she said, "Oh, no, really, I'm fine. Barely a scratch. How's your mom?"

"Oh. She's great. She even power-walked this morning with Bernice."

"Awesome!" Celia said. There was too much chirpiness again. Barry didn't seem to notice.

"She has something she wants to tell you, but...well, it can wait."

Celia wanted to say, 'I have something I need to tell you, too,' but the words wouldn't come out. Instead, there was a long silence.

"What I was thinking," Barry continued, "is that I'd rent a car, drive up to where you are, and we could head home together."

"Oh. Yes. Good. I'm not supposed to do much moving of my neck for the next couple of days anyway."

"Great. Because Mother wants me to take her up to Gainesville."

"What's in Gainesville?"

"Her sister's kid...my cousin Sabrina? You remember. With the husband and the Ponzi Scheme?"

"Oh yeah," Celia said because she vaguely recalled him talking about it a while back and had hazy memories of Sabrina's long red nails, large breasts, and very small hips. "Whatever happened with that?"

"Well, the Feds couldn't convict him because of lack of evidence or something, but he had to declare bankruptcy. Sabrina left him. They lost the big house with the pool, and she's raising three kids in a tiny little apartment."

"Yikes," Celia said, suddenly imagining herself in a similar situation, knocked up, jobless and alone, and what would she do?

"Anyway, mother promised we'd look in on her. I'll take her up there, and then we could..."

The call suddenly dropped, either on Celia's end or Barry's. She tried hitting redial but got no signal. Part of her was relieved because it meant she could put off making a decision about what to say and how to say it. She called out for her mother but got no response. Hanging heavy in the air just outside her window was the sweet smell of hickory coming from the smoke house. She couldn't remember when she last ate. Suddenly, she was famished.

At first, she moved tentatively; she wasn't sure how her neck would feel, and she was more than a little afraid there would be pain. So she was surprised to find when she hauled herself up to a sitting position that it didn't much hurt. Maybe a little achy at the back of the neck and a little twinge when she turned a certain way. She pulled back the covers.

She noticed a large black and blue mark, like a smudge, on one thigh, just above the knee. She must have hit it on the dashboard. She touched it gingerly. It felt tender and made her wince. She swung her legs around and pushed herself to a standing position. Okay, well, a little woozy, but she was on painkillers. She made her way to the window, passing her reflection in the mirror over the bureau—since her nightgown had burned up with the rental car, she was wearing a weathered T-shirt and a pair of gym shorts Dante had dug from a drawer. She looked disheveled. She pulled the curtains back and peered out. Customers were leaving the barbecue shack, plodding slowly toward their cars with the heavy gait of a post-food orgy. She could see Roberta closing up inside.

Celia made her way out of the bedroom, but nobody was in the kitchen or the living room, or in Penelope's room. She heard metallic clanking coming from below. She headed down the stairs. At the bottom, she found that the old tarp that was covering what appeared to be a vehicle in the corner of the barn lay in a crumpled pile. There indeed was a vehicle. It was a dusty old convertible. She noticed a badge on the hood. *Triumph,* it proclaimed, although right now the word did not seem to apply.

Underneath the car, making that clanking noise, was Dante, on one of those wheeled contraptions, although she could only see him from the waist down, so all she really saw were bare feet, faded torn jeans, and just the hint of contoured belly which made her...

She stopped herself and cleared her throat.

He wheeled himself out from underneath the car. He had a wrench in one hand and was a little sweaty. There were globs of grease on his T-shirt and his nose. An awkward moment passed where neither of them said a word.

"Hey," he finally said. "You supposed to be out of bed?"

"I'm okay. Where's my mom?"

"In town. Lester took her and Penelope to buy you some things."

"Oh," Celia said.

She could only imagine what her mother might choose for her to wear.

He sat up straighter, tugged free the rag tucked into a belt loop, and used it to wipe grease off his nose. He cleared his throat. "So...about what happened..."

"You know what?" Celia began, "How about let's forget it. But—just so you know—I don't do things like that. I don't want you to think I'm that kind of person because I'm not."

"What kind of person would that be, exactly?"

"Well, you know, um, kind of a slutty one. One who has no morals."

"Right. Okay. Well, just so you know, I'm not all that slutty, either," Dante said. "And, just FYI, I do have morals."

"Right. Of course you do."

"You know what I read somewhere once, though?"

"I sense you're going to tell me either way."

"It was that sometimes," Dante continued, "when you meet a person, and you jump into the sack, and you have that fast, furious kind of romp—even if you have a connection that's sort of electric and that will get stuck in your head forever so that you'll think of it at the oddest times—maybe it means what you're really doing is running away from real intimacy. That you fear genuine closeness."

"Oh, brother," Celia said, rolling her eyes.

"What? Too heavy? Too deep from some poor slob who smokes meat all day long?"

"You think I fear real intimacy?"

"Well, Forget all about it? Really? Is that what you want to do?"

Celia said, "I have a lot on my plate right now."

"Right. Mentioned you're getting hitched, didn't you?"

"Well, we haven't set an actual date, but yes, I am engaged to be married."

"Uh huh."

"What is that supposed to mean?"

"Did I say anything?"

"You had a tone. To that 'uh-huh'. What, you don't believe somebody would want to marry me? Is that it?"

"Not what I meant at all. Not in the slightest."

"Then what did you mean?"

"Okay. How long you been with this dude?"

"For your information, Barry is not some random dude. He's a very respected Ear, Nose..."

"Yeah, yeah. And Throat. I got it, I got it. But how long you been together?" Dante asked again.

"What's that have to do with anything?"

"Well, maybe if he really wanted to marry you, you'd be married already."

"How come you're not, if you're such an expert on the subject?"

"I wanted to marry Penny's mom," Dante said. "I asked her several times. Once on bended knee even. But she wouldn't have me." This seemed to bring up a bad memory, or at least a far from happy one. He frowned, examined the wrench in his hand, cleaned bits of grease off it, and set it down.

In the awkward silence, Celia looked away. Her eyes landed on the car. Upon closer inspection, it had a pleasing, sleek shape that suggested motion even though it was standing still. Or at one time it did. It appeared as if it might have once been a shade of red, although it had faded to an orange sort of pink. The fenders were covered with a patina of rust. The convertible top was riddled with rips and tears. She peeked inside at the cockpit. Here was a dusty mess that smelled of mold. She could see protruding wires and lumpy-looking worn leather seats. Genuine wood lining the dash was pitted and cracked. Still, something about it made her smile.

"I wanted something like this once," she mused.

Dante shot her a confused look.

"A convertible. A red convertible. Or, well, I should say somebody I once knew wanted one like it. A friend."

"It was my mom's," Dante said. "I need something to drive since you wrecked my truck and all."

"What? Me?! It wasn't my fault. In fact, if you hadn't been following so close and going so far over the..."

He held up a hand. "Chill out, lady, I was yanking your chain."

She laughed a little. Then it dawned on her. "This is the car Lester told me about. He said he once tried to fix it for Mary Rose."

"Yup," said Dante. "That's true. Anyway, with my truck out of commission, and I'm not exactly flush with cash these days, I thought I'd try and get it up and running instead of letting it sit here gathering dust. What happened to her?"

Now Celia shot him a confused look. "To your friend?" he clarified.

"Oh. Well, actually, she didn't exist. I made her up," Celia said. She had to stop herself from laughing again. "It's a long story. Never mind."

He regarded her for a moment with a crooked smile, his eyes crinkling at the corners. "Okay. I'm just guessing here, but it was you who wanted the convertible?"

"Yup. Something like that." His expression changed to something like bemusement."I know what you're thinking," Celia said.

"What am I thinking then?"

"You're thinking, 'Who is this crazy girl and her imaginary friend?' But it wasn't like that at all really, like I'd talk to her or anything. Well, not out loud anyway. Or, well, most of the time not out loud. It was more like this image I had of my grown-up self, of adult me. Does that make sense?"

"Yup. I had one too. A made-up best bud."

"Seriously? You did?"

"Didn't everybody? Anyway, he was way cooler than me. He rode a Harley. He could talk to girls. I'd trip over my own feet and walk into walls. My grandma made me button my shirt all the way to the top and bought my sneakers at Sears. I was really just a big dork, to be honest."

He frowned at the memory. More silence. This time, gurgling from her stomach filled it. Celia flushed crimson. "You hungry?" Dante asked, suddenly brightening. "Because you sound it. Sound hangry, in fact."

"Actually," Celia said, "I can't remember the last time I ate. I'm starving."

"Come on, then."

He stood, brushing dirt and grit from the floor of the barn off his jeans. She followed him to the barbecue shack, which was now closed. Inside, she waved at Roberta, who had ear buds in and was dancing to some unheard tune as she filled salt shakers and wiped the tops clean with the towel tucked into her waistband.

Celia headed with Dante into the kitchen where a large platter covered in foil sat on the counter. He removed the foil. A rich, meaty, fragrant steam rose from the platter, only stoking her hunger. There were racks of baby back ribs, a mound of pulled pork, and a few sausage links, charred on the outside, really blackened in spots, and bursting from their casings, juices pooling at the bottom of the platter. Not only was Celia's stomach still gurgling, but her mouth actually started to water as Dante fixed her a plate. He set down a rack of the ribs along with a pile of pulled pork and a sausage link. He turned to the stove behind him where something was burbling away in a large cast-iron pot. Out came a spoonful of long-simmered collards. He grabbed a knife and, from a pan over the stove, sliced a hefty hunk of corn bread. From the refrigerator came a serving of creamy slaw. He placed the plate in front of her along with a couple of squeeze bottles of house-made sauce. "This one," Dante said, pointing at one bottle, "is more vinegar based. It's tart, and it's got a peppery kick to it from jalapeno—not too peppery, but take note of that. The other is sweeter and more tomato-based."

"I know. I've tasted all of this."

"No. You tasted Roberta's version. Each pitmaster's will be different. Different nuances and such. Mostly because of the way you tend to the fire and adjust the amount of smoke and the level of heat. You'll see that my food's way better."

"Screw you!" This came from Roberta, who apparently was no longer listening to her music and had heard Dante.

"Anyway," Dante said, "dig in."

Celia picked up a rib, which came away from the bone with barely a touch. The meat, with a dark ring of smoke at the edges, was highly spiced and extremely porky. It seemed to melt in her mouth. "Wow," she managed between bites. "It's really good."

"You think?"

She was downing a forkful of creamy slaw now. "Yes. I do."

"Because I'd been resisting something, but Roberta's been nagging at me about it, and I think now maybe we're finally ready."

"For what?" Celia asked, now cutting into the sausage, which oozed more juices onto the plate. These she soaked up with a chunk of warm cornbread. She briefly wondered if she was making too much of a mess but forgot the thought because everything tasted so delicious and she couldn't stop shoveling food into her mouth.

"For a barbecue competition down in Macon on Saturday. This is pretty much the exact plate I'm going to enter. First prize is ten grand."

Celia would have commented on it, but she was busy savoring the pulled pork, with the little burnt ends of crust mixed in with small chunks of creamy pork fat. She took a sip from the tall glass of iced sweet tea he had set in front of her. "Fact, maybe you could do me a favor," Dante said.

Celia now found herself embarrassed to be actually gnawing on a rib bone in order to get at the last shred of meat that was stubbornly clinging to it. She set the bone down. She dabbed at her lips with a napkin, then started wiping her hands. "A favor? What kind of favor?"

"I have to submit pictures. Of each dish. Plus one of myself. And some of the shack, inside and out. They need to be emailed by the end of the day. I was going to do it the afternoon you showed up, but we know what happened after that."

"Okay. And...?"

"Penelope showed me the pictures you took of her while I was locked up."

"Oh! Well, those?"

"Yeah."

"Honestly," Celia said, "we were just goofing off. I only started taking them because I had to bargain with her into changing into actual clothes for school."

"Otherwise she was insisting on going in her pj's?" Dante asked, smiling.

"She's done that before?"

"Um...yeah. Like eight days out of ten? It's either pj's or some old Halloween costume she digs out of the closet. Welcome to the daily joys of being a parent, I suppose. Everything is a battle. Fun never stops!"

Celia smiled, remembering similar little wars with her own mother.

"Anyway," Dante continued, "the pictures are really good, actually. I feel like you captured something about the kid. Her personality seems to come through in a way that it doesn't when I take her picture."

Somehow, during those few days when Celia had been in charge, it became a morning ritual. It helped that Penelope was a big ham. She loved posing for the camera. Celia wondered if acting was in the girl's future, or maybe directing, as she had an instinct for how a shot should be framed. She hoped there would always be somebody to encourage her.

Celia would snap off a few shots before they left the house. Then one morning, on a whim, she took the camera with her, first to breakfast at Belle's, and then when she and Lester headed out on her route of sales calls. She took a few pictures inside the coffee shop, of an intensely focused Belle balancing a tray full of breakfasts in one hand while pouring coffee with another, of Miss Nedra and her wheezy old dachshund almost nose to nose – or nose to snout – looking as if they were deep in heavy conversation over bowls of steaming grits.

There was one photograph she actually did find interesting. The image had been captured in a doctor's office outside Atlanta. Celia had finished up her sales call quickly and was heading back to the waiting room. She spotted Lester Brenneman, his chin resting against his cane, looking fast asleep, surrounded by a bevy of chatting blondes awaiting appointments for Botox or hormones or both. Something about the scene struck Celia, Lester at dead center, the chatty women in orbit around him. She got the picture before anybody noticed. She liked it even more when she later switched over from color to a black and white filter because it emphasized and deepened the contrasts. It made her smile, as did a few others she'd taken through the day. She'd point and shoot and then move on to the next, and then she'd amuse herself later, in a quiet moment after Penelope was asleep, scanning through the pictures to see if she caught anything decent.

Now Celia said to Dante, "Look, it's not like I'm a professional. Not even remotely close. I mean, years ago, yes, when I was a kid, and then again in college, I was interested in photography."

"Yeah? So what happened with that?"

"It was a long time ago."

"And...?"

"And I gave it a try. I dabbled in it. Then I...well, I just moved on, I guess."

"Maybe it's time you took it up again."

"I wouldn't want to screw things up for you. This sounds too important."

"I'll take my chances. Hey, and in the end, the competition's about the food, not the pictures. Plus, I don't have time to hunt anybody down. Like I said, they're due today."

"Well, I'll think about it."

He smiled. "So you want to finish?"

"Um, eating?"

"Our talk. About what happened. What if I have something more to say?"

Celia took a big bite of cornbread. She wasn't ready to talk about it because she wasn't sure how she felt. And she figured she couldn't answer with her mouth full. That wouldn't be polite.

THE FOLLOWING MORNING, Celia hired the one local cab (no Uber or Lyft in Hodges Creek. Not yet, anyway). This was an ancient dented Chevy Impala, which was owned and driven, rather recklessly it turned out, by a suddenly chatty Miss Nedra, with her dachshund riding shotgun, so Celia and her mother had to sit in back where the floor was littered with crumpled 3 Musketeers wrappers and crushed cans of Yoohoo. The cab, which also carried the odd, competing odors of wet dog and menthol cough drops, was taking them into Blairsville because Celia had to return all the clothes her mother had purchased. The slacks, for instance, practically slid off her waist and were a good three inches too long. The blouses were just, well, wrong. Daisy had selected one in gingham that made Celia look like somebody's grandmother. The other top was all lace and frills with a big bow at the neck. Worse was that both hung on her like old sacks. An exasperated Celia had protested, "Did you really think I was going to wear these?" and "How big do you think I am, mother?"

"Well, I just wanted to be sure they would fit, dear. I can always alter them, of course. And as for the blouses, I think they're adorable."

Celia knew better than to argue. She and her mother had been having fights like this for as long as she could remember, her mom bringing home outfits for her and her sisters and Celia and Bernadette and Rosalie rolling their eyes or, worse, throwing tantrums and refusing to wear them until their grumbling father would tell them all to pipe down already and work it out. Would the situation ever change, Celia sometimes wondered, or was this another of those annoying looping arguments that mothers and daughters would have for eternity?

The boutique – somewhat funky for a small, conservative town in the South – didn't have the most extensive selection, but Celia managed to find a pair of jeans that fit through the hips and tapered slightly at the ankles, and a couple of cute simple tops, a pink scoop-neck, and another in a jazzy shade of red.

Done with clothes shopping, they headed back to Hodges Creek, settling in to one of the weathered red booths at Belle's for lunch. They ordered cheeseburgers and Cherry Cokes, and while they were waiting for the food, Celia said, "Something's been bothering me." She thought she detected an eye-roll from her mother, but pushed on. "Why did you and Daddy always refer to me as 'the middle one'?"

"What on earth are you talking about?" asked Daisy.

"I was telling Penelope a bedtime story a couple of days ago, and I remembered this one Daddy used to tell me and

Rosalie and Bernadette. In the story, we were all princesses, and you were the Queen."

"Wait," Daisy interjected, "I was the Queen?"

"Yes."

"Ha!"

"Why is that funny?"

"Well, I can't remember the last time your father treated me like a queen. Maybe when we were first dating, I guess. When he was trying to impress me the way men do, pretending they know all the answers and paying for every little thing and holding doors open and being all polite and never burping in front of you. But years later? And I mean, really—Queen of what, I'd be afraid to ask."

"Anyway," Celia continued, "he said Bernadette was Princess such-and-such and Rosalie was Princess this-or-that and I was always just 'the middle one.'"

"Oh, for goodness sakes, sweetie. How on earth would I know what your father meant by that? Most likely he was just distracted by work or being lazy about coming up with some interesting name."

"Well, you were married to him for thirty-something years, so I thought you might have some insight."

"Yeah, well. He said all sorts of things that didn't make sense if you want to know the truth."

"Is that how you thought of me, too? Oh, she's just the middle one?"

"Don't be silly, Celia."

"I'm not. I just would like to know if my own mother thinks I'm a big bore. A big zero. A loser."

Daisy clearly wanted to change the subject. She said, "A more important question might be what you're planning on telling your fiancé?"

"About what?"

"Really, do I have to spell it out?"

"Yes."

"Okay, for starters, let's talk about your neck. There is clearly bruising of some kind there—like an abrasion—and your new friend appears to have a pretty thick beard. Hmm-mmm. What could that possibly mean? However, I must add that there was a time your father grew a beard. It was a stage of course—starting with just a mustache—a slightly strange one for him, and like all of his stages it passed. But I walked around for months with all sorts of burns and grazes on my neck. Really, it was quite embarrassing. Although, I'll admit there is something sexy about a beard."

"There is," Belle echoed as she dropped down their Cokes, which came in tall, frosty glasses filled to the top with cracked ice. "Always beware of a man with a beard. T.R.O.U.B.L.E. I'm just saying. Food'll be up in a jiff!"

Belle flitted off. Celia felt her cheeks beginning to flush. She started to sputter a response to her mother.

"Oh, don't bother with some excuse. I could tell the minute I saw him looking at you in the hospital. I may be ancient, but I can remember that look men get."

"Really? What look is that?"

"That hungry 'I want to rip your clothes off' look. I remember it well. I was young once, too, you know."

"Okay. I think we're venturing into too much information territory."

"So you're not denying it?"

"What happened between us...it was a mistake," Celia insisted. "It won't happen again."

"So you're going on with the wedding plans?"

"What? You think I should call it off?"

"I'm not going to tell you what to do, Celia. You're a big girl. You're not an infant."

But her mother said this in a clipped, mincing way that made Celia feel as if she were five, and it annoyed her to no end.

"Well, maybe it's the tone you're taking."

"What does that mean?"

"You don't approve of Barry. You never have. Why don't you just say so."

"That's crazy. I adore Barry. It's just...well, never mind."

"What?"

"Well, you never really explored other options."

"What other options?"

"I mean, you know, played the field."

"You're saying I should have had more hit and runs? Hooked up like the kids all do now? Swiping this way or that way on Tinder? Like that? Have a bunch of Friends with Benefits. Or just, maybe an F-bud who texts me randomly asking if I'm horny or I'm naked? Been more, well, slutty?"

Now Daisy started sputtering. Flustering her mother was part of the plan, so inwardly Celia smiled. "Talk about too much information," Daisy finally managed.

"Well, you started it!"

"And that's not what I meant at all," Daisy said. "I mean there's a difference between having a few boyfriends, or even lovers if you'd prefer that, and being a slut, which is just a horrible word anyway, and never a fair one because you never hear of a man being referred to as a slut, do you? Maybe it's time that changed already. I mean, it takes two, doesn't it? Anyway, I just always got the sense you fell into this thing with Barry, and quite frankly, it seems like you're in a rut – that you have been for a while—and you're not even married. Ruts are for married couples, dear. Couples that have been married forever. So if you ask me – and your sisters and I have discussed this – you're going about the whole thing in a backwards sort of way."

"Great. I'm sure you and Bernadette and Rosalie all have had a fine time dissecting my life when I'm not around to defend myself."

"Oh, get real, Celia, we do it around you, too. Right in your face!"

"Did you and dad get into a rut?"

"Of course we did. Every couple does. It wouldn't be natural not to. Everything about life becomes something of a rut if you want to know the truth. You turn around, and before you know it, life seems like nothing but loading the dishwasher and emptying the dishwasher, and moving the trash bins to the curb one day and then dragging them back the next, and trying to keep track of all your stuff and, my God, all those horrid passwords, and trying to keep things clean and organized, although that's a losing battle, let me tell you. But, anyway, what isn't natural is being in a rut from the get-go. That would be an issue. Because it leaves you with nowhere to go."

Celia was quiet a moment. She looked away from her mother, out the window at traffic lazily drifting past the diner, at people in town going about their business—popping into the drugstore or feeding the meter with quarters—while her own life seemed to unravel at an unnervingly rapid rate. Had she been in a rut with Barry from the start? They were always comfortable with each other as if they had known each other forever. Should that have been some sort of warning sign, too? She was thinking this over when her mother proceeded to get on her nerves about another subject. "And then, you know, it's the same with your work."

"Now there's something wrong with my work too?"

"Well, since you mention it, honey..."

Celia had to interrupt: "I *didn't* mention it. You just did."

"Right. Whatever! Anyway, it always seemed to me like you just drifted into your job. Just sort of fell into it. And now how many years have passed?"

"Oh, my God..."

"And do you ever stop to think about the ethics of it all?"

"Mother, what are you talking about?"

"For starters, since when are women my age supposed to have the sex drives of teenagers? What if we're just all done with that part of our lives and we're okay with that? You know, we can look back on it and maybe even smile a little if we were a bit wild here or there, but it's just in the past. But no, you make us feel like we're some kind of failures if we're not attracting hot mature men – or even better, some studly young thing – and jumping into bed with them at the drop of a hat. As if we might not break something, or pull a muscle. Or have a stroke. Older—or more mature I should say—people should not be jumping in or out of anything if you ask me. It's a recipe for disaster."

"Hell-to-the-yeah," said Belle, who had arrived with their order—nicely charred burgers smothered in grilled onions and melted American cheese, with pickle chips and pert squiggles of ketchup and mustard on top, all on buttered, grilled buns. A tangled pile of crisp, well-salted fries were on the side. "You tell her, hon!"

Daisy was delighted to have an ally, which only encouraged her. She tipped her face up toward Belle. "I'm right, aren't I?" she asked. "Is it so awful to just want to wash your hands of all that sex business at some point? Just be all done with it?"

"Amen, sister," said Belle. "I mean, naturally I was sad when my Ernest passed, but on the other hand, having the bed – heck, having the whole house *and* the bathroom, which is probably the best part—to myself was sort of a blessing."

"It's not just husbands who hog the bed, either!"

This had come from Ms. Nedra, who had taken a booth at Belle's for coffee and a peach fritter while waiting to ferry Celia and Daisy back home. "This one," she continued, pointing a finger dusted with powdered sugar at her old dachshund, "practically sleeps right on top of me. You would never think such a small dog could take up so much room, but half the time I'm falling off the bed, have just this little teeny corner of space. As long as he's comfortable, I'll deal with it, though. On the other hand, his issues with flatulence..."

"Oh, don't get me started with Ernest," Belle threw in. "Sometimes I'd consider sleeping in a gas mask. Or in another room entirely!"

Celia, mortified at the whole conversation, waited for Belle to hustle back to the kitchen and Ms. Nedra to go back to her fritter before she said to her mom, "Whoever even broached the idea of you jumping into bed and having sex with anybody?"

"Oh, come on, Celia," Daisy said, "have you not seen the ads for the very same products you're pushing on vulnerable, unsuspecting people? From the very company you work for? You know exactly what I'm talking about. They tell us—with the silliest of images I might add—old folks walking on a beach actually smiling at each other and holding hands for god's sakes—tell us to reignite our sex lives and never mind about the possible tumor that might show up or whatever other horrible side effect might kill us. Or they tell you in a bunch of gobbledigook at the end, speaking so fast that who can possibly fathom what they're saying? And fat chance any man will look at a woman like me..."

Celia attempted to interrupt, but her mother was on a roll.

"...At the supermarket, for instance. I mean, for goodness sakes I've turned into that lady who gets excited when she gets to use a coupon for Metamucil! Or I'm stocking up on the high-fiber cereal where you might as well be choking down shredded cardboard, but it helps you poop, so you put up with it. What man is going to be interested in all that? But that's the reality, dear. And to be honest, at this stage of the game, I have to say that most of the time when I'm in bed, I'd just rather read a good book."

"First of all," Celia said, "okay, fine, maybe I kind of did 'fall into this job.' But I've worked hard for a really long time to get where I am."

"Just where are you then?"

Celia gaped at her mother with blank astonishment. She opened her mouth. Nothing came out. Suddenly, she wasn't sure the answer to what did seem like the simplest question, so she nudged the argument in a new direction. "How about this? Where were you when I needed you?" she asked.

"Meaning?" Daisy managed with a mouth full of cheeseburger, burger juices dripping down her arm.

"Meaning maybe when I needed encouragement. All I remember is you with the 'Get a nursing degree, Celia', or 'Brush up on your tech skills'. Always with the 'something to fall back on.' It was as if you never believed I had the talent for anything else or the grit to follow a dream."

Daisy dabbed at her arm with a napkin. "Oh, so it's my fault? Why is it always the parents' fault when something goes wrong in a child's life? Besides, I'm your mother. You're not supposed to listen to me. Not one word that I say. You're supposed to go off and do whatever you want regardless of what I might think while I sit back and worry myself to death." Here she took her napkin and wiped some grease off Celia's chin.

"Right on, Sugar, right on!" said Belle, who had come back to refill their drinks. "Like my little Ernest Jr.," she clucked, "Always blaming me when everything goes wrong, which for Little Ernest it often does. Why that boy can't get his life together is one of those little mysteries I'll never understand. But it's always momma's fault, isn't it?"

"Yes, indeed it is," Daisy answered, and then had something else to add, but Celia didn't hear it as, suddenly, she felt she couldn't breathe, needed air, and was already headed for the exit.

Outside, she paced the sidewalk in front of the diner, her mother's words ringing in her head—where exactly was she in her life? Suddenly, she wasn't sure of anything. She felt adrift, like that time when she was a kid at camp; a lake was a central part of camp life, so they were always boating or swimming or diving off a board built on a raft. On one outing, Celia had tumbled from a canoe. She flailed for something to grab onto and found nothing. She felt panicked in those seconds, utterly and terrifyingly alone, until rescue came from the strong arms of a counselor, who plucked her from the water and placed her safely back in the boat. Then, as she sat in Miss Nedra's cab to wait for the ride back up the mountain, she remembered something she had once heard—from where, she couldn't remember. But it was about spotting opportunity and then jumping on it without thinking, without too much analyzing—it was really about instinct and trusting your gut—otherwise, that chance might just forever slip from your grasp.

A SHORT TIME LATER, Celia found Dante out behind the barbecue shack. He was splitting logs, the ax arcing down and striking its target with a loud crack that echoed off the nearby mountain. When he paused to add the fresh-cut log to an ever-growing pile and brush wood shavings off his jeans, she said, "Okay. Let's do it."

"What? Now? Right here? I mean, that is kind of kinky, but, why not?" He started to pull his T-shirt over his head.

"No! What are you doing? Stop!"

"Okay, I can leave the shirt on. It's all good. Jeans off, though? Socks, too? Because I've met women who've been into socks-on for some reason I've never sussed out. Sometimes boots, too. Which is for sure some sort of fetish."

"Shut up! I meant I'll take some pictures like you asked. Jesus. You can be a real chatterbox, you know that?"

The last words she threw over her shoulder as she stalked off and returned to the house. She grabbed the camera from Penelope's room. Having it in her hands suddenly seemed like the most natural thing in the world, and briefly she wondered about the meaning of it, as if the urge to explore this territory had in fact always been there, like it was years ago, but had laid dormant, waiting for her to catch up. She thought of the crocus bulbs her mother religiously planted every fall and the springtime blooms that erupted in a welcome riot of color so many months later. Is that what it was like? Having patience to see something through?

Dante was waiting in the kitchen. For a moment, Celia eyed him critically. "What?" he said, clearly sensing disapproval.

"Well," Celia began, "you're going to be in some of these pictures, I'm thinking."

"Okay. And?"

"For starters, that T-shirt is filthy. So are the jeans. Also, your beard and your hair are a mess. Your fingernails are just gross. And you're covered in sawdust."

Dante inspected his hands and smiled sheepishly. "I've been working. Before splitting that big pile of logs, I had to shimmy under the Triumph to pry out the oil pan. I don't work behind a desk, remember. I get grubby."

"Well, go clean yourself up."

"Aw, c'mon," Dante protested. "Do I have to?"

For a moment, they seemed at loggerheads. It struck her that through her whole life, Celia would be the one to cave. She'd have an idea or she'd make a suggestion about something, and the person she was trying to help would put up a protest. Celia would let it drop. Maybe the idea wasn't really good, she'd worry, or maybe the other person would like her more if she didn't push. But now, she didn't feel like ceding territory. Celia said, "If you want me to do this, I'm in charge. I will make the decisions."

She grabbed his hand and marched him down the hall. She ordered him into the shower. While he was in there, she took a look in his closet. It was, as expected, a chaotic jumble—T-shirts and sweats wadded into bundles on one shelf, jeans and shorts shoved into another, boots, shoes, and sneakers in a willy-nilly pile on the floor. She found what appeared to be a clean button-down plaid flannel shirt on a hanger and a pair of jeans that smelled of fresh laundry. Dante emerged from the bathroom in a haze of steam, a towel cinched at his waist, slick as a wet seal, his hair shining, and his beard trimmed. Celia tossed him the fresh clothes and said she'd wait back in the restaurant. When he joined her, he shifted from one foot to the other, unsure where to put his hands. "What do I do?" he asked. "Where do we begin?"

Celia wasn't sure, either. Truth was, she didn't have a clue about what she was doing. She felt awkward, too aware of how she might look, as if she was an actor playing a part but hadn't learned the script. "Well," she said, "let's keep it simple. Why don't you start with the beginning of the process. We can try to turn this into a series so it sort of tells a story. Beginning. Middle. End. How does that sound? That seems okay, doesn't it?"

Dante nodded. "Yeah. Right on."

He reached for the big battered stainless steel bowl. He grabbed canisters from shelves. He started filling the bowl with his secret blend of spices (he was apparently far more trusting than the overly suspicious Roberta, Celia thought, as he didn't make her turn and face the wall while he mixed it up). She started snapping off shots. She put her squeamishness aside and photographed him as he carried a large hunk of carcass from the walk-in. He sharpened a cleaver and then a couple of knives and then broke down the slab into smaller pieces. She caught his face, his brow furrowed in concentration as he made precise cuts. She moved in tighter for close-ups of his hands as they massaged the blend into the various pieces of meat. She began to remember technical things she learned long ago about shading and light and shadow, and so she began manipulating those elements. At one point, she paused and dragged an old white sheet out of Dante's closet and used it as a backdrop for some shots. For others, she enlisted Penelope to hold an umbrella just so.

Celia followed him to the smoke house. She stopped along the way to capture what seemed a wry composition of the ax now angled into a tree stump surrounded by the freshly cut stack of hickory. Turning the camera toward the smokehouse door, she snapped something moody, wisps of smoke slowly curling out through a jagged crack, drifting lazily up into deep blue sky.

Inside, as Dante explained the ins and outs of tending his fire and the low, very slow process of smoking the meat, she photographed different cuts at various stages. She thought about her own experience with what she thought was bar-becue but learned was actually just grilling – there was only one, a time she and Barry had selected a gas grill for the yard and threw on some chicken, which they proceeded to tinker and fuss with so much it wound up overcooked, turning into something resembling shoe leather.

Back in the kitchen, she was preparing to set up a shot when Dante snatched the camera from her hands. Celia tried to grab it back, but he pointed the lens at her and started firing off shots. For as long as she could remember, Celia hated being the subject of photos. She looked chubby. Or too short. Or her hair was just wrong. Or her sisters out-shined her. She tried to grab the camera back. He kept elud-ing her with fakes and dodges. She'd grab at his arm, and the coarse hair running its length would brush against hers, and she knew from the jolt she'd feel deep inside that she might be moving into dangerous territory. So she backed off and let him take some pictures. Later, when she was alone, she studied them. There she was, with no make-up and her freckles exposed, her hair pulled back and tied in a simple ponytail, in jeans and that vivid red scoop-neck top she had picked up in town. She almost didn't recognize the smile, and what seemed like athleticism long missing from her life, as she tried to lunge for and catch the dodging Dante. In fact, she thought, she looked younger, as if using the camera was somehow turning back time—hurtling her backward toward her college years.

By the end of the day, she had photographed finished racks of ribs, piles of pulled pork, squares of cornbread, the simmering pot of collards, and a fresh batch of slaw. She had taken several of the outside of the shack—of the long porch with its rickety chairs and oil-cloth topped tables—and once it opened, a few of happy diners digging into the food.

Dante and Roberta were cleaning up after the place closed when Celia realized one piece of the puzzle was missing. "But what about dessert?" she asked.

"What about it?"

"Didn't you say you needed to serve one? What do I photograph?"

"Oh, crap."

"Why don't you have dessert here, anyway?"

"I've only asked that same question, like, one gazillion times," said Roberta. "Folks want dessert. They crave something sweet at the end of the meal. They expect it. I've even shown him Instagrams and blog posts and tried to get him to listen to all the pods where people lament the fact that we don't have one. Just go on and on about that very fact."

"They can go into town and get ice cream at the drug store. That should suit them perfectly fine if you ask me."

"Now, that's the kind of attitude that's not going to win us any awards," Roberta insisted. "You have got to give customers what they want, don't you agree?" She addressed this to Celia. "I mean, you're a salesperson. You know all about marketing, I presume. What happens when you don't give customers just what they want."

"She's right," Celia said. "They go find it somewhere else."

Dante grumbled.

He went to check the rules of the competition. Indeed, dessert was a requirement, he told them, when he came back. Then he appeared to sulk, hands shoved into his pockets, eyes cast to the floor. Celia, without really thinking it through, said, "My mother makes a pretty good coconut cake."

He looked up at her.

"The icing is amazing, actually."

"Is it really?"

"If you must know, I occasionally have dreams about it."

"Dirty dreams?"

This got Roberta's attention. She tilted her head at Celia.

"Shut up. Filthy minds. Both of you."

Dante said, "Well, it must be good, then."

"Yep. I bet she could whip up a cake in no time if you ask her nicely."

"Oh, I couldn't do that. I barely know her."

"I can ask if you want."

"Okay," Dante said. "That would be good."

Together, they headed inside where they found Daisy, perched on the sofa, a book open in her lap, reading to Penelope, who was nestled under an arm. Already, she seemed to have fallen into a grandmotherly role with the child, who seemed to crave this sort of attention; Celia briefly wondered whether this was a positive development. Then, when she brought up the idea of making a cake, Daisy instantly put up a protest. "Well, dear, I don't have my recipe. How could I possibly?"

"Mother, how many times have you made that cake over the years? You know it by heart, I'm sure."

"Baking is a very exact science, Celia. You would have no idea about that, of course."

"Meaning..."

"Nothing. Goodness gracious, you're so touchy these days. What do the kids say? Chill out! You just hardly bake at all is what I meant. Or, really, ever. You always were too busy. You and your sisters. But if you ask me, the truth is you do sort of seem to look down your nose at such things. The economics of running a home, I mean. It's not so easy, you know. It looks easy, effortless if you know what you're doing, but it's not."

"I do not look down my nose at anything you do," Celia protested.

"Of course, it never stopped you from tasting the fruits of all *my* labor."

"Are we now circling back to my weight?"

"I never mentioned a word about a weight gain. Again, you take things way too personally."

Celia knew exactly what was going on here. Her mother was still peeved that she had ditched her at lunch. She wondered how long this snit would last, wondered when it would pass and her mother's mood would change for the better. That's when her eyes settled on Fionnula's cookbook, which had found a new home on the kitchen counter where it had sat since its arrival. She picked up the book that long ago had belonged to Dante's grandmother and was again surprised at its heft. She flipped to the index and scanned it. Not only was there a recipe on page four hundred and fifteen for the somewhat curiously named Aunt Dan's Delightful Coconut Cake Supreme, but when Celia turned to the page, there was a message. She held up the book and pointed it out to Dante, who had joined them. "*Mary Rose loved. Definitely make again*" was written in the margin next to the recipe in bright red ink and then underlined twice.

"Well," Dante said, "hmmmmm." He traced a finger over the letters his grandmother had scribbled so many years earlier.

"Some might take that as a kind of sign," Celia added.

"I suppose," Dante mumbled. "Maybe."

He didn't seem convinced. She handed the book to her mother. Daisy glanced at the recipe but kept her mouth clamped shut. Celia said, "If I offer to help, will you make the cake?"

Now Daisy folded her arms across her chest. "By help, do you mean waiting until I'm done doing all the hard work and licking the bowl? Because that's really no help at all."

"C'mon, Mom."

"I'm a little tired, quite frankly. I am getting old, you know."

"Really, mother? Seriously?"

Celia could see the corners of Daisy's mouth curling up into a smile as if this had been one more battle in some endless line of little wars that had begun when Celia was born, and she had notched a small, if temporary, victory. Daisy turned to Penelope and said, "We could use an assistant cake baker. I wonder who we could get?"

"Me! Me!" Penelope shrieked.

Daisy laughed, took Penelope's hand, and led her into the kitchen. She began an inventory of ingredients and soon sent Dante into town for shredded coconut, insisting that he make sure it was fresh - *'you must check the date!'* - or it would taste like sawdust. Celia used the few free moments to log onto his laptop. She was certain – absolutely one hundred percent sure of it – that her emails would have been piling up like crazy. She sat at his desk, and in an instant, Mrs. Whiskerson appeared out of nowhere and leapt silently into her lap. She absently stroked the purring cat's chin while the computer booted up.

She waited with a strange combination of eager anticipation and dread. But there was no pileup of unread mail. It was a little shocking; word of her hiatus seemed to have spread so that she was no longer important. There was, however, the typical onslaught of spam, numerous messages from Rosalie and Bernadette, all with the subject line in FULL CAPS with way too many !!!!!!!!!!'s demanding information about their AWOL mother, and a lone note from Sonya wondering how she was doing, heavy on grinning emojis. Celia sent back something a bit too cheery. She assured her sisters that their mother, despite the nuttiness of running away, was safe and sound and would be back home shortly.

But where were her clients checking in? It was as if all those years of hard work and toil for the company had vanished into the ether. She had to wonder: she was at the top of her field. She had won awards for her sales, had them lined up on a shelf behind her desk. Junior reps looked up to her and tried to emulate her results. What would happen if that was suddenly gone? Should it bother her that, deep down, it didn't seem to matter?

She tried Barry's cell. It went straight to voicemail. "Hey," she said, "Where are you? Well, okay, I just wanted to check in. Call me."

She stood, sending the cat skittering to the floor and scabbering away. She joined her mother and Penelope in the kitchen. Penelope was perched on a stool. She watched as Daisy measured out dry ingredients and handed them over, cup by cup for the flour, then teaspoon by teaspoon for the salt and baking powder ("*He makes his own!*" Daisy marveled). Penelope stirred them with a whisk in a big bowl set before her on the counter. Then Daisy flicked on the mixer and began to cream together butter and sugar. "Nobody misses me, it seems," Celia said as Daisy handed her eggs and told her to crack them gently into a bowl.

"What, dear?"

"At work. It's like I might as well be dead or something."

"That's a little dramatic, Celia."

"I've been gone from the office a week. I was in an accident, what could have been a really bad accident, actually, when you think about the fire and all that. Is it too much to ask that people at least check in?"

"Oh. Well, you know how that goes."

"How what goes?"

"You leave a job, and everybody promises to stay in touch, but after a couple of lunches and phone calls, and maybe a card for a year or two at holiday time, that's that."

"How do you know? You stayed home."

"I had jobs before I married your father, Celia. I had a life. After, even. It was when I got pregnant with Bernadette that I stopped working. Outside the home. Don't you start in on trying to tell me raising three daughters wasn't work because it most certainly was. Still is. More than you'll know until you have daughters of your own. And why is it, can you tell me, that children don't realize their parents had lives before they came along? Because they did!"

"Okay. Fine. But I didn't leave my job."

"Right. You were suspended or whatever. Maybe people think you're not coming back, so they're just writing you off. You know people are busy. They get all caught up in their own lives, and it's just not worth the effort."

"Nice. Thanks, Mom."

Celia had finished cracking the eggs into the bowl. She reached for a fork and was about to start beating them but a loud "NO!" from her mother and she froze, the fork stuck in mid-air just above the bowl.

"What?"

"Oh, for Goodness sakes, Celia. Really," Daisy said.

"What did I do?"

"Don't beat the eggs."

"No?"

"No! Have you ever paid attention when I'm baking? Ever?"

"Um..."

"They get added, one at a time. Slowly. We're not scrambling them. I'll let you know when we're ready. Put the fork down. Step away from the bowl."

"Okay, okay."

Celia backed up, hands in the air, trading a secret smile with Penelope, who had been watching their back and forth like a tennis match. Meanwhile, she wondered: was this really the case with people from work? Did they assume she was never coming back? Of course, Celia knew her mother was right—when other reps or supervisors or assistants at the office moved on, they'd swear to stay in touch. They rarely did. Before, that had never bothered her, but she was never the one who had gone. It was always somebody else—this one to have a baby, or that one got a better offer somewhere, or another was getting married and moving to a new city. Okay, she had to admit, sometimes she envied these people, especially if what they were leaving for sounded foreign or exotic. But she'd put those thoughts out of her head and focus on her work, and soon that person would be forgotten. In fact, with some, she could recall a name but couldn't even conjure up a face. Had this happened with her already?

"Okay, now we're ready," her mother said. "Bring over the eggs."

Celia joined Daisy and Penelope at the mixer. In the bowl, the butter and sugar had been creamed and looked light and fluffy. "Now we're going to pour in one egg at a time. Slowly. Can you handle that, Celia? Or should I have this child do it?"

"I can do it," Celia sighed, "but Penelope, you can help if you want."

"Okay," said Penelope.

So together Celia and Penelope added the eggs, slowly, one at a time, just as directed—wait for the yolk to drop, then the next. Daisy turned her attention to Fionnula's cookbook, tapping a fingernail against the page while biting her lower lip as she slipped her reading glasses from her forehead down to the tip of her nose to more closely inspect some handwritten note. This image Celia had been seeing half her life, it seemed, her mother inspecting a recipe in some book, and it felt so achingly familiar and comforting it almost made her want to cry. Then Daisy headed back to the mixer to double-check their work. She switched the machine to a higher speed, and the loud whirring intensified. Soon, Celia was helping her mother to combine other wet ingredients and add them to the bowl (buttermilk, "well-shaken!", melted butter, real vanilla extract, and something Daisy had insisted Dante also search out and buy, pure coconut extract). Penelope was allowed to stir one final time with a big wooden spoon – but not too much – "*just until blended, or the cake will crumble!*" (this was a message Fionnula had written in the margins, so a message from beyond the grave, really, as if she was hovering over them all, watching warily). Daisy, who claimed her hands were no longer steady, insisted that Celia pour even amounts of the batter into the three pans they'd prepped with butter and flour and then smooth the tops with a rubber spatula. The pans went into the oven while they started on the icing, which consisted of tons of soft butter and cream cheese whipped up with confectioner's sugar, coconut extract, and the shredded coconut Dante brought back from town, Daisy whacking Celia's hand every time she dipped a finger in for a taste while they waited for the cakes to come out of the oven.

Then there was another seemingly endless wait for the cakes to cool on the wire rack Daisy dug from a cabinet.

"Now?" Penelope kept asking, stilted up on tippy-toes at the counter so she could get a better view.

Daisy would lightly touch the top of one cake and shake her head in the negative. Penelope would frown, tapping a foot.

To pass time, they escaped the hot kitchen and headed outside. Where earlier the air had been dense, humid, and thick, a fast-moving shower had brought a cool breeze blowing down the mountain, rustling the branches and needles of the pines that surrounded and loomed up over the barn. They took seats on Penelope's swing set, and while Penelope swung herself in higher and higher arcs, her legs straight out in front of her in a rigid line, her little hands tightly clutching the ropes, Celia and her mother moved lazily back and forth, their feet grazing dirt with each pass. Suddenly, there was the sound of what seemed like a thousand songbirds as they took flight from a nearby oak. Daisy stopped swinging and took in the sights and sounds. "It's nice here," she said after a moment. "I didn't know what I was in for when I got on that plane, but I must say a person could get used to this view. Maybe I should sell the house and move to a place like this. To a more peaceful place. To the country."

"You've been in that house forever, Mother."

"Exactly. Maybe too long. Change of scenery might do me good."

"You have rubber bands from, like, twenty years ago in the junk drawer in the kitchen. Paper clips, too. Rusty paper clips. Not to mention that desk in the study. You know, mom, you don't have to keep tax returns from forty years ago, right? And that's just the tip of the iceberg, I'm guessing."

"Do you want to know what else I've saved?"

"I can only imagine."

"Every letter you ever wrote to me and your father. From camp or wherever you went on a trip. Every postcard. Every report card too, from every grade. Every book report and every badge and medal you earned from I'm not even sure where anymore. Not just your stuff. Bernadette's and Rosalie's too. All of this is in the attic. And more. For instance, I have the original outfit from when Kim arrived at the airport that night we all went to pick her up, that teeny pink onesie..."

Here Penelope giggled. Celia and Daisy turned their eyes to see her at the top of the arc of a big swing. "I had a pink one, too!" she said.

Daisy smiled and turned back to Celia. " I just couldn't bear to part with that, it was so cute. Do you remember that night? How excited we all were?"

"I do," Celia said.

"And let's not forget the pictures," Daisy continued. "From the time when we all printed every last one. Ones of your father and me before you all even came along, on a beach or a hike up in the mountains. Sometimes I find myself in the attic, and I'll open a box and pull out a handful. There's you, all swaddled up as a baby, and there's one of *my* mother holding newborn Bernadette. How long is my mom gone now? Gosh. And then I'll just wonder how all this time passed. Where could it possibly have gone? It really is like the blink of an eye. People say that, and you never believe it when you're young, but it turns out to be so frighteningly true. Anyway, I must have thousands of pictures. Oh, boy."

Celia didn't admit that she was gratified to hear all this, that little things from her past actually mattered to her mother. She said, "Are you ready to get rid of it all? Just let it all go?"

"Well..."

Daisy suddenly seemed unsure—or she was just flat-out horrified at the prospect of having to tackle the years and years of clutter and mess she knew she had accumulated and socked away. She went quiet and started swinging again.

Finally, it came time to finish the cake. Back in the kitchen, Celia watched as her mother and Penelope began the complicated process of icing the three layers, Celia noticing for the first time that her mother's hands trembled as she used an offset spatula to spread the icing in nifty little swirls. Was this something new? She wanted to ask; a small part of her was afraid to, and so she didn't. Once the cake was iced, her mother patted more shredded coconut all over it, so it resembled a giant snow ball. She grabbed a knife and was about to cut into it when Celia said, "Wait! What are you doing?"

"Well, we have to do a taste test, dear. I've never made one from this recipe, and you never know for sure until you taste it."

"Yes," said Penelope, eyes like saucers focused laser-like on the cake. "We must. This is very, very important."

"But Dante can't bring a half-eaten cake to the competition."

"Of course he can't," Daisy agreed. "I have enough ingredients. Good bakers plan ahead, you understand. We'll make another one. In fact, it will be better the second time around, I'm sure. Good cooking is all about repetition, really. Now, go get him so we can try it."

Celia found Dante downstairs, now with Roberta and Lester Brenneman, who apparently had dug up the repair manual for the Triumph he had told Celia he ordered all those years ago. She couldn't imagine how he might have found it, but he and Dante and Roberta had the book open and their heads under the hood. Various parts of the engine had been removed and these were laid out on the floor while the three seemed to be arguing about the best way to fix whatever had gone wrong. Celia wondered how they could possibly put it all back together and make it work again.

"It's time for cake" was all she needed to say.

All instantly dropped their tools. They trundled up the stairs at her heels and took places at the table to sample the cake, Celia first snapping a cross-section picture. They began with reasonably-sized slices, then just a tad more to make sure of the flavors, then a little more just to even things up until before they knew it, a major hunk was gone, and everybody had frosting on their fingers. As Celia figured, it was marvelous, the cake moist and light but rich and sweet, the icing like coconut-flavored clouds. Dante turned to Lester. "What do you think?" he asked.

Lester eyed his fork critically and licked off the last few crumbs. "It's a mighty fine cake," he said. He helped himself to yet one more little piece.

"And you?" he asked Roberta.

"It's bomb-ass," Roberta blurted out. Penelope tittered, and Roberta covered her ears playfully.

"I agree wholeheartedly," Dante said. "This will be perfect, Mrs. Bernhart. And I want to thank you, ma'am. I do appreciate the effort."

"You're very welcome," Daisy said with a satisfied smile.

Dante turned to Celia. "And I'd like to thank you."

"Me? For what?"

"For bringing the cookbook in the first place."

"Oh. Then you're welcome."

"I mean," Dante continued, pointing at Lester, "at first it just pissed me off because of all the business with this old dude you opened up."

Celia sat up straighter and opened her mouth to mount a defense. Lester seemed taken aback at being called an old dude and opened his mouth. But Dante held up a hand.

"Let me finish, will ya? Both of you?"

Celia closed her mouth. Lester snuck in a last bite of cake.

"Anyway, then I sat down and really looked through it. Page by page. I didn't want to miss anything. There are all sorts of notes penciled in the margins, notes between my mother and grandmother, like for years they were sending this book back and forth, which is another thing I never knew about them. 'Try this recipe, Sugar' or 'Loved that one, Mama, but added too much salt.'"

"I used to do that with my own mother," Daisy interjected. "I'd try it with Celia, but she doesn't have the time for such things. Neither do my other daughters. Everybody's so busy these days with their whatnot—I don't know—but just, apparently, they're swamped every minute of the day, so they have no time for the little things that make life nice. "They have an app for that stuff" is what my girls say—just push a button thingy on your phone and get whatever you want whenever you want it—they have one where a person will come and clean up your dog's poop for goodness' sakes. Since when are people too busy to clean up after their dogs? If that's the case, if you want my opinion, they shouldn't have dogs anyway."

Celia rolled her eyes.

Dante continued, "The fact is, I don't really have much else left of the two of them—my grandmother and mother—especially of them getting along sort of nicely and not hollering at each other. Or at each other's throats over this or that."

"They did a whole heck of a lot of hollering," Lester put in. "I can attest to that."

"They sure did," Dante agreed, "But now, in a way, it's kind of like I can hear their voices. It's not like looking at a picture—it's more like following some long-ago conversation that would have just up and been forgotten." He turned to Celia. "So I appreciate you bringing it here. It's nice to have it, after all."

Celia smiled. She took another bite of cake while her mother leaned over and wiped away a dollop of icing off the end of her chin with that little slip of Kleenex she had forever tucked in her sleeve.

VII.

Celia was having the strangest dream. She was at a wedding. Her wedding, she surmised, because she was standing at the altar in a blindingly white dress. But this dress had the kind of extremely long, fussy, and complicated train she never would have selected. She had in mind something more sleek and modern. Like the ones she had circled or bookmarked in all the magazines and catalogues she'd been scanning for years. The church, which she also didn't recognize, was decked out beautifully. Rose petals in a vivid red were strewn up and down the aisle. Okay, that was a little cornball, so this had to be a dream. And wait, there was Penelope, a basket full of the petals in one hand, one of her hens in the other. What was she doing there? With a chicken? Music burbled from an unseen organ. It sounded somewhat somber. *Could this be a funeral?* But then there were perfect rays of bright sunlight streaming through stained glass windows. The pews were filled with expectant guests, all dressed in their finest. But upon closer inspection, something was very, very off.

For instance, yes, the guests were dressed up, but they weren't people. They were pill bottles. Prescription pills, complete with expiration dates she could read. Sonya, her maid of honor, in a puffy powder blue dress, meanwhile, appeared to have the body of a syringe. And the justice of the peace was a stern-looking Danielle Chan, who was muttering something in her native Mandarin. Celia couldn't make heads or tails of what she was trying to say. *This is all very odd,* Celia thought in that funny way you try to make sense of things when you know you're in the middle of a dream but you're sort of curious to see what's coming up next, even if it might be scary, like a fall from a cliff or down a flight of stairs, so sudden it makes your heart flutter. It occurred to her that she should turn and face her groom. She did so.

It wasn't Barry. Bert Pitoniak stood there. He was wearing a loincloth, which didn't suit him at all. "Told you," he said in that annoying, smirky way he had.

"Told me what?" Celia tried to ask. The words came out muffled, in that bizarre dream like way, as if she had a mouth full of marbles. "Mmmmf mmm wmmmf?"

She tried to say it again, louder, but there was something stuck over her mouth. It was a patch—an HX III Hormone patch. She tried to pull it off and couldn't. She tried harder. She mumble-screamed some more. Her whole body shook as she tried to wrench off the patch. *Wait,* she thought, again in that odd dreaming and still asleep way. *I'm really shaking.*

Then she realized somebody was poking at her, trying to shake her awake. She opened her eyes. Dante was sitting on the edge of the bed. "Whoa. What?" Celia mumbled, groggily, confused also because he had been sleeping on an air mattress in Penelope's room.

"I need a favor." He whispered. Her mother was snoring away in the bed beside her; there had been nowhere else to put her.

It was still dark outside, although a sliver of moon was visible through the window. "What time is it?" she asked.

"Five."

"Oh, jeez..."

"Roberta's flaking on me."

"Flaking...What?"

"So I need a favor."

"A...huh?"

"I need you to come with me."

"Come with you? Where?"

This came out loud. Her mother stirred, threw out an arm in a haphazard way, snorted, and rolled over. Her snoring began again.

Celia climbed out of bed. She was groggy and disoriented from the dream, but she tried to focus as she followed Dante into the kitchen. The first thing she noticed was that her replacement phone, which had arrived during the night, sat on the counter. She ripped open the box, pulled the shiny new device from its plastic case, and plugged it in to get a full charge as quickly as possible. Then she noticed Roberta perched on the counter, her eyes narrowed, her brow furrowed, and her mouth set in a grim frown. "I don't care what, I'm not going," she said to Celia.

"Um...Not going where?" Celia asked.

"To Macon," Dante said. "All of a sudden, she's refusing to work the festival. I can't do it without a second pair of hands."

"Why won't you go?" Celia asked.

"The last time I was in Macon, I got harassed."

Celia looked at her blankly.

"I was with my girlfriend at the time," Roberta continued. "We're no longer together, btw, because she turned out to be, like, insane, or at least bipolar for sure, and not taking her meds. But anyway, we were just walking down the street, and I took her hand is all, and I held it. Okay, and maybe we kissed once. Or twice. Who can remember these things? It wasn't like we were making out or there was tongue involved. So, there was this group of rednecks. Good old boys, some people call them, although somebody tell me what's good about them. Anyhow, they followed us. We were called terrible, terrible names, and I felt fear like I never felt anywhere else. I said then that I'd never set foot in that town again. As a sort of protest, right? I was up all night wrestling with this, and I decided I just can't."

"If you stay away, the bigots win," Dante said.

"Who says I gotta be some damn bellwether for equal rights?!" Roberta practically shouted, then lowered her voice to a loud whisper when she realized people were sleeping. "I never signed up for that crap. I'm just trying to live my friggen life."

"I'm just saying," Dante said.

"I've spent a lot of time in Macon," Celia added. "I have a bunch of doctor clients. I've always found it to be lovely."

"Thanks, Straight White Woman. That's a real help," Roberta said.

"Oh, you think I've never experienced harassment?" Celia asked. "Ever have some gross doctor with a huge sense of entitlement come after you in an empty office? There are so many skeevy ones it'll make your skin crawl."

"Oh, poor you," Roberta said. "I'm not going."

She threw a final glare at both of them, leapt from her perch on the counter, and stomped out. They heard her Harley fire up and roar down the driveway.

Dante said, "See? She's stubborn as an old ox if you ask me. Will you come? I'll have you back by tonight. But I really need a helper."

Celia considered her options. Barry wasn't due until the day after tomorrow. She could stay and let her mother drive her up the wall with whatever might get in her head. She was feeling better, with little stiffness in her neck and that bruise not feeling so tender.

"No funny business?" Celia asked.

"Funny ha-ha, or funny some other way?"

"You know what I mean," Celia said. "There will be no monkeying around."

Monkeying, she thought. How was it that he kept bringing out the stern schoolmarm in her? Well, she knew the answer to this, really. It was because he was a bad boy. This was the simplest explanation. He was one of those devilish men she had long ago learned to stay away from, the kind of guy she'd lust after in secret, and didn't lust always lead to something that would end in heartbreak? *Still*, she thought, *a bad boy who needed a good spanking and a good*...She stopped herself because, again, she was slipping into dangerous territory.

"Okay," Dante promised, "No...um...monkeying, even though I'm not exactly certain what that means. Scout's honor, ma'am."

He said this with a wink. Celia ignored it.

"Plus," she added, "I find it hard to believe you were a boy scout."

"I was. Sort of temporarily."

"What? They kicked you out?"

"I guess you could call it that."

"What happened?"

"I didn't like uniforms and being told what to do. Or how to think. Anyway, no fooling around. I promise."

IT WAS ONLY A MATTER of hours, it turned out, before promises were broken. And here Celia was once again, next to this man—out in the open air, in the dark of night, under actual stars and constellations she could make out and still identify, which was kind of shocking—both of them naked, gasping for breath and slicked in a fine sweaty sheen after a fast, frantic romp that left her feeling as if she had been flung into outer space—into those very constellations—had orbited the planet, and crashed back down to earth. What was it about him that made her do these crazy things, and how would she ever atone for them?

It had started out business-like and polite.

She agreed to accompany Dante to Macon. Before they left, Celia stood under the shower. She towel-dried her hair, pulled it back, and tied it into a damp, slightly messy pony-tail. She dabbed on a little blush, added a bit of lip gloss, and thought about powdering over her freckles but decided against it. She slipped on her new jeans, the ones that fit, and pulled the low-cut crimson top over her head. For a second, she stood before the mirror and assessed how she looked. Different, she thought, but she couldn't exactly pinpoint how.

They left the house as Daisy was fixing Penelope break-fast—softly scrambled eggs and nicely buttered toast slathered with fresh strawberry jam—and they drove south from Hodges Creek. They did this in Mary Rose's old Triumph, which Dante and Lester had put back together and got up and running. Celia rode shotgun on a weathered and cracked leather seat that had springs poking her in the ass. Her mother's coconut cake was perched on her lap. The trunk was packed full of prepped barbecue and supplies. Dante had to fold his long, large frame to fit behind the wheel. It looked almost comical, as if he was driving some child's toy car. His knee bumped the steering wheel every time he went to use the clutch until he said, "Can you drive a manual transmission?"

"It's been a while, but yeah. My dad taught me and my sisters. He always wanted us to be prepared."

"Prepared for what?"

"You know," Celia had to admit, "I'm not exactly sure."

He pulled over. They switched seats. Celia fit far better behind the wheel while Dante had more room for his long legs in shotgun, even with the cake now on his lap, which he had to struggle to balance because the car bucked, lurched, and shimmied at first as Celia, admittedly rusty driving a manual, made the gears grind like mad.

"You sure you know how to do this?" Dante asked, a look bordering on terror in his eyes that Celia found amusing.

"Chill out, dude," she said. "I'm on it."

Soon it was all coming back, including the voice of her father explaining in a slow, gentle tone how to ease off the clutch while slowly pressing down on the gas. After a short time, she was shifting like a pro. And the little convertible had kick; it leapt forward when she hit the accelerator, a throaty roar emerging from the exhaust. It rolled confidently into turns, its steering tight and precise. It was simple, low-tech fun, something so rare in cars these days, she thought, and she understood why Mary Rose would have wanted it. Because there was only an AM radio that refused to produce anything more than ear-splitting static, they were forced to talk. Dante, an only child raised mostly by a stern and curmudgeonly grandmother, was curious about what it was like to grow up with two sisters and both parents at home. "Oh, it could be hell," Celia said about the sisters part.

"Really?" he asked. "Because I kind of always wanted a sister. Or a brother."

"We'd fight like cats sometimes. You could say lots of the time. I mean really nasty fights. Which sometimes would even get physical."

"Oh, come on. Seriously?"

"Yup. We'd pull each other's hair. Or poke each other in the eyes. Or kick each other in the shins."

"That's pretty nasty."

"There's more. We'd frame each other for some infraction or whatever we didn't do so the other one would get blamed. My father would yell like crazy at us, or my mother would threaten spankings even when we were too old for anything like that, and she'd never follow through on the threat, anyway. My mother can be kind of flighty, which I'm sure you noticed."

"But you love each other, you and your sisters?"

"Yeah," Celia said. "Of course."

This was true. Sometimes she hated her sisters and she knew there were times they felt the same about her. Often, they got on each other's nerves, or one would say something mean, and another would resent it for days on end, or longer. Indeed, resentments—or perceived slights of even the smallest kind—could stretch back decades, only to be dug up and revisited, if needed, to slam home a point. But she'd do anything for either of them, she told Dante, if it came right down to it, and she knew they'd do anything for her. And if something happened to either of them, and suddenly one or the other was gone, she didn't know how she would handle it.

"Kind of like how I feel about Penelope. I'd step in front of a train for her if I had to. I never thought I'd feel that way about another human being, but I guess you don't know these things until you become a parent, and then everything changes."

Celia felt a pang somewhere deep inside because she didn't know that feeling. She was beginning to realize she wanted to understand it, especially after the last few days looking after Penelope, as if this had awoken some maternal instinct that had lain dormant, and this brought her once again to the idea that time was running out, and what was she waiting for? She tried to put these thoughts out of her mind.

"Does she miss having a mom, you think?" Celia asked.

"Well, she does have a mom."

"I mean one who's around all the time."

"Was your mom?"

"Yeah. She was always there for us. Every day when we were kids. I sometimes wonder about how she feels, about the choices she made—you know, to stay home and not work at some other job—I mean, she did, like volunteer stuff—but I don't think she really regrets anything."

"Well, yeah, I guess Penelope misses it. I've told Luanne she needs to do more than just send all these gifts and things. She needs to be there in person. Be a real mom to her. But she doesn't want to listen. She just goes off and does her own thing. Just like always."

"Can I ask you something?"

"Yeah."

"Is she really a stripper?"

"Well, she dances. Sometimes around a pole. And, well, she does take off her clothes."

"I don't get it. Why do men fall for that?"

"Don't know. Maybe we're just hard-wired that way."

"Hard-wired to drink shots of tequila or beers or Jager or whatever it is you drink in those places, and scream like banshees, and have women grind their asses into your lap? And don't give me any nonsense about how these women have the power, or that the job is empowering. That's a load of bullshit," Celia said.

"Is it?"

"You don't think so?"

"The whole thing is carnal, for sure. There's something primal about it, you might say."

Celia was pondering that idea when Dante added, "Or maybe the thing is this: men are basically dogs. Just filthy, dirty little animals."

"That's it!" Celia said, smiling. "Now you're making sense. Why do you men feel like you have to lie about things like that?"

"Don't know. But can we talk about something other than my ex, please? It's not a subject I'm particularly fond of."

"Okay. Why barbecue?"

"Well, I like to eat."

"But is it what you always wanted to do? Did you go to school for it?"

"There's no school that can teach you to be a good pit-master. You have it in your blood or you don't. Sort of like a gene. Then you just have to practice. Endlessly. It becomes an obsession, you might say, because it requires almost constant attention and care. To do it right, you're checking things every couple of hours, all night long most of the time. You can forget about a normal night's sleep. So yeah, obsession is the right word."

"And you got it from your grandfather?"

"I suppose, although I don't really remember him too well. But he was the one who built the place and ran it for years. Although from what I hear, he originally put the shack together as an escape from my grandma. Sort of a man-cave, I guess you might call it these days. Anyway, aside from being into eating it, I was always just naturally good at making fires."

"Yeah. I heard that from Lester. But you didn't always do this."

"Nope."

"What did you do before?"

"A lot of things."

"Like?"

"Construction mostly. Down in Florida. I did carpentry. Building kitchen cabinets, or bookshelves, which nobody really used for books. They'd mount a flat screen in them. Or they'd go off and buy books by the yard at some second-hand store and never ever read them, which confounded me, actually. Want the covers a certain color to match the sofa or the rug. Which is wrong, but everybody says no one reads real books anyway. They do it on their phones or whatever. But I like books. Real ones you can hold in your hand when you read them. So you can turn a page, and then turn it back and reread a sentence. Like my grandmother's cookbook—how she and my mom wrote notes in the margins. Sure, it's kind of old and musty, but it has a history. You know what I mean?"

"Yeah. Although to be honest, I always swear I'm going to read more, and then the plan gets away from me. There's always a stack of books I'm meaning to get to. Sometimes it's like they throw me guilty looks even."

He let out a chuckle at that. "Anyway," Dante continued, "I did some electrical, too. I can rewire just about anything. Something Lester taught me. No plumbing, though. Fixing dirty pipes always sort of grossed me out, although you can make a shit-ton of money. Work was great until the market went bust and housing tanked, which was about the time my grandma started to decline, so I brought Penny back home. At first, I wasn't sure what I wanted to do, so again I did a little bit of everything for folks around here. Construction stuff. Worked with Lester on a lot of jobs. But all the time, that shack was sitting there staring at me, looking all broken down and forlorn."

"So it was like a calling?"

"Don't know if I believe in that. I just knew one thing: I didn't want to spend the rest of my days putting up drywall in some stranger's house. I mean, maybe if I build my own house someday. We probably can't live in that barn forever. But anyway, I was searching for something else, like a purpose, if that makes any sense."

She thought about that as she drove, for a moment focusing on finding the right gear to pass a truck that had slowed in front of them. Sometimes, she wondered what her own purpose truly was in life and whether she was fulfilling it. Occasionally, it would keep her up at night, this musing, and she'd have to find some other way to get to sleep, to quiet the whirring in her brain. "It makes sense," Celia said.

"And you know, barbecue, it's kind of an art. I mean, I won't nerd out on the subject too much even though Lord knows I could, but what I'm saying is there's an art to getting it just right—what kind of wood, and what temperature, and how much smoke and how many hours will it need? And, well, there actually is some science, which appeals to the geek in me. It takes a lot of doing it wrong at first, for sure, but there's something really satisfying about the process, too, especially when you start to really figure it all out. Also, there's something nice about making folks happy, filling their bellies and leaving them with a smile, you know? It's gratifying. Instant gratification, which I figured is very hard to find in actual life."

"I can see that," Celia said.

"What about you?"

"What about me?"

"You happy doing what you do?"

She was contributing to making lives better, wasn't she, some small part of a person's healing process? But...was that actually true? Did she still really believe it? She was feeling so unsure about the subject, she decided to change it. She asked about the man he thought was his father and about Lester Brenneman and what was it like to have things change so abruptly. Dante said he always suspected something was off about his ties to Brooks Zebulon, who had pretty much vanished from his life anyway. He never felt close to him, bonded, the way a son was supposed to feel about a father, but he always did have some odd connection he couldn't quite pinpoint with Lester. Penelope had bonded with Lester, too, he added, as if she somehow sensed a deeper connection. "Maybe that's why I took a swing at him after you brought the letter," Dante said.

"I don't see your logic."

"Harbored up resentment. Left it festering for too long. That's not a good thing, from what I understand. I took it out on him, I guess."

"Well," Celia said, "it just means you have strong feelings for him, maybe, when you have a reaction like that."

Dante nodded as if he agreed while slowly stroking his fast-thickening beard .

THE FESTIVAL WAS BEING held along the banks of the Ocmulgee River in downtown. Gateway Park, Celia learned it was called, because although she'd been through Macon many times, she rarely detoured from a prescribed route deemed by some algorithm the company devised to be the most speedy and efficient.

Now, spread before them like a vast green carpet, was a lush lawn with sweeping views of the water. Small smokers had been set up in booths for each entrant. The smell of various woods already burning and sending out scent in the crisp morning air was intoxicating. They made their way to Dante's booth, and there lining the walls were enlargements of the high-resolution photographs Celia had taken. She stepped back and eyed them critically. She decided they looked somewhat decent for an amateur.

Dante began unloading supplies from the trunk of the Triumph. "Go ahead and get a fire going," he threw in Celia's direction, apparently forgetting he wasn't talking to Roberta, who knew what she was doing in these types of situations.

"I....Hmmmmm," Celia answered.

She looked around, her hands fluttering vaguely. She finally set them on her hips, arms akimbo, as if striking a confident pose might make it seem like she was up to the task, that she was capable and ready.

Dante regarded her for a moment, a smile turning up the corners of his mouth. "My bad. You don't know how to start a fire, right?"

"I don't have a clue," Celia admitted.

And so he set about demonstrating. First, he grabbed some newspaper from a small stack in a corner. He crumpled a few sheets into balls and stuck them in the underside of the chimney, which he then filled with charcoal that was piled up nearby next to a small stack of hickory. He handed her a book of matches. "Light it up."

Celia looked down at the matchbook and was suddenly filled with a memory of three or four girlfriends lighting an illicit cigarette behind some alley when they were in middle school. She pulled out a match and struck it. She threw it at the charcoal and jumped back. Dante's eyes widened, and then he burst into laughter. Celia joined in even though she wasn't sure what was so funny.

"Okay," Dante said, "First thing to keep in mind is that we're not using gasoline here, or any sort of accelerant. It will not, like, instantly explode, I promise you. It's the newspaper underneath—you want to light that. Just a corner or two is fine. The rest will take care of itself."

"Oh!"

This time, she got it right. He coached her through waiting as bright orange flames licked up through the chimney and ignited the coals, through waiting some more until the flames died out and the coals were nicely covered with ash. Then he stepped in to dump the coals from the chimney, spreading them in an even layer in the bottom of the smoker. She watched as he set down a few chunks of hickory that had been soaking in apple juice. He took his time, explaining how to tell when the temperature was just right, occasionally placing a hand over the coals to test the level of heat, waiting until he could let his hand hover there for a few seconds without being burned. Soon, he was arranging in the smoker the racks of ribs and cuts of shoulder that had been rubbed with his secret spices. The door shut with a clank. Fragrant smoke chugged through the vents.

Dante pointed at a sack full of bunched greens. "If you wouldn't mind, how about prepping those collards?"

"Right. On it."

"You know what I mean, right?"

"Uh..."

"Just remove the stems, then cut the leaves into neat thin ribbons."

Celia eyed the collards warily. She reached in and pulled out a large bundle. They were an inky dark green, almost leathery to the touch, with lighter veins running throughout. Had she ever cooked these with her mom? She was pretty sure she hadn't. She set them on the small cutting board. She picked up a knife, but the handle was slippery. An "Oh, oh!" squeaked from her mouth as she fumbled with it. The knife dropped to the ground, barely missing Dante's foot, the tip slicing into dirt.

He picked up the knife and set it back on the table gently. "Or," Dante said, "You know what? Why not go into town. Get yourself a Starbucks or something. You like Starbucks, don't ya?"

"Okay!" Celia said, relieved. "You want one?"

"I'm good."

She could tell he wanted her out of the way for prep, that he'd get through it faster on his own.

She did something she hadn't done for as long as she could remember; she took some time just for herself. She didn't rush through the park as she headed back to downtown as she might have done if she were working, running madly from one appointment to the next as if she were in some sort of race. She didn't have her mother or her sisters on her case for this or that. She took a seat on a bench, tipped her face up to the sun, and just enjoyed the warmth on her skin, the expansive view of the river, and the sounds of life in the park. She heard birds—a chorus, maybe hundreds of them—none of which she could identify if her life depended on it. On another bench nearby, a mother scolded a young boy who had waded into the water and got mud all over his pants. There was the annoying canned music of an ice cream cart. After a few minutes, she couldn't resist the urge to check her new phone. Again, there were no work texts or emails, which was, frankly, annoying. There were texts from Rosalie and Bernadette, along with one from Barry.

"Barry!"

She said this so loud that people nearby turned to look.

"Sorry," Celia said. She felt her cheeks flush. "It's nothing! All good!"

The mother nearby gathered up her boy and scurried off. A hipster glanced up from his phone, then averted his eyes. Did they think she was unbalanced, or even crazy?

Was she crazy? How would she explain the last few days to the man she was supposed to marry? She had to come clean, she knew, but the idea filled her with dread. Would he forgive her? Should he even? If the positions were reversed, she wondered, how would she feel? Accepting? Angry? There were a few times when she suspected Barry might be fooling around. He was, after all, surrounded by nurses and patients, some of whom she knew had that savior-complex sort of thing for doctors. She never dug hard enough to find any evidence, though. Maybe she didn't want to know. She wondered now—could they find a way to get through this? She had no answer for these questions, and for now, she put the inevitable confrontation out of her mind.

She left the park and wandered the streets of downtown Macon somewhat aimlessly, poking her head in one little shop after another. She didn't see a Starbucks but found a small café and treated herself to fresh-brewed coffee and a rich, buttery croissant, which shattered into flaky crumbs the instant she bit into it. She brushed the crumbs from her lap and polished it off. Usually, if she stopped in the middle of the morning like this, she'd be entering her orders on her laptop or getting in touch with clients, shooting off thank you notes to some, setting future appointments with others. Now she just observed the people around her and wondered a little about their lives.

And then, at a table on the opposite side of the cafe, she recognized a face. It was a client, a dermatologist originally from Jaipur, a handsome man with an easy smile and blazingly white teeth, whose order was always heavy on fillers and collagens although today he wasn't in his white doctor coat, but golf clothes. She rose and crossed to the table. "Well, hi, Dr. Nawali," she said, extending a hand.

"Uh..."

He looked confused. This was disconcerting.

"It's me. Celia!"

"Oh! And I know you from....?"

Out of her typical work uniform—outside the familiar confines of his office—did she really look that different?

"Celia Bernhart! From AxCelacron? I've been your dedicated rep for several years."

"Ah..."

He still looked confused and vaguely trapped but was about to shake her hand when they were interrupted. "What are *you* doing here?"

Celia turned. Here was Bert Pitoniak, also in golf clothes, carrying a tray piled high with pastries, which he set on the table before the doctor. "There you go, Pradeep," Bert said. "One of everything because I wasn't sure what you prefer."

"Thank you, Bert," said the doctor.

Bert turned to Celia. "Danielle was a little cagey with details," he began, "but I heard you were on vacation. Rather suddenly." This last was said in his smirky way.

"Well, what if I am on a little break?"

Bert didn't respond. He sat and took a big bite of an eclair.

"I am using some much needed me-time, Dr. Nawali, but it's temporary," Celia said. "I'll see you again very soon."

Dr. Nawali would have answered, but his mouth was stuffed with pastry.

LATER, AS CELIA HEADED back into the park, the aroma of barbecue was overwhelming. She found Dante chatting with a man and woman in matching T-shirts and visors, who seemed to be surveying the booth. "Here she is now," Dante was saying as she approached. "You can ask her yourself."

"Ask me what?" Celia said.

"We were admiring your pictures, my husband and I," the woman began. She was very tall and stick thin, with a shock of frizzy red curls framing a long, narrow face.

"They're terrific," added the man. In contrast to his wife, he was short, stocky, with a shiny bald dome of a head and wide bright eyes. "You really captured the mood of Dante's place."

"Oh," Celia said, a smile forming. "Well, thank you."

"Our booth's over there," the woman said, pointing to a spot nearby. "As you can see, the photographs we sent in suck."

Celia looked. Their pictures were basic shots of food plunked down on plates. They were flat. They had no composition. The colors were off. They didn't make the food look appetizing. "Well," she said, "they don't, uh..."

"No, they stink," the man said, "There's talent involved with taking good food pictures, and we do not have any! So we were wondering if we could get you to come out to our place down by Charlotte."

"Down to your place?" Celia asked. "For what?"

"To take some pictures. Ones like these. We need them for the new website we're putting together. Just name your price," said the woman.

"Within reason, of course," added her husband.

They pressed a card into her hand and left. Celia looked down at it, somewhat shocked that people would actually offer to pay her.

"Didn't I say you were good?" This came from Dante, who then vanished into a cloud of smoke as he stoked his fire and rotated the meats.

"Oh, well," Celia said, "I mean...how do we know these people are actually sane? They could be raving lunatics. They could want to lure me down to Charlotte for God only knows what reason."

"Yeah, right. They looked really nuts. Couples in matching visors. Who most likely drive a mini-van. Watch out!"

"Besides, it doesn't even qualify as a hobby at this point."

"Does that matter?"

She shrugged. She pocketed the card and pitched in to help for the remainder of the afternoon. With a weathered wooden spoon Dante had said belonged to his grandmother—a good luck charm, he hoped—she stirred the collards, now simmering with onions and a meaty ham hock in a pot resting on a small portable Weber. She measured and handed ingredients over as Dante mixed up a large batch of batter for the cornbread that would be baked in well-seasoned cast iron skillets.

The festival officially began at dusk as a big orange sun first hovered low over the river like an absurd giant balloon and then began a lazy descent, until it sunk into the distant horizon. A bluegrass band twanged away on a small stage. There was dancing. There was a glittery Ferris wheel that fast filled with shrieking children and furtive-looking teens, who were either making out or tossing items from the uppermost reaches and craning their necks to see where they landed below, clapping and whistling if they hit their intended targets. Hungry crowds descended on the booths. Celia helped to dish up food and pass out plates. She wished she had brought the camera, for here were faces with barbecue sauce smudged on cheeks in an almost comical way. Customers licked their fingers clean or belched in satisfaction as they rubbed their bellies. Others posed for selfies with the pitmasters or carefully snapped pics of their dinner.

Later, Dante put together one perfect plate for the judges, along with a nice big hunk of the second coconut cake Daisy had baked, which was just as perfect as the one they had all sampled. For what seemed like an eternity, they held their breath while plates were sampled and rated. The judges—a serious, well-fed-looking lot—poked and prodded at the food; they leaned in close, so close their noses were almost touching the meat as they inhaled its heady aroma. One savored each bite with his eyes closed and seemed to be experiencing a kind of bliss. Finally, all pitmasters were summoned to the Judges' Table and stood before it in a line. Celia watched as Dante fidgeted nervously. Earlier, he had insisted he didn't care how it would all turn out, but she could tell he did, that this mattered.

He didn't win.

But he did take second runner up. And, Celia gathered, since this was his first competition, it was something to celebrate, which they did later over ice-cold beers as they packed everything up and stowed the gear in the trunk of the Triumph.

The car refused to start. It wasn't the battery, Dante was quick to surmise as he poked his head under the hood. The ignition was turning over, but something wasn't catching, and because Celia, in the driver's seat, kept hitting the gas, the engine flooded, which meant they'd have to leave it be until the fuel resettled or some such thing.

They decided to wait out the car over another beer. Dante dug out an old plaid blanket that was buried behind the seats. She followed him down to the banks of the river where first he shook the dust out of the blanket, then let it flutter to the ground. They sat side-by-side and for a moment they watched as ribbons of water rippled by under the glow of a fluorescent orange moon. Dante said, "You know, I've been on my feet all day over that smoker, and I damn well reek of hickory."

"Yes," Celia agreed. "You do. And sweat. You stink of that, too, if you must know."

"Well, I was nervous about the outcome, so flop sweat I guess you could call it."

Celia smiled.

"What do you think I should do about it?"

"Um...well, there's any number of..."

She didn't finish the thought. He sprang to his feet. He peeled off his T-shirt. He dropped his jeans. Off came his briefs, which was somewhat shocking to Celia, that he seemed so comfortable in his own skin. He sprinted down to the river's edge, and without a second's pause, he plunged beneath the surface. When he came up, he let out what sounded like a howl. With his beard wet and glistening, he resembled some wild, exotic beast.

"It's awesome!" he shouted to Celia. "Come in."

"I am so not jumping into that river," she shouted back.

But...from a small corner of her brain came a thought: *Lisa would do it. Lisa would throw off her clothes and just get it done.* Celia wished she could quiet that little corner of her brain. All it did was get her into trouble.

"C'mon!" Dante said before dunking under the water once more and giving Celia a flash of naked butt.

She stood. She sat back down. She stood again.

"Water's real nice," he said. "Not too cold. Not too warm. Just right."

"Turn around."

"Look, I already saw you with your clothes off, so it's not like you got anything I haven't already laid eyes on."

"I'm not coming in unless you do."

"Okay."

He turned and faced the opposite way. Celia removed her blouse and her jeans but considered keeping on her bra and panties. That would be the right thing to do. She felt all grubby and sweaty, though. She unhooked the bra and wriggled out of the panties. She ran to the edge of the river, hesitated for a moment and took the plunge. The water was cool and crisp, instantly invigorating. She reveled in that, and the welcome thick underwater silence that muffled the outside world. Her foot touched the murky bottom; she paused there briefly, then shot back to the surface. She found herself a little too close to Dante, and so she paddled backward until they were a decent amount of space apart. A respectable space.

"See?" he asked. "Refreshing, isn't it?"

"Yeah, yeah. Just keep your distance, bub."

Dante grinned, his head slightly tilted and his eyes crinkled at the corners. He drifted a little closer. Celia backed away. She noticed again those tattoos, the ring of fire on his chest and the symbol she couldn't quite identify on his arm. "What's the meaning of that?"

He glanced at his biceps. "Well, I was a little plastered when I got that."

"That's often the case, from what I hear," Celia said.

"You never wanted to get one?"

"I thought about it once. I'm too afraid of pain. Rosalie has one. She and her wife got them together — interlocking hearts—which I guess was kind of sweet, and sort of hopeful.... you know, that everything will work out, like, forever."

He nodded.

"So what is that second one?"

"It's a piece of punctuation! It's a semi-colon."

"Okay, why would you get a semi-colon tattooed onto your arm?"

"Well, the way I understood it at the time, and again keep in mind I wasn't remotely sober, it's a symbol—it has to do with unfinished business. When you're writing, and you have something to add to a sentence, you use it, not a period. Get it?"

"I guess it kind of makes sense," Celia reflected. "What sort of unfinished business?" she added.

"Oh, you know, take a pick. With my mom, I guess. With Lester for sure, and the man I was told was my dad. With Penelope's mom. Who doesn't have unfinished business, by the way? Don't you?"

He drifted even closer, bobbing along with the slow, gentle current. He smiled.

"Of course I do," Celia said. "And wipe that smile off your face."

"Can't help it."

"Yeah. Uh huh."

"You want to hear something crazy?"

"No, I don't."

"Well, I'm going to say it anyway."

"Really. You don't have to."

"Here's the thing: I think I'm falling for you, Celia."

"No, you're not. That's absurd."

"Yes, I do believe I am. It's only been a couple of days. I know that. Sometimes that's how things happen, though. In an unexpected sort of way. Life throws you a curve. Anyway, I got it bad."

"No, it's the moonlight, and being in the water, and the beer talking. Plus, it's been a long day, and you're tired. When you sober up, and after a good night's sleep, everything will look different. It always does."

"I don't think so. In fact, I believe it's fate. You and I. Us. We were fated to meet."

"What?! How do you figure that?"

"I mean, some mail person delivers a package to you—a package that rightfully should have showed up forty years ago—and what do you do? Did you scribble across it 'Not At this Address?' or 'Mis-delivered?' and shove it back in your mailbox?"

"Well, no..."

"No, you didn't. But you easily could have."

"The thought did cross my mind, though. And, well, I haven't mentioned this, but I did bring it back to the post office."

"Yeah? And how'd that go?"

"The lady basically told me it would wind up in the garbage."

"Which brings me to this question: did you toss it in the garbage? Especially after the post office—lots of people would have just done that. Just thrown it out without a thought because they've got too much else to do."

"Well, to be honest, I did consider throwing it out."

"Did you?"

He paddled closer. Celia could see little wisps of steam rise from his bare shoulders. In the moonlight, his blue eyes seemed inky black. She suddenly noticed he had a small diagonal chip in one tooth. She wondered how he got it as she back-paddled, putting a safer distance between them again.

"As a matter of fact," she said, "I actually did toss it in the trash."

"Really?"

"Yes. And maybe that's where I should have left it. I did fish it out, though."

"And why did you do that?"

She thought about what her reason could possibly have been. She honestly didn't have an answer.

"See. It's like it was calling to you. And you held onto it, like some unseen force was your guide."

"Well, that's just nuts."

"You don't believe in fate?"

"I didn't say that."

"Well, I believe in it. I believe there was a reason you personally went out of your way to deliver it. First to my grandmother. And then, after they told you she had passed, and you could have given up on it again, to me. What are the odds?"

They were both kicking their legs to stay afloat, treading water. For a brief second, his leg brushed up against hers. Her teeth started to chatter. She could feel goose bumps all over, her skin tingling. She wasn't sure if it was because the water was cold. She said, "I'm getting out of this river right now. That's what I'm doing."

Before he could say another word, she turned and dunked back under to the solace and quiet beneath the surface. She was determined to be good, determined to do the right thing. Without breaking the surface, she held her breath and, scissoring her legs, powered back to shore.

When the Triumph still refused to start, they polished off the beers. They wound up falling asleep on the blanket a good distance apart because she insisted it be that way. But later, Celia woke to find out that somehow her back was pressed up against his. She wondered who inched up against whom? Was it her? She could feel his bare skin through her shirt and, along his back, rigid contours of muscle. He felt solid, like he was carved from stone. She wondered if he was really like this as a man—solid and dependable. His life seemed chaotic, really—more than a little messy considering all that unfinished business and all those loose ends.

She moved to put distance between them. But something sharp poked into her thigh. She dug into her pocket. She pulled out the card the couple at the festival had pressed into her hand when they had asked if she'd consider photographing their place. She sat up and stared at the card, which suddenly became a blur because she realized she was looking at it through tears. She was crying. Not just a little. Heaving sobs, coming from God knows where, but it felt good at the same time, like a release. And then Dante was there next to her, folding her into his arms.

"Hey," he said, "Hey! What's this?"

She thought about explaining why she suddenly felt so sad. She thought about saying that there was a time once, all those years ago, when she would have killed for a chance like the one that was in front of her, to be paid to do something she actually loved. She might have told him how she wished she had more confidence in herself. Because the truth was that she had none, and she regretted that. Now, even though when she held that camera and looked through its lens it made her feel alive in a way she hadn't felt in a long, long time, she was sure it was too late, that too many years had gone by, and she wouldn't possibly know how or where to begin again. This made her angry at herself for being so timid, and also sad, as if she was mourning. Words to explain this didn't come, but the longer he held her, the less she found she could resist the warmth of his embrace. She tried to push him away, but the sobs kept coming, and when he put his arms around her again, she didn't resist.

"Oh, hell," was what she finally said before her lips found his and she pulled him closer.

VIII.

They didn't make it back to Hodges Creek until late the next morning, after a mostly silent ride. This suited Celia just fine since she didn't want to talk about what happened, again, or analyze what she was going to do next. She focused on her driving. She did her best to ignore Dante and his attempts to initiate conversation. Eventually, he turned to stare out the window, occasionally sneaking glances at her.

Back at his place, she left him unloading the trunk of the Triumph while she headed up the stairs the barn. But at the top of the stairs, she stopped short.

"Oh, my God!" popped out of her mouth.

Gathered before her in the kitchen, next to her mother and Penelope, were Rosalie and Kim, a squirming twin in each arm, and Bernadette, who, pen in hand, was adding something to what looked like a list. Kent, her painstakingly fit, angularly handsome husband, impeccably dressed as always like his wife, impeccably groomed, too, with not one hair out of place, was sprawled on the couch, his nose in his iPad. Seeing them all before made her feel dizzy and disoriented as if again she had slipped through a crack into some new strange universe.

"Well," said Daisy, affixing Celia with a long, appraising glance, the kind she might have thrown at her if she was a teenager and stayed out all night, "Well, well, well. Hmmm-mmm."

She walked right up to Celia and inspected her neck where there appeared to be fresh marks. "Uh huh," Daisy muttered, and moved away, shaking her head dramatically.

Rosalie said, "You couldn't have texted, Celia, about where you've been? So we all wouldn't have to worry ourselves to death?"

Bernadette added, "Or called? How hard would that have been considering how much effort and time it cost us all to fly down here on such short notice. It's a good thing Kent and I have all those airline points. Otherwise, it would have cost a fortune, too. Right, Kent?"

Kent nodded from behind the iPad.

"Okay," Celia began after she had gotten her bearings although she still felt a little woozy and off-balance at seeing them all, "who exactly asked you all to fly down here?"

"We couldn't reach you or mom," Bernadette said. "You sent one measly email that didn't explain the situation at all."

Rosalie said, "We were worried sick, Celia. Anything could have happened. You might have been kidnapped for all we knew."

"Or staying with some maniac," added Bernadette, "who might murder you all in the middle of the..."

An actual scream from Rosalie interrupted Bernadette. She was pointing at the top of the stairs. Everybody turned to look at what startled her.

There stood Dante. His jeans, which were from the previous day, were rumpled; his T-shirt was smudged with soot. His shaggy hair was a mess, his beard even scruffier. Plus, he had the ax from the woodpile in his hand. They all gaped up at him, all six feet and three inches, somewhat disheveled, and carrying what might be considered a weapon, and even Celia realized what it must look like.

Dante just smiled sheepishly and took a step back. "Sorry," he mumbled, "Blade needs an edge."

He fished in a kitchen drawer and removed a whetstone, then stood awkwardly, shuffling from one foot to another, waiting for an introduction. Penelope materialized, shimmied up first his leg, then an arm, until he hoisted her up the rest of the way so she hung off his neck.

"This is Dante," Celia said. "This is his house. He's Penelope's father."

Bernadette said, "Oh!"

Rosalie shifted her eyes down to her Birkenstocks and inched closer to Kim. "Sorry for screaming," she practically whispered.

He went around the room shaking hands.

"Anyway," Bernadette continued, "we've been very concerned about Mom. Do you know, Celia, when she took off out of the blue like she did from Rosalie's, she once again left a kettle on a lit burner."

"I did not!' Daisy insisted. "Did I?"

There was a brief pause, where a shadow of doubt appeared to flicker over her face, and all sorts of possibilities seemed to be rolling through her mind. "If I did do it," she finally said, "then I'm sorry."

"Well, get this," Celia added, "When she got here, she was wearing her sweater inside-out."

Bernadette said, "Mother, again? Really? Did I not implore you to check a mirror before you go anywhere? Do I need to put a note on your front door reminding you? Or do you want people to think you're careless and, well, I just have to say, slovenly?"

Daisy said, "Oh, this is nice. This is great. So, now you're going to all gang up on me? Let's pile on the demented old person to deflect everybody's attention from the real issue?"

"What is the real issue again?"

This came from Kent, who was intermittently looking up from whatever was on his iPad, a Words With Friends game, it turned out, and not one of the major venture capital deals he always seemed to be working on.

"Well, I don't know," Daisy continued. "But we could start with how Celia's life has gone completely off the rails."

"Yeah, we heard you got put on suspension from your job," said Bernadette. "Which is really quite shocking because you've been at it so long. How many years now? Like forever?"

"And you wrecked a car," added Rosalie, "You've always been such a careful driver, too. It's odd."

"Oh, I hope you took the extra insurance," Bernadette put in. "You most definitely don't want to get stuck with that bill."

Her mother turned to her sisters, pointed at Dante, and mouthed the words, *And the best part is she slept with him.*

Rosalie said, "She what?"

Bernadette just stood there, her mouth open but no words coming out.

"Oh, Good Lord," Celia snapped, exasperation rising. "Here we are, a thousand miles from mom's house, and once again everybody's picking on me? It's just like a typical Sunday Supper."

"What's a Sunday Supper?" Dante asked, still shifting from one foot to the other, Penelope hanging off his neck but watching the back and forth between Celia, her mother, and her sisters with what appeared to be some amusement.

"It's when these four women get together and cluck like a passel of hens," Kent said from the sofa. "You generally want to steer clear of them is my advice. I hit my man-cave when that goes down."

"Passel of clucking hens?!!" Daisy said, then seemed to realize it sounded something like a squawk.

"What exactly is that supposed to mean?" Rosalie asked while Kim sent a glare in Kent's direction. "I've heard plenty of men cluck like chickens, you can be sure," Rosalie added.

Kent opened his mouth to protest, but Bernadette interrupted: "Kent, shut up and go back to your game." Then she added, "And by the way, when he says man-cave, he means cushy den with giant flat screen TV, which he parks himself in front of and doesn't move from for hours. He makes it sound like he's some Neanderthal, but he's just a big softie. Take away his grooming kit, Postmates, and God forbid, good WiFi, and he'd be lost."

Kent grumbled something, but they all ignored him.

"Actually," Daisy continued, back on subject, "it's funny Celia should mention Sunday Supper. That's exactly why we've been putting together a list."

"What?" asked Celia. "Here?"

"Well, it's Sunday, and we do have to eat, don't we?" Bernadette said. "After all this traveling. Even with all the miles, we could only swing economy tickets on such short notice, and God forbid they should throw you a peanut."

"Or a glass of sparkling water. And not from an aluminum can, for God's sakes," Kent said.

"And have you forgotten Kim has babies to nurse?" Rosalie added. "Did you happen to think about these children?"

"Well, I..."

Daisy interrupted, "I'm going to finally make my Oriental Casserole!"

This brought silence as everybody contemplated that. Daisy smiled as if she had won yet another battle that only existed in her head. Celia wondered for a second how her mother would cook without a recipe until she remembered this casserole involved mixing a whole bunch of canned things—cream of celery soup, water chestnuts, those crunchy fried noodles–with sautéed celery and onions, copious amounts of soy sauce, and chunks of poached chicken. The dish was all baked together and served over boiled rice. No recipe needed. What was Oriental about it she never could quite figure out, although, she had to admit, it tasted delicious, especially with more crunchy noodles on top, more soy sauce and, in recent years, lots of Sriracha, which Daisy had inexplicably come to adore and started to glug on almost anything.

"Have you even thought of asking permission to take over somebody's kitchen?" Celia asked.

"I'm good with it," Dante said. "I was just trying to figure out how I'd feed you all. Now, I don't have to cook."

So they all piled into the mini-van Kent and Bernadette had rented and made a trip to town, stopping first for a late breakfast at Belle's. They filled up the one large booth at the back, and while Belle took their orders and marveled at the little baby twins, Kent and Bernadette couldn't take their eyes off Ms. Nedra, who was breakfasting as usual with her dachshund, until Ms. Nedra finally said, "What? He's partial to grits because they're easy on his little old teefers!"

"His....huh?" Kent asked, the precise features of his face forming a perfect question mark.

"Teeth! Jesus, have you never had a pet?"

"Uh...no," said Kent while Bernadette smiled one of those frozen smiles she put on when she addressed a crazy person in the city. Surreptitiously, Kent removed a small bottle of hand sanitizer from Bernadette's bag and left it there on the table in a way that seemed to reassure them both.

Belle started sending out food. First came platters of those fluffy biscuits, steaming hot from the oven, split down the middle, with peppery cream gravy laced with chunks of spicy sausage ladled all over. After that came soft, custardy scrambled eggs alongside crisp bacon and a basket of warm buttered toast, a dainty pot of homemade strawberry jam nestled inside. All of this was washed down with just-squeezed orange juice and strong hot coffee.

After breakfast, Celia gave them all a tour of the town, or what she had learned about it in the past—what was it...a week?—although to her, it suddenly felt longer, as if she'd settled there ages ago. She pointed out the statue in the town square and the sheriff's station and jail. They hit the market so Daisy could get the items she needed. But when she learned they stocked none of the crunchy noodles—a necessary part of the dish—she pivoted to her beef stew, which Celia was happy about because she liked it better. Daisy selected a boneless chuck roast big enough to feed an army. She sent Bernadette and Kim to find beef stock and wine while Celia tagged along to grab first carrots, then new potatoes and little pearl onions, and finally a bag of frozen petite peas.

Back at Dante's, the women commandeered the kitchen while Kent sprawled on the couch for a nap and Dante headed outside to tinker underneath the Triumph. Bernadette cranked up some of Daisy's favorite jazz—Ella and her trademark scat, and, as always, Daisy began doling out assignments while they unpacked and sorted groceries; soon they were working together like a well-oiled machine: Penelope, plunked down on a stool with a peeler and a bunch of carrots, slowly and methodically began scraping, focusing so intently on the task her face was all scrunched up; Rosalie was given onions to dice, an always weepy endeavor she seemed to enjoy; Bernadette potatoes to scrub; Kim mushrooms to quarter; and Celia, parked next to her mother, flour to season. Daisy dusted beef chunks in the flour and tossed the meat into a pot for a good long even browning. Then the diced onions were caramelized in the hot fat. She measured ingredients for the broth in which the stew would slowly bubble. This braise would take time—the longer the better, Daisy insisted—and over the next couple of hours, the house would fill with what always seemed to Celia like a cozy, wintry aroma.

While dinner was bubbling away in the oven, Kent and Bernadette took Kim, Rosalie, and the Twins into nearby

Blairsville to check out of the motel rooms they'd stayed in the previous night since they planned to fly home after they ate. Daisy took her turn on the sofa for a nap. Celia surveyed the mess they'd made—it was like a storm had blown through the kitchen—and so she started putting it back in order. Then she began to set the table for dinner. She was laying down place mats when Roberta appeared at the top of the stairs; next to her was a shorter version of Roberta, another squat muscular woman in clunky boots with lots of ink, piercings, and her hair in a severe mohawk.

"Oh!" Celia said, startled.

"This here's Noreen," Roberta muttered.

Noreen stared at her boots. She said something, but her voice was so low and soft Celia couldn't be sure if any words actually came out. She continued setting the table, plonking down silverware on top of napkins. "If you're looking for Dante, he's probably underneath that convertible."

"I already saw him. I wanted to talk to you a minute. Noreen, give us a sec?"

Noreen nodded. She turned and clomped down the stairs so fast and loud it sounded as if she might have tumbled down them.

"I came to apologize," Roberta began. "I shouldn't have ditched Dante and made you get out of bed and go to the festival in my place. It wasn't right."

"It's okay," Celia said, although the truth was it might have saved her a heap of heartache and trouble.

"What happened," Roberta continued, "was I let fear get in my way, and the more I thought about it, the madder I got at myself. Sat home all day at Noreen's just being angry at myself. Sometimes when I get mad, I punch things. Oh, don't worry, not people or animals or some such. Bric-a-brac mostly. Or it's walls. Made a nice big hole in Noreen's mom's living room! Then, naturally, she and Josephine—that's her mom—got sore at me for being a big stupid grump. Told me I needed to attend those anger management classes like I was ordered to do. So it was just a bad situation all around."

"Really," Celia insisted, wondering about the implications of the 'ordered to' part. "It's okay."

Roberta gave her a crooked smile. "You know, I was kind of hard on you when you first showed up here. I gave you some shit, thought you were just gonna be another big city snot. But you know what?"

"What?"

"You're kind of dope, Celia. You stepped up with Penny. With Lester too. Most wouldn't. So I hope I wasn't too much of an ass. I get that way sometimes with people I don't know. Sort of a defense mechanism you might say."

"You were fine."

"Anyway, here's my advice: whatever it is you're afraid of, try and get over it. You'll feel worlds better. I know I do. And also, get things off your chest. No good keeping shit bottled up. It's not healthy."

"Got it," Celia said.

Roberta gave her a thumbs up and clunked down the stairs after Noreen.

LATER, THEY ALL GATHERED around the table to dig in: Celia, her sisters, her mother, her little twin nieces, Kent

carefully smoothing a napkin over his lap, Lester Brenneman, who had dropped by to help Dante with the Triumph
and who Daisy asked to stay, and finally Roberta and
Noreen. Dante and Penelope looked somewhat startled to
be surrounded by this big noisy group, as if their home had
been invaded by some strange foreign army. Even a rattled
Mrs. Whiskerson had scrabbled to the furthest spot under a
bed and refused to come out for her insulin shot, so Celia
and Dante had to actually move the bed to get it done. But
Penelope and Dante seemed pleased to have them all there,
especially Penelope who, like all children her age, was the
center of attention.

Celia helped her mother spoon out bowls of the stew,
aromatic now after its hours-long braise, the meat meltingly tender, the vegetables soft and comforting. Chatter went
down to a minimum as they ate, so everybody looked up as
the sound of wheels crunching up the dirt driveway broke
the silence. Then came the noise of a car coming to a stop.

Kim, who had dashed back to the kitchen counter for
bibs for the twins, glanced out the window and said,
"Uh...Celia...?"

Celia looked up, her mouth full of stew.

"I can't be one hundred percent sure, but, um, I think
Barry's here."

Her fork clattered to the table.

"Also, if I'm not mistaken, that's his mother in the car."

"Gloria's with him?" Celia said, nearly choking as she
swallowed a last bite of a potato.

"And," Kim added, "an African-American woman I don't
recognize is in the back seat."

Celia stood. She felt light-headed as she approached the window on rubbery legs. She peered out into the dusk. There, indeed, was Barry, moving around to the passenger side to help his mother. Out of the car came Gloria, with her deep tan, complicated updo, and big jewelry. She, in turn, swiveled and was saying something to the woman in the back. Barry looked up, saw Celia in the window, and waved. She felt pangs of guilt, like sharp little jabs, when she realized he was wearing a shirt she'd picked out for his last birthday. Before she knew it, Penelope led them up the stairs, the scent of Gloria's Charles of the Ritz perfume arriving before them like the cloud of an approaching storm.

The unknown woman trailed them all. She was short, solidly built, bosomy, crowned by a close-cropped frizz of an afro flecked with gray, and eyes that seemed to dance with mischief. She smiled shyly and held Gloria's hand to help her up each step. Introductions went all around. The mystery woman was, of course, Bernice, the new home health aide Celia had heard about. While Dante and Lester started shuffling everybody to make room for three more at the table, Celia took Barry's arm and started to lead him toward the stairs. "Um...we need to talk," she began.

"Oh, crap," he answered, suddenly blanching. "You already know?"

She paused. She had no idea what he was referring to. "Already know what?"

"That there was something I wasn't telling you."

"You weren't telling me something?"

"Maybe you should sit down."

"I don't need to sit down. Just tell me."

"He's been avoiding mentioning that I'm moving back to New York," Gloria said. "With Bernice."

Celia looked at Barry. He gave her a little shrug. Gloria sank into a chair at the table with a loud sigh of some kind, or was it a groan?

"You're what?"

"I'm leaving Boca."

"You're moving?"

"Yes. Because of my health scare. It was a wake-up call. While I enjoy Florida, of course, and I do not miss winter one bit, I shouldn't be so far from my only child."

"Health scare?" Celia repeated. "I thought you had indigestion because you ate a Cuban sandwich for lunch."

"It wasn't a Cuban sandwich. Cuban food. I had the Ropa Vieja with fried plantains on the side. And, boy, was that a mistake."

"Okay. Plantains but..."

"...And sure," Gloria continued, "I just needed to pass gas. But God only knows what horrible thing might be coming up next. Just ask your mother, dear. She'll know what I'm talking about."

"Oh, don't look at me. I'm fit as a fiddle," Daisy burbled.

This earned skeptical looks from all three of her daughters.

"Well," Gloria said, "maybe for now, but you know what Bernice says?"

"What?" asked Daisy.

"She says 'Getting old's a bitch.' Isn't that what you say, Bernice?"

"Yes, indeed. It sure is," Bernice said, nodding her head, "A bitch." But she had one of those Caribbean lilts, so it sounded smooth and inviting, like an ice-cold piña colada on a hot summer day.

"I can second that," added Lester Brenneman in a thoughtful tone. He was the only one who hadn't stopped eating and, in fact, was helping himself to seconds of the stew. "The human body starts to betray you in Lord knows how many ways. Not all at once generally, but little by little, part by part. Or organ by organ, maybe, is a better way to put it. Until before you know it, you can't even go into the mens' room and step up to the..."

A nudge from Dante, and Lester fell silent. But suddenly, all eyes were on Kim-Cuc, who had a hand clamped over her mouth and seemed to be trembling. She might have been choking; it turned out she was overcome with the giggles. Flushing crimson, Kim bolted from the table, throwing apologies over her shoulder.

"Anyway, no reason to panic, Celia," Gloria continued. "We're not moving in with you and Barry. We'll take an apartment, Bernice and me, so I won't be alone, and she'll be closer to her cousin, who lives in Jersey."

"West Caldwell!" Bernice put in, grinning. "Nadine is my cousin. She's a pistol, that one!"

"Not too far from you," Gloria continued. "Walking distance maybe, because I'm not schlepping on any damn bus."

Celia attempted to form a response, but no words came out.

Barry said, "So that's what you wanted to talk to me about then? You had a hunch Mother was coming back?"

"Well, actually no."

"Then what was it about?"

Celia was about to tell Barry they needed to talk in private, but Gloria interrupted: "Is that Daisy's famous beef stew I smell?"

"It is," Rosalie said, "And it came out very delicious tonight. Can I fix you all a plate?"

Gloria looked both eager and skeptical as if she might be calculating if that would give her gas too, but they all squeezed in at the table. With the rearranging, Celia found herself between Barry on her right and Dante on her left as everybody dug back in. Conversation suddenly veered into the safe territory of how the trip up from Florida was, what route they took, what they saw, and where they ate. Gloria was in the middle of describing the unexpected cleanliness of the ladies' room at a rest stop near Tallahassee when Dante, who had been antsy and shifting restlessly in his seat, leaned across to Barry, nodded toward Celia, and declared, "By the way, I am in love with her."

"I'm sorry, what?" Barry said.

The din of conversation and the clatter of silverware against plates came to an abrupt halt. For a second, the thought passed through Celia's head that if somebody did drop a pin, she'd hear it land with a plink on the wood floor.

"I am in love with your fiancé," Dante repeated, louder this time.

A look of confusion passed across Barry's face. His mouth fell open.

Dante kept going: "I feel this love in my bones. I will emphasize that I am sorry. Truly sorry. It's not my way, and it was never my intention to tread into another man's territory. Although that doesn't sound quite right, does it? You don't own her. And how she feels about me, to be honest, remains a mystery. But, anyway, it's the truth. And if she'd have me, I'd marry her in a hot second."

Every eye in the room was on Celia. Even Penelope seemed suddenly drawn into the drama. The first sensation to hit Celia was one of utter mortification as she looked around the table. Gloria gasped and clutched at her chest. Barry, who had started to ask her if she had slept with Dante, turned to his mother, while Bernice handed Gloria a water glass and fanned her with a plate. Celia's sisters were trading glances with Daisy. Kim, quietly making her way back to the table, was half in and half out of her seat. Even Kent had looked up from his iPad. So she was mortified, yes. But Celia was also feeling this: for maybe the first time in her life, it was like she was no longer the random middle one, the bland sister everybody took for granted, or often seemed to ignore. She knew it was wrong, but for the moment, with growing chaos all around her, she reveled in the sensation of being the center of attention, and she wondered whether the two men might come to blows – over her! – and wouldn't that be something?

CELIA WOULD SOON LEARN there were only so many ways to say she was sorry for what she had done, and that it probably wouldn't make a difference.

"It happened. I wasn't looking for it. I swear," she began when they stepped outside so they could escape all those prying eyes. For what seemed like forever, Barry just looked at her. All at once, she couldn't look back.

"Why did you do this?" he finally asked.

"I don't know. I didn't mean for anybody to get hurt. It was stupid. A mistake."

Barry just shook his head.

"I could blame the alcohol, I guess, although that would be lame," Celia continued. "But when you didn't show up for my birthday, I was alone. I was a little sad, I have to admit. I got hammered."

"Are you saying he took advantage of you? Because you were drunk?"

"No. He tried to do the right thing. He tried to stop it."

Barry put his head in his hands. "We had it so good. We had it all planned."

"Did we?"

He looked right at Celia, a pure piercing gaze that seemed to penetrate her soul. Again, she had to look away. After a short tense silence, he said, "Oh, you are not putting any of this on me. You broke us. Now at least own it."

He was right, of course. She had no good answers. She expected him to yell some more. She braced herself for the onslaught she knew she deserved. But Barry had always been even-tempered, so she wasn't entirely surprised when he turned and walked away. All she could do was watch him go. At the same moment, she noticed her mother and sisters peering out a window of the barn, straining to see what was happening. They speedily withdrew the instant they noticed her looking.

She felt drained. She sank into a seat on the porch. A question nagged at her. Why had this happened? If that cookbook had never popped up, uninvited, after nearly forty years of being missing in action, she silently reasoned, wedding plans would have continued uninterrupted, she was sure, and the marriage itself would have eventually taken place. She did love Barry. But now she had to wonder: had they waited too long to solidify the relationship, to make it permanent—with vows and in front of witnesses—which was maybe more important than either of them thought? Was necessary even. And had their moment, without either having realized it, somehow passed?

Before she knew it, Barry, Gloria, and Bernice were gone. She watched, unable to move from where she sat, as they piled back into the rental and tore off down the road. Now the enormity of what she had done finally hit her. She felt heavier, almost drugged, as she stood and headed back inside. She stopped her mother and sisters before they had a chance to utter a word: "Not now," was all she said before walking into the bedroom and shutting the door. Sure, it wasn't her room, but she needed a space of her own, at least for a bit. At first she just stared blankly ahead. It seemed suddenly dark in the room and she switched on a lamp. But then it seemed too bright and she switched it back off. Silence enveloped her. A while later, there was knocking.

"Honey...?"

It was Daisy.

"Go away, Mom," Celia said.

There was murmuring—a consultation between Daisy and her other daughters, and some talk about them all soon leaving for their own flights home—and then they all moved off, and it was quiet again.

A short time later came another soft rap. Dante whispered her name, but she didn't answer. Instead, she climbed into the bed, at first focusing on a small sliver of moon visible through the window. She pulled the covers over her head. In time, she fell into a restless sleep that made the night feel like an eternity. She woke in a damp tangle of sheets and blankets. She slipped into the bathroom and showered quickly. After toweling off, she caught a glimpse of her face in the mirror, and it made her pause—she had that trapped, frozen look you might get when you're caught in the middle of a choice, unsure which direction is best but unable to make the decision.

Dante was sleeping on the couch, but he roused when she emerged from the bathroom. He sat up and rubbed sleep from his eyes. "Well, finally we're alone," he said.

"No, we're not. Penelope's here."

He gave her one of his crooked smiles, but Celia was having none of it.

"Listen," she said. "I'm not staying, either."

"You don't have to leave."

"Yeah, I do."

"Why?"

"You really need to ask that? Seriously?"

"I do."

"Okay," Celia said. "I need to figure some things out. A lot of things, actually."

"Like...?"

"I don't know how to explain it."

"Try."

She sat at the counter and rubbed at her temples. After a moment, she said, "All right. The other night, in Macon, when you found me crying? Well, I think it had suddenly dawned on me that somewhere along the line, I disappeared."

"Hmmmmmm," Dante said. He stroked his scruffy beard. He filled a kettle with water for coffee, lit a burner, and set it down on the flame before turning back. "I see you just fine."

"Well, I said you wouldn't understand, and I was right."

"So make me understand," said Dante.

Celia thought about how best to explain. "You know," she began, "a long time ago, when I was a kid, maybe the same age Penelope is now, I had these fantasies—these visions—of what my life would be like. When I grew up, I mean. When I'd be an adult."

"Yeah. Well, who doesn't? Everybody has those."

"Except nothing turned out the way I thought it would, the way I dreamed it would."

"You're not alone there, either," Dante said. "My guess is it's probably true for a good portion of the world. A majority, even. But, hey, also you're not dead yet, are you? If you're unhappy about something, you can change it. It's not easy, but you can try."

"I get that."

"Then what's the problem?"

"When that couple at the festival asked me to take pictures for them, it reminded me of something. When I was in college, for a photography class, I had this final project to do. I poured my heart and soul into it. But the professor ripped my work to shreds. I don't remember all of it. But he said something like I needed to disappear in order to take the kind of pictures I wanted to take. Anyway, now, after all this time, I did it. I captured some images that those people responded to. So that must mean, somewhere along the way, I disappeared. I vanished."

"But wasn't he saying that would be a good thing? It would be an asset?"

"Yeah. I guess maybe he meant it that way. But I can't get this idea out of my head—that I lost what I wanted out of my life. And I'm wondering how that happened, and why."

Dante was quiet a moment. Then he said, "Maybe you shouldn't be looking at what you lost."

"Yeah? What should I look at, then?"

"Maybe you should look at what you found."

She paused. But she continued to gather things and throw them into her bag.

IX.

O n Celia's first day back at headquarters, Danielle Chan summoned Celia to her office and began what felt like an interrogation: "You're absolutely sure there's no permanent damage?" was the first question fired her way.

"Danielle, I'm fine," Celia insisted.

"You're absolutely positive about that?"

"I could not be better. It was a minor accident, really."

"Minor? I heard there was an explosion. A very massive one!"

"Well, yes, the car I rented did, in fact, burst into flames—but I had the extra insurance, so no worries there!—but I'm not certain if I'd categorize it as a massive explosion. That's a little dramatic, in fact. And by the way, where did you hear about it?"

"From what I gather, you told Sonya. Bert Pitoniak may have, in passing, overheard the conversation."

"Ah. Of course. And he couldn't wait to tell you. Nice."

Danielle seemed a little obsessed with the accident. "Still, we should maybe schedule you an appointment for a complete physical."

"Really, there was no damage. To me. I mean, in a physical sense. Permanent damage, I guess."

"Car crashes can be very debilitating," Danielle continued. "Sometimes, you don't know the true extent of the injury until much time has passed."

"Not necessary, really."

Celia insisted all was great – terrific even –- but it wasn't. Not even remotely close to great. Things didn't even seem close to so-so or even fair. Actually, nothing was right. She felt adrift and disoriented, as if she were moving carefully but fitfully through a world that had suddenly been enveloped in a thick, dense fog.

She felt this from the moment she woke up the morning after she flew out of Atlanta and landed in New York because she opened her eyes in the room she had when she was a child, in her mother's house, and at first, she had to wonder how she got there. Also, Daisy hadn't touched the room since Celia left for college, so it was like being in some strange time capsule—her 21 JUMP STREET poster was still on the wall, Johnny Depp gazing down at her smolderingly, as was her poster of the Go-Go's on a stage somewhere, all glamour and rock and roll. She pulled open the drawers of her desk. In one were old journals and diaries. In another her old school yearbooks. Underneath them was the camera from her college photography years. She wiped off the dust and set it on the desk, then got distracted by all the old cassettes and mix-tapes she supposed were now useless. Lined up along a windowsill were dolls and all the stuffed animals she hadn't thrown away even after she knew she had outgrown them. These were lumpy now, the insides turned to sawdust, and they smelled damp, musty, and stale. Everything had layers of dust all over it, making her wonder about what had been going wrong with her mother's housekeeping. Daisy was always a huge fanatic about these things – she would always complain about tidying up—but Celia and her sisters had been noticing glaring lapses. Celia's old room seemed to be evidence of even more slippage, but they were all over the house really, Celia had noticed—the tops of picture frames were dirty, windows were streaked, and in one little-used bathroom, mold was clearly visible on the tiles in the shower. When she or her sisters would suggest Daisy bring in help to clean the house, she would flat-out refuse to even consider it.

But before showing up at her mother's, after landing at JFK, Celia first had parked down the street from the house she shared with Barry. It was office hours, so she knew Barry would be gone. She wasn't sure if she could face Gloria, so she sat in the car and waited, watching the house. The rhythm of the block seemed undisturbed by her absence. Next door, elderly Mr. Pickler slowly rolled his garbage bin to the curb, methodically placing it just so before putting his arms akimbo and stretching his back. The harried mother at the corner—Celia could never remember her name—pushed one toddler in a stroller while a baby was strapped to her chest. Claire from across the street, with the always-perfect garden that shamed everybody else, walked her jittery German Shepherd toward the park. Soon, an Uber slid into the driveway of her house. Bernice helped Gloria into the car and got in herself.

Once they had gone, Celia slipped inside, feeling stealthy, as if she were doing something illegal. It was dead silent in the house. It felt like an eerie rebuke. She looked around at all the furniture and the appliances she and Barry had picked together—they seemed to look back at her with reproach. So, too, did all the knick-knacks and framed photos of the two of them in happier times, one all smiling faces as they clinked wine glasses together in a vineyard, another at the base of a snow-capped mountain, almost comically bundled up, bodies pressed together. She inspected the pictures more closely, tapping the glass with a nail, searching for clues as if maybe there was something that could tell her how it all would go so wrong. Also, she wondered, what would happen to the pictures now? Would they get torn up? Stored in boxes and forgotten?

In the bedroom, she opened her closet. There were her blue skirts and blue blazers and her white blouses, all in a precise line. She packed them up, along with all her other clothes. She gathered her make-up, her jewelry, her books, and all the other little things she had accumulated and felt an attachment to. She sat on the bed, and for a moment, its familiar lumps and bumps were like a tug. She put her head back on the pillows, then sat up and pulled open the drawer of her nightstand. Inside was a jumble—a dry cleaning receipt here, knotted-up cords for a long-discarded phone there, an old tube of Chapstick, a few stray pennies, many pens—most she was certain didn't work—and a key for some lock that was a mystery. Uncertain what to do with what was basically garbage, she slid the drawer closed again.

She was heading with her bags to the front door when she spotted the stack of mail. Right on top was a big envelope with her name on it. She ripped it open. Inside was a slick brochure from one of the wedding venues she and Barry had contacted. Well, she had made the contact, but she was planning to tell him. It was an old white clapboard restaurant with a nautical theme, perched jauntily by the sea, so if you picked the right date and the weather cooperated, you could have your wedding on the sand, with waves crashing nearby and the welcome scent of brine. Celia sank onto the couch and leafed through it. Here were examples of gorgeous, happy couples of every stripe—bride and groom, groom and groom, bride and bride, and here, too, were their devoted families and delighted friends, all perfectly coiffed and dressed beachy-casual, some barefoot even, in the middle of toasting the newlyweds. She realized she was looking at these pictures through a hot blur of tears, and then the door burst open, and there was a shriek!

It was Bernice. She had deposited Gloria at the hairdresser and had a couple of hours to kill until it was time to collect her. "Good Lord," Bernice gasped when she caught her breath, "Girl, you scared me dang silly!"

"Sorry," Celia said. "I'm really sorry."

She started crying harder. In the last few days, these uncontrollable sobs seemed to be coming out of nowhere. Bernice stepped closer and pulled her into a hug. Celia felt strangely comfortable nestled against this unfamiliar woman's soft, ample bosom. Also, Bernice smelled comforting—like she carried with her the gentle, intoxicating scent of a soft island breeze. As Celia continued to sob, Bernice gently patted her back. "There, there," she murmured in that sing-songy Caribbean lilt. "It's okay, honey. Nothing like a good cry sometimes. You go on and let it out. Big problem people have these days is they just don't cry enough. They hold it all in, and it just makes things worse! Causes illness, in fact, if you want my opinion."

Celia untangled herself from Bernice's embrace and blindly fished in her purse for a Kleenex. Bernice, apparently one of those women prepared for any and all sorts of emergencies, pulled a wad from inside one sleeve and pressed it into her hand. Celia dabbed at her eyes. "I don't know what's happening to me lately," she confessed. "I'm very confused."

"Oh, course you are, honey. Don't you know we all are, really, when it comes right down to it. Oh, we may pretend we're not big balls of confusion—put on big strong facades and brave faces and all that—but it isn't even remotely close to the truth. The truth is, we all just blunder from one mistake to another and then muddle through as best we can."

Celia snuffled and wiped her nose. She detected another unfamiliar aroma—this time something spicy and delicious. Bernice seemed to pick up on it. "Well, I been jerking chicken," she said.

"Um...what?" Celia asked. It sounded vaguely dirty.

"Jerking! It's a spice blend. Everybody does it a little different—some like more allspice, some less habañero; although, if you ask me, heat's important in jerk; although, granted, you might pay the price in the morning—they don't call it 'ring of fire' for nothing! But my blend is the best. I'll tell you that. I'm bringing chicken to a barbecue at my sister Jeanette's in Jersey tomorrow. It's not for Mrs. Kepler or Barry. No, ma'am. Not with them tummies. The both of them." She made a tsk-tsking sound and shook her head gravely.

Celia nodded. "They probably both hate me. Does he hate me?" she asked.

"Well, I can tell you this: he isn't happy," Bernice admitted.

"We were supposed to be like these people," Celia said. She pointed to the couple being happily married in the brochure.

Bernice scanned the pictures and let out what sounded like a snort. "Everybody looks like that at the start, honey. It's only later that it starts to go sour, once all the shininess wears off."

"You're married?" Celia asked because there was a gold band on her ring finger.

"Ah, this?" She held up her hand. "Stuck there. From husband number two. Or was it three? Girl, my fingers got so fat I can't get it off. Some doctor offered to saw it off, but I didn't think that was a particularly good idea." She chuckled heartily and held her hand out to gaze at the ring for a moment.

"How many husbands are there?"

Bernice gave her a cagey grin and shook with more laughter. "Five!"

Her smile was infectious. Celia couldn't help but smile back. She could barely manage one man. She couldn't imagine having to contend with that many husbands.

"And not one worth a dang cent," Bernice continued. "This one stole money. That one gave me an STD. Another had an affair with my cousin. My very own cousin! I mean, really? In fact, every last one of them I caught cheating. But that's a man for you. I asked one once—why do you cheat? He just shrugged and muttered something about getting this ooogy feeling in his groin."

Celia gave Bernice a puzzled sort of look.

"Exactly! I go, Oooogy? What's ooogy? And he says, you know, just warm and tingly and moist and maybe a little sweaty down there, and like you gotta just screw or you gonna bust and you can't think about nothing else—you go into a kind of stupor, or a trance I guess—until you just do it with the closest thing you can find. Anyway, that's men. Ruled not by their brains—if they lucky enough to have any—but by their peckers."

Celia's mouth opened but nothing came out.

"Of course," she added knowingly, "women stray too. It's a fact of life. I've been tempted, yes ma'am I certainly have, but mostly it's men, I've found."

Bernice had children, Celia was to learn, grandchildren, and even a great-grandchild, although she didn't seem old enough. Some of them were still in her native Barbados, others scattered up and down the East Coast. It all sounded very complicated, and apparently somebody was always mad at somebody else, or bearing some sort of grudge. Bernice offered to make her a cup of chamomile tea, swore up and down it would soothe her jangly nerves, but Celia, suddenly feeling like a stranger in her own house, felt the need to get moving.

Once she was settled back into her car, she realized it was the first time in what seemed like forever that she didn't know where to go. For a few moments, she sat there wondering. She thought about a hotel, but didn't she spend enough time in hotels already? Nearly half her life, it seemed. She could call one of her sisters, but did she really want to stay in Bernadette and Kent's apartment in the city? Sure, they had an extra room, but it was set up as a library with a pull-out couch, and she knew she'd just be in the way, or they'd get on her nerves with all their fastidiousness. Rosalie and Kim's was just too crowded and, with the twins, too chaotic and noisy. Plus, if she stayed with either sister, there would be the requisite judgment and criticism. She could call a friend, she thought, until she realized how few friends she actually had. Sonya from work would take her in. Wouldn't she? She debated renting a place of her own. She hadn't had her own apartment—a space she could call her own—in years; there was something intriguing about the idea, a blank slate where she could start fresh.

It didn't matter. Later, she came up against the force of her mother, who often seemed flighty but just as often had a will of iron. Daisy insisted Celia move home, at least until she could get her bearings and, despite her saying over and over that all was fine, there was admittedly something nice about being at her mother's again. She knew this house inside and out, its creaky stairs and pipes that groaned if you ran the hot water too long, and all its familiar smells. She didn't have to worry about a thing. She didn't have to pay bills. She didn't have to vacuum or dust. She didn't have to do the laundry. She didn't have to grocery shop. She didn't have to plan meals, cook, or do the dishes. Daisy seemed pleased – almost eager in fact – to do it all, seemed to relish having somebody to do it for, even though all the years when she did do everything for Celia and Rosalie and Bernadette, she seemed to complain endlessly about how nobody ever pitched in to help.

That first morning, she fixed Celia the same breakfast she'd often make for her and her sisters when they were small: French toast, crisp on the outside, almost custardy inside, with sizzling sausages, and lots of warm maple syrup to pour over it all. Daisy washed, folded, and ironed her clothes. She kept the room tidy, especially after Celia finally called her out on all the dust. Daisy, while not admitting fault, made a big show of pulling out extra rags from an over-stuffed bag under the kitchen sink and shaking them with a crisp, audible snap while shooting Celia a tight-lipped smirk. Part of Celia wondered if she might never ever leave. She'd stay right in her old room and become one of those extremely testy, high-strung women who live with their mothers for life. Well, there was no comfort there as she then imagined them becoming crazed incessantly-bickering recluses who dressed like eccentrics, ate out of cans, and had tons of cats as their only company.

Still, she continued to insist to herself that all was fine that first morning as, after breakfast, she showered and dressed in her uniform—the narrow blue work skirt, blazer, and blouse. *Did this outfit always feel this stiff and itchy?* she wondered. No, she was imagining this, too. Certainly she was. It must be just that she'd spent the last week or so in jeans and T-shirts, and so she just wasn't used to having it on. She told herself all was great as she pulled her hair back and secured it with a ribbon, then brushed powder over her freckles and rolled on some lipstick.

All was just excellent, she claimed out loud a few minutes later as she backed the car out of her mother's driveway, even if her teeth were gritted tight and she backed out a little too fast and aggressively, earning a stern, disapproving glare from the next door neighbor mom, a new arrival Celia had never actually met, who was pushing her helmeted and comically padded toddler on a tricycle. She drove down the street, cranking up the tunes to crowd out negative thoughts when she caught sight of a tall, shaggy-haired bearded man walking a dog, and it brought back a vision of Dante stripping off his clothes and diving into the river in Macon. She turned the music louder and started to sing along with the song even if she knew she was mangling the words. Didn't matter.

And so, back at headquarters, she insisted to Danielle that she couldn't wait to get to her territories, was really raring to go (until she realized that her enthusiasm suddenly sounded slightly demented). Then she arrived at her first appointment. Something odd happened as she launched into her pitch. "Picture your mother *before* the HX III Patch," Celia began, just like she had rehearsed, pointing to the image of the old lady on her PowerPoint presentation. "She looks...."

She broke off and really examined the picture for the first time.

"...Well," Celia said, "she sort of looks like my mother, actually."

The resemblance was uncanny; it suddenly hit her. The doctor, a prominent dermatologist who was preoccupied with something on his computer, didn't seem to notice, so Celia continued, the filter in her brain apparently turned off. "And, the fact is, what's wrong with the way my mother looks? I mean, yeah, she's a little wrinkled, and God only knows what her hair would actually look like if she didn't make those weekly trips to the salon with Lois from across the street, but there's something comforting about that face, I would have to say."

Now, she had the doctor's attention. He stopped clacking away at his keyboard and fixed her with a quizzical look. "I'm sorry, what?"

"I was just saying that the more I think about it, I don't really believe there's anything wrong with the 'Before' picture. Do you?"

"The picture of the old lady?"

"You don't have to say it like that."

"Like what?"

"In that sort of disparaging way. Or dismissive. Condescending, you might even say."

"Oh. Well..."

Celia could not seem to stop herself. "In fact, some people might appreciate a picture that accentuates the wrinkles. I mean, I'm starting to realize something - let's face it: getting through life is no picnic, is it?"

"Well, Um..."

"Maybe a few wrinkles here and there are concrete evidence that you've been winning the battle – or at least surviving from one day to the next—and that isn't such a bad thing. I'm just saying."

She was ushered out of the office without closing one sale, a first for her, or at least something that hadn't happened in too many years to remember. She stepped onto the elevator going down; it was packed with reps just like her, but it was as if the others could smell her defeat. Nobody met her eyes, and there was silence until they all reached the lobby and scattered, the only noise the squeaky wheels of their black cases trailing behind them. That all of this didn't bother Celia made her realize that something drastic had changed. It was as if somebody had flipped a switch, and she no longer believed in what she was selling, and if she couldn't believe in it, how could she do it? She could change accounts and just take on benign products like anti-itch creams or hand sanitizers or over-the-counter cough remedies, but was that how she wanted to spend her life? Would she look back when it was all over and think it was worth it, that she'd contributed?

So in what she best could describe as a trance-like state—her mind felt like a complete blank—she drove back to headquarters. She parked her sedan in its assigned spot. For a time, she just sat and stared at the hushed campus — beige, windowless buildings squatted against a cloudless blue sky. The whole place suddenly had an ominous look. The car window was open, but she noted a distinct absence of sound as if even birds and squirrels in the few surrounding trees knew to keep clear. Finally, she got out of the car, chirped the alarm, and headed inside. She marched directly to Danielle's office and quit.

"Are you still mad that I let Bert Pitoniak temporarily take over your territories?" asked a shocked Danielle.

"No, I'm not mad."

"You're sure? It would be understandable if you were. I am the boss, and you are the employee, so it's normal for there to be friction, and perhaps even a touch of jealousy, even though our relationship has always been so cordial."

"I am definitely not mad."

Danielle pursed her lips. She fiddled with a pen. "Are you crazy, then? You've been here forever!"

"Yep. Exactly. It's the only job I've ever really known. So maybe that's part of the problem. Time for a change, I could argue. I will argue."

"Okay. But I will argue this: you actually have it pretty easy, Celia. You understand that, don't you? I would say yours is a somewhat cushy position. On the other hand, most people are miserable in their jobs. They drag themselves out of bed and toil away for hours at a time, dreaming of nothing but getting home into that bed again."

"And you know this because?"

Danielle ignored that. She leaned closer. She paused and lowered her voice. "Is it something hormonal, Celia? Really?"

"Um..."

"Because you know how it is, right? Sometimes when our hormones are out of whack, we make bad, very emotionally charged decisions, decisions that we later regret. I told you to take some time away because I thought you needed it, but now perhaps I was mistaken because maybe you've had too much time on your hands, and you're not thinking clearly. Are you sure you want to make a change—a momentous life change, I might add—that may be very difficult, impossible even, to unwind?"

"I don't think it's hormonal. Although even if it was, wouldn't that be ironic?"

Danielle looked confused. "I don't know where you're going with this."

"Well, like some kind of karmic payback? Now, that would be something, wouldn't it?"

Danielle apparently didn't see the karma or the irony as she didn't even crack a hint of a smile.

Celia left the office with Danielle still trying to convince her to stay, Danielle in fact shouting offers of more money! A bigger year-end bonus! A Tesla! Celia ignored it all. She marched down the hall to her own office. She said good-byes to her assistant, to Sonya, and even to Bert Pitoniak.

"You can have my territories. You win, Bert," she said as she headed for the elevator, a small box of her belongings (yes, everything from her office fit in a small box, and what did that say, she suddenly wondered), and Bert just stood there staring at her, slack-jawed, unable, for once, to come up with a response.

Outside, she realized her sedan was a company sedan. The company owned it. Barry owned the house they lived in. They always talked about adding her to the title, but somehow it kept slipping away. How, she suddenly wondered, did she arrive at a place where she had what felt like nothing?

So she Ubered back to her mother's house and crawled into bed.

Oh, she knew the psychological implications of all of this. She was feeling lost and confused—feeling sorry for herself when she knew deep down she really had no right to—and was reverting to a childlike state. But she decided not to fight it. For the first few days, she let herself be waited on by her mother, who seemed to relish having a job to do, which made Celia wonder about how Daisy had filled her days since her nest emptied.

Simultaneously, there was all the second-guessing. She should have fought harder to win Barry's forgiveness. Should she beg for it? Wouldn't she deserve the humiliation? Didn't he deserve to have her put up a fight? But then this thought—would he ever really forgive her? Truly? Would she spend the rest of her life unsure whether or not he trusted her? Should he trust her after what happened? Thoughts like these began to crowd her mind.

There were other pressing issues. Like money. How exactly would she make a living now, and how long could she last on the savings she had banked? Could she go back to school? Was she too old? Was it too late? Then images of Dante would interrupt. She wondered why he hadn't texted, or called, or emailed. Okay, well, she had ordered him not to when she left, but still. She tried to sort out how exactly she felt about him. She missed Penelope, too, but figured a kid that age would have forgotten about her already. Wouldn't she?

Her mood seemed to change by the hour, and her mother decided to give her space, calling up from downstairs that she was headed to the store or to town with Lois, who had returned from her rehab stint in Texas, and calling up again that she was back and did Celia want anything to eat? Mostly, she said no, but up the stairs her mother would come anyway with comforting things on a tray, and Celia would manage to eat after all, meals like a grilled American Cheese sandwich with a cup of tomato soup, or a slab of meatloaf with gravy and mashed potatoes. Yes, Celia suspected this acting like a child all over again was getting out of hand, but she didn't seem to have the strength to fight it even if she kept worrying that she might keep regressing and regressing until she was in diapers again.

After a couple of days, her mother began finding little things for her to do, just to get her out of bed and out of the house. Could Celia accompany her to the dentist, an old pro who had faithfully tended all Bernharts for as long as Celia could remember and who now had cataracts, used a walker and could barely hear. Was sticking with him a good idea, Celia wondered? Or could she haul a box of old clothes to the Salvation Army? And get a receipt? One morning, Daisy placed a hefty envelope in Celia's hand and asked her to take it to the post office. Celia glanced at the label. It was addressed to Dante. Celia just fixed her mother with a puzzled look.

"Something wrong, dear?" Daisy asked.

"What are you sending him?"

"Well, he seemed to appreciate that recipe for the coconut cake so much, I thought he might like the book that has my original recipe. Because while the one in his grandmother's book was perfectly good, this one is better, if you ask me."

"You couldn't just write it down and email it? Or shoot him a text with a picture? Haven't we told you enough times, nobody mails things anymore!"

"You have. And I have chosen to ignore you. Plus, don't you think there's something much nicer about getting an actual book?"

"Well..."

"Something you can hold in your hand and leaf through? There's a lot of good recipes he might appreciate. I sat down and really looked through it again. I even noted in the margins a few he might find interesting, so he can't miss them. But I don't need the book at this stage of the game, so I copied the one recipe I need. In pen with my hand, if you must know. Unless of course you or one of your sisters might want it? Although I must say I could imagine once I'm gone, all my old recipes will end up being tossed on the trash heap. I don't think you girls value them."

"And now a guilt trip, Mom? Really?"

Daisy simply gave Celia a vague smile.

She decided not to argue further. She showered. She put on clothes. She brushed out her hair. She grabbed her mother's keys and got in her ancient Wagoneer. It turned over roughly and idled like a truck, bucking and shimmying and belching ominous black smoke from the tail pipe until it warmed up. She looked down and noticed not just holes in the floor mats but holes in the actual floor, the metal rusted clean through, so she could see the driveway, which also was pocked with oil stains, so the beast must be leaking, too. *Was her mother losing her mind,* she wondered as she drove into town, because crumpled notes littered the car, little lists and reminders about just about everything, some more cryptic than others. For instance, what in the world could 'Beans beans corkscrew candlestick' scribbled on a post-it possibly mean?

She stood in line at the post office because the one machine where she could get the postage herself was, of course, not in service.

"You again, huh?" said the lady behind the counter when it was Celia's turn, and she realized it was the clerk she had talked to when she tried to return the mis-delivered package belonging to Dante's grandmother. "This one's not forty years late too, is it?" she grumbled, rolling her eyes theatrically as if thinking *here comes that difficult one again, the lady with all the complaints.*

Celia couldn't help a little laugh, which felt oddly liberating after several days of barely showing emotion. "Not this time."

The postal lady placed the envelope on the scale and punched some numbers into her keypad. "What'd you do with that envelope anyway? Toss it in the trash?"

"No," Celia said. "I actually delivered it."

The lady cocked her head and raised an eyebrow.

"Hand delivered it, actually" Celia added. "To an address in Georgia."

"Really? How'd that work out for ya, then?"

Celia truly wasn't sure how to answer, so she just shrugged.

ON SUNDAY, HER SISTERS descended on the house for supper. Daisy had been cooking all day, and Celia knew the aromas from memory, knew her mother had prepared an old standby, spaghetti and meatballs, a dish she, her sisters, and anybody who also might have eaten it over the years, actually adored and devoured with greedy abandon. First, the smell of simmering sauce came wafting through the house, onions and garlic sizzling in olive oil, soon to be joined by crushed tomatoes, oregano, and freshly torn basil. Once the sauce was bubbling away on the stove, Celia could hear her

mother humming her way through the mixing of her meatball ingredients, a top secret blend that Celia vaguely knew
included bread crumbs (fresh ones), milk (whole, not skim),
grated parmesan cheese, tons of chopped parsley, more garlic, and an egg or two and, if she wasn't mistaken, a little bit
of ricotta, and then the slow, careful browning of the meatballs, these aromas only stoking Celia's anticipation.

Rosalie, Kim-Cuc, and the twins were the first to arrive,
Celia could tell from all the noise and commotion downstairs (she was still ensconced in her room). Then came
Bernadette, by herself as usual because Kent always concoct-
ed some excuse to stay in the city. She could hear her sisters
pitch in, Rosalie putting together a salad ("These radishes
are organic, non-GMO, and from the farmer's market, right,
Mom? You're sure?") and Bernadette setting the table
("Mother, these placemats are coming apart at the seams.
Won't you ever get new ones?"). Soon, they insisted she
come downstairs and join them, which she would have done
anyway because by dinner time her stomach was actually
grumbling. Even more so when it turned out Daisy had decided to toss garlic bread into the mix, and the rich fragrance
as it browned and crisped in the oven was nearly making her
crazy.

She threw a bathrobe over sweats and made her way to
her spot at the table just as plates were being passed around,
each one piled high with spaghetti, topped with a couple of
meatballs and sauce, with more grated parmesan showered
all over. It felt so warm and cozy, with the steam rising off the
plates and the twins happily situated between Rosalie and
Kim, but then her sisters started in on her with the unsolicit-

ed advice: "You know what you should do?" Rosalie began, "You should come to my office and volunteer. We can always use people helping out at the food bank. Or you could work in the thrift store. Because I know you're feeling sorry for yourself, Celia, but you need to see that there are people who are in way worse shape. Like they're homeless for real. Or paralyzed. Or mentally unstable and have no access to good healthcare or the proper medications."

Bernadette picked up the thread. "No, she should come to the firm. Since that last blip in the economy, we're hiring again. She could enter a training program. I don't imagine she's too old yet. Although, frankly, she might be. Anyway, she could bank some real coin instead of that salary plus commissions she's been slaving for all these years."

"Maybe money isn't important to her. Maybe helping the less fortunate is what matters," Rosalie countered, and Kim nodded along in agreement while breaking off a tiny sliver of bread and passing it into the groping hand of a twin.

Celia's mother said, "She could go for paramedic training."

This seemed to come from left-field and caught everybody's attention. Daisy noticed them all staring. "What? I was just reading about a big need for paramedics. It's a very short course, apparently, and then you can ride around on one of those nifty big red trucks and help save lives. What could be more meaningful than that?"

Kim said, "No, what would be best for her to do is..."

Celia interrupted: "Really, people? Seriously? Must we do this?"

There was a chorus of "Do *what's*?"

"Have your weekly criticize Celia time?"

"We're just trying to help," Daisy insisted as she dropped another meatball onto Celia's plate.

Celia pushed the plate away. "You know what?" she continued, "How about if, for once, I pick your lives apart?"

Her sisters and her mother all shot her blank stares. Celia took that as an opening. "Let's start with you, Rosalie: this do-gooder thing? Yeah, we all get it, you're going to save the world and all, and we all thank you for that—really we do because none of us have the time—but would it be so horrible to put on some make-up every once in a while and maybe some chic and stylish clothes and not some old thing that looks like it came from a rag bag? And God forbid, a splash of something nice-smelling. And, you know, once in a while, let yourself have a little silly fun? Just quit being so damn serious and let go! I bet Kim would love it, wouldn't you?"

Kim-Cuc pivoted toward her wife. "Now that Celia mentions it, sweetie, you can go a little far with the drab. You look so pretty when you wear a pop of color. Or show off your legs. Or, well, even shave them."

"I don't like to spend money unnecessarily on frivolous things," Rosalie protested. "It's wasteful, and it's bad for the planet! Like with the straws everybody uses once and throws away. All that damn plastic. You all understand dead whales are washing up on beaches with stomachs full of plastic? It's a horror."

"I get it. We all get it, honey." Kim said. "But still..."

Rosalie started to protest more, a fast-escalating tirade that circled back to leg shaving and the evil patriarchy, but

Celia turned her attention to her other sister. "And you, Bernadette," she said. "Guess what?"

Bernadette suddenly looked nervous. "Um, what?"

"One day, you're going to drop dead. It's not going to matter how many dollars are in your brokerage account or how many pairs of Louboutins are in that giant walk-in closet you're always yakking about. So just chill out with the money fixation and the square footage of your co-op and the names and the labels on everything, okay? Because in the end, none of it will matter. You're not taking it with you."

"Well, I never implied that I..."

Celia didn't hear the rest of her sister's retort because already she had swiveled around to face their mother. "And you with the non-stop nit-picking."

"Me?!"

"Yes, you. All my life! 'You've gained weight, Celia.' 'You're too old, Celia.' 'Your fingers are fat.' 'Your job stinks.' 'Why are you *still* not married?' 'Where are my grandchildren?' Do I find fault with every little thing you do?"

"Yes!" Daisy sputtered. "All the time. You and your sisters!! Especially lately. You don't have to watch my every move. Like I'm going to burn down the house or spend all my money. I have every last one of my marbles!"

Bernadette said, "Oh, Mother darling, we're not finding fault."

"That's right," Rosalie agreed, "we're expressing concern."

"Because to us," Bernadette added, "with the forgetfulness, and all the flighty, sometimes questionable decisions, it does, occasionally, seem like you're going a little gaga."

Rosalie and Kim nodded in support.

"Nice. Great," Daisy said as she leaned closer to the twins. "I can see the writing on the wall now. Your mothers and your aunts are going to lock me up."

The Twins smiled simultaneously and stretched their rubbery arms toward their grandmother, who slipped a strand of spaghetti in each of their hands.

"They'll call it assisted living or some such thing," Daisy continued, "and it will have this pleasant-sounding name like Riverview, or Shady Acres — but that isn't really what it is. It will be a nice room, but if you look beyond that one door at the end of the hall, it turns into a hospital. Or worse! And it's filled with all these old people in wheelchairs staring into space. It will be like a jail, that's what it will be like, and they'll keep me there until I'm carried out in a box." She dabbed at drool on the twins' chins. "Do you two babies think I'm a nutball, too? Do you think Grandma needs to be put out to pasture?"

"Oh, puhleeeese?!" Rosalie squawked. Then Bernadette chimed in. Their mother retorted, all their voices rising at a steady pitch and blending into a kind of chorus that was making Celia's head throb. She wondered how long it took them all to notice she'd simply gotten up and left the table.

In fact, she left the house altogether because suddenly she needed fresh air.

Outside, a damp, chilly, noise-muffling haze had descended over the neighborhood, leaving fuzzy glowing halos around lamp posts and making the world seem hushed and quiet. Soon, sounds pierced the silence—the random dog barking, the stern, almost dire tones of a TV news show, and a horn honking, followed by a sharp screech of brakes. She started to walk. She wasn't really paying attention to where she was going, but it felt good to be in motion. Before she knew it, she had walked all the way back to Barry's.

For a few minutes, she just gazed at her former home. In the den, everything seemed the same, except all the furniture had been rearranged. Beyond her own reflection in the glass of the sliding doors, she could see Barry, Gloria, and Bernice on the couch, all eyes fixed on the big flat screen. They were laughing, so the show must have been a comedy. It felt bizarre to feel like a total outsider, but she kept rooted to the spot until Barry turned—like somehow he'd sensed she had arrived—and their eyes met. He headed for the door. Soon, he was right in front of her, giving her an odd look. Celia realized she had marched out of her mother's house in her bathrobe and slippers, not even pausing to grab her phone. She said, "What's wrong with people? You'd think somebody might have stopped to ask if I was okay."

"Are you?" Barry asked.

"I don't know. Are you?"

He was quiet a moment. "I have to say, I've been better."

"Yeah, me too."

There followed an awkward, almost painful silence. Celia broke it with, "I quit my job."

"You did? Why?"

She paused to find the right words. "I'm honestly not sure. You know there's that old cliche….like my heart just wasn't in it anymore? It's kind of that. But maybe it's because it's all I've ever really done, and I just need to try something else. Because it kind of feels like if I wait any longer, I never will."

He nodded. "But you and me—we were good once, weren't we, Celia? I mean, for a long time, actually."

"Yes."

"You know what I was thinking about on the drive back up here? I was thinking of that morning we met when we rode up the elevator together in my building."

"We pretended like we were two crazy old people," Celia said, and the memory — about a time when it was okay to be goofy and awkward — made her smile.

"I thought we would get there, you know, you and me? The years would pass so fast our heads would spin. We'd have kids—our own little family—and they'd grow up and leave home, and then there'd be grandkids—we'd be that old couple going to the doctor with each other, or like the ones you see in the grocery store arguing over coupons or finding exact change while holding up the line."

Celia started to say she was sorry, but Barry held up a hand. The air had grown chillier. Little puffs of condensation wafted up from his mouth. He shoved his hands in his pockets and shifted from one foot to the other.

"I said the other day this was all on you. That you broke us. And it does hurt, Celia. I'm not going to lie. But now, I'm not so sure that was totally right. Or that I was totally innocent. I don't know when or where, but somewhere, I guess I started to take you—to take us—for granted. Somewhere, I forgot I needed to put in work to keep us together. So, I guess I'll shoulder some of the blame."

Celia nodded.

Now they were both quiet.

"I'll drive you home?"

"No, I'm good."

"You're in slippers and a bathrobe."

"It's okay. Nobody seems to notice."

Neither of them knew what to do. Barry looked like he was going to hug her, but then he thrust out a hand, and Celia knew this was truly an end.

SHE WASN'T HALFWAY down the block when she spotted the car. They must have followed once they realized she was gone. It was Rosalie and Kim in their Prius with her mother and Bernadette in back with the twins. They were still squabbling, she could hear, from half a block away, about whose fault it was that Celia had walked out and how they could get her to regain her senses and come home. Rosalie was taking one position on the subject, Bernadette another, and their mother a third. From what she heard, it all sounded slightly demented, and it hit Celia that like it or not, she was stuck with these women for life. But she was smiling a little as she headed for the car.

X.

Somehow, when Celia wasn't paying attention, a whole new way of doing business had sprung up. For instance, when she first visited the offices of SayCheeeeez!, the app that matched photographers with potential clients, she was disoriented to find nobody had offices or even cubicles of their own. The space was a huge old refurbished warehouse in Williamsburg, with exposed steel beams, brick walls, and a scuffed wooden floor that seemed to date from a hundred years earlier. Loud hip-hop thumped through unseen speakers. Employees (at first she didn't realize that's what they were, or indeed if that's what employees were called at a place like this) all lounged on low-slung sofas in front of laptops. Some had slumbering dogs by their side. A tall man with cornrows had a cockatiel perched on his shoulder. All seemed a good ten years younger than Celia, or more—she tried not to notice, and the tattoos, body piercings, and hair styles were off the charts. This place was nothing like the doctors' offices she was accustomed to visiting, all solidly cemented in previous century office design, or even her own old office space, which now seemed to be hopelessly out of date. At first, the whole vibe threw her off.

"Oh, you'll find work I bet," said Minnie at what was called Celia's 'onboarding' session.

All Celia could think of was how some people so perfectly fit their names. Minnie was a teensy sliver of a thing, thin-boned, pale, and very, very delicate, as if she were constructed out of nothing but air. If it wasn't for a shock of inky black curls piled willy-nilly atop her head, you might even miss her, Celia mused.

"Even though I don't have a....well, a whole lot...of professional experience," she asked. "If any, really?"

"Well, keep in mind we don't make judgments on your past experience."

"You don't?"

"Nope!"

"Then if you don't mind my asking, what exactly do you guys do?"

"Think of us as facilitators."

"Okay. Um..."

"We provide a link between two interested parties. Kind of like Tinder, but for pictures! And not dirty ones. No naked selfies. No nip slips. Definitely no bulges in underwear. No piercings in places you don't want to know about. We have a strict policy against that type of deal. There's plenty of other platforms for those kind of shenanigans. Too many if you ask me. I mean, really."

"Okay. Right," said Celia, who suddenly wondered if an app like Tinder would be in her future, too. She put that frightening thought out of her mind.

"Now, don't get me wrong, professional experience isn't a bad thing," Minnie continued, "although everybody has to start somewhere, right? But this is more about a visceral reaction. People will look at your posts and either respond or not. And let's face it — much of photography is just dumb luck. You point, shoot, and if you're lucky, you get something amazing! Anyway, if you get pinged, you'll have to sell yourself as best you can. You can do that, right? Hustle a little? Because, let's be honest, in this day and age it's all about the hustle. And btw, we do sell ad space on the site in case you hadn't noticed. Just FYI. Although people can upgrade to the ad-free version, but that'll cost them. But the bottom line is that it's up to you to sell yourself, ultimately."

Celia nodded in the affirmative even though she was far from sure about anything.

She had stumbled on the app while perusing job listings on Craigslist while sitting in the Starbucks down the street from her mother's. The place was filled with people like Celia, earbuds in, tapping away at laptops or squinting at their phones. She wondered if they were actually working, looking for jobs like her or just playing games or checking social media. "Photographers? Looking for Gigs?" was the headline that caught her eye, so on a whim, she clicked on the link and entered the necessary information.

In the few weeks since quitting the only job she'd ever known, Celia had signed up for extension courses on photography at her old university. Some of the material she already knew, but there was so much to learn, a never-ending process really, but it was a step. She also began to assemble a meager portfolio. She started by texting Dante and asking him to send all the pictures she had taken of the shack and the food. He did it right away, along with a selfie of he and Penelope making sad faces. It was around this time that her phone rang. When she glanced at the caller ID and saw a Georgia area code, she figured it was a former client.

"Hi!" said the voice she instantly recognized as Penelope's when she answered the call.

"Oh, hi!" Celia answered, flustered. "Does your dad know you're calling?"

"No, he's not here. This is his phone. He forgot it when he left. Guess what?"

"What?"

"I tripped! I scraped my knee! It bled, and I got a band-aid."

"I'm sorry to hear that. Are you with Roberta?"

"Yup! She says to say hi."

"Okay, say hi back."

"Okay!"

There was a burst of giggling, some static, and then, suddenly, jarringly, Dante's voice. "Hey," he said.

"Oh! Um..." was all Celia could come up with, totally caught off guard.

"I came back to get my phone. I didn't expect to find you."

"Well, thanks for sending me those pictures."

"I'm gonna text you something else," Dante said. "No response necessary," he added. "Although you can if you want. I would not object."

"Okay. Thanks."

The call abruptly ended. Celia felt a little tug from somewhere inside.

Her phone buzzed. She saw there was indeed a new text from Dante, along with a picture. She debated what to do.

Look? Delete without looking? This seemed to be the option that offered far less complication.

But her curiosity got the better of her. First, she read the text. "Thought about our conversation, and I took care of some unfinished business," it began. "With Lester. With my other dad. With some memories of my mom and grandmother. You were the push, and I thank you. These things needed to be done."

She expanded the picture. It was the tattoo of the semicolon. He had it altered. It now appeared to be a heart, and no longer a symbol for unfinished business.

She took a deep breath. She closed her eyes and just sat silently for a while. She didn't delete the text, but she closed her messages so she could move forward with the day and not obsess over it.

She had another mission. Her old college-days camera required actual film—35 millimeter, difficult to track down these days—so Celia left it in the desk drawer (not that she wanted to abandon film altogether, but for the time being, it would be back-burnered) in her room at her mother's house. She used a chunk of savings to invest in the newer digital version along with a good selection of other equipment she would need, a couple of lenses and filters, and a few lighting accessories. While the salesperson rang up her purchases, she wandered into the section of the store that held darkroom equipment. Could she set one up somewhere down the line? Darkrooms were always something intriguing as there was inherent promise in developing an unseen picture. Newly outfitted, she spent a few days roaming aimlessly around town, photographing whatever caught her eye, a rusty old pick-up truck in a weedy front yard here, a mother pushing a stroller of triplets while walking three rigidly groomed Schnauzers there. She explored corners of the area she had long forgotten. She discovered pockets she didn't even know existed. After Minnie texted her to come in to meet (what they really wanted, it seemed, was her approval to run a background check and get their own picture of her for the site—an ordeal in itself, as in some she looked drably serious, in others too casual, until they finally settled on one Celia liked), she uploaded the work and waited for offers to come in.

And waited.

And waited some more.

Celia checked the app constantly. She deleted and reloaded it because she thought, *Well, maybe it's got a bug, or it's not functioning.* She spent much time setting up a website, wishing she wasn't so technically challenged when she couldn't get the site the way she wanted. She started to wonder if she had made yet another awful mistake. Would Danielle Chan give her her old job back?

Finally, there came a query. Celia borrowed her mom's Wagoneer and headed to a meeting with a super-nervous bride and her equally jittery groom. They looked dubious when she hopped out of a creaky old car with holes in the floor, its tailpipe belching ominous dark smoke. Things only got worse when they learned this would be her first wedding gig; she never heard another word and, frankly, who could blame them? There were a few more dead ends, another nibble or two, and then she reeled one in, which, okay, was through a connection, but still. It came from Sonya, whose niece was having a Bat Mitzvah. She had seen Celia's postings on one of her new social media sites. "I told my sister you were the best Bat Mitzvah photographer ever," Sonya said, Face-timing while out on a sales call, Celia could tell, could even recognize some of the nurses in the background.

"But," Celia protested, "she knows you're kidding, right? That I'm an amateur. That even if she considered actually hiring me, she's totally taking a very big risk?"

"No! Do not worry, Celia. I know you can handle it."

"Um..."

"You've heard the saying, 'Act as if'?"

"Uh..."

"Act as if you know what you are doing."

"Hmmmmmm," Celia mused.

"It works, trust me. I do it all the time, in all sorts of situations. Best advice I ever got. For instance, when I got this job. They asked if I spoke Russian fluently because they thought it might be a help with foreign sales. A vast untapped market is what they said, for big pharma. Well, I don't. I'm from Ukraine. There is a difference. I mean, really. People need to take the time to learn a little bit about geography. And culture. But, anyway, I said I did, and I got the job!"

Celia thought about that. Before she knew it, she had accepted the gig.

When the day arrived, she carefully selected an outfit, something formal enough with, she hoped, a hint of style, but that would also allow her movement and fluidity. She chose the pair of slim black slacks she had bought down in Georgia that flared a little daringly at the ankle, a muted cream blouse, and a blazer she could remove if need be and still seem dressy. A simple beaded necklace and small hoop earrings completed the look. She put on a bit of make-up, tied her hair back tidily, secured it with a clasp, packed up her equipment, and headed down the stairs.

She couldn't get through the front door, though. She looked at it, but felt suddenly frozen with a kind of paralysis she couldn't quite pinpoint. She set down the cases of equipment and sank into the sofa. A few moments passed, and then Daisy came into the living room, a cup of hot tea in one hand, her daily newspaper in the other. She stopped short when she saw Celia. "Shouldn't you be on your way?" her mother asked.

"Yes."

"Well...?"

"Maybe this whole thing is just crazy. Maybe I'm kidding myself. What if I screw it all up? One wrong picture, and I could scar that poor girl for life. I mean, she's only thirteen, and the way things go viral these days! I'm not sure the odds are in my favor, the more I think about it."

Daisy set down her tea and sat next to Celia. She took her hand. She hadn't held her mother's hand in years. In fact, she couldn't recall the last time. But it felt strangely comforting how easily their fingers interlaced as Daisy said, "I've been thinking about something you mentioned to me the other day when we were in that coffee shop down in Hodges Creek."

"I probably said a lot of stupid things."

"No, you didn't. You said I never encouraged you, that I always only cared if you had something solid to fall back on, like a real job."

"Mom, I..." Celia interrupted.

"No, let me finish, honey. Because you were right. I didn't encourage creativity or urge you to follow a dream. I guess because I was afraid you'd get hurt. I got hurt when I was that age, and I tried to do something out of the box. I've never admitted it. So I just wanted to protect you. That's just part of being a mother, a part that never, ever goes away. But now that I look back, it was wrong. So you have this second chance. I want you to go for it. Just grab it. Because I have this feeling you'll be just fine."

Celia smiled. She squeezed her mother's hand, then leaned over and gave her a kiss on the cheek.

Soon, she was on her way. Oh, she was still moving as if on auto-pilot, determined to keep all the fears and doubts from thrumming around her head, trying hard to, as Sonya said, act as if. Luckily, Sonya was a guest and provided moral support, and so when Celia arrived at the Temple, a low-slung discreet beige brick rectangle set in a grove of dense pines and sycamores, and began setting up, Sonya introduced her as the esteemed photographer, and Celia almost burst into tears at the show of confidence.

She began by capturing arrivals, the first group a noisy gaggle of pre-teens and teenagers. The girls were a good foot taller than the boys and looked more like poised young women while the boys were gangly and awkward, already tugging at their ties, already with shirts half untucked and hair going every which way. The teens clamored into the temple and plunked into seats in chatty, flibbertigibbet cliques. Then came groups of adults, first what appeared to be parents and parents' friends, the women ultra-chic, the men in sleek dark suits, some of them murmuring softly in their native Ukrainian, others shouting loudly and slapping each other on the backs. Finally, in a painstakingly slow procession, came the elders, the grandparents and their set, some moving with jaunty ease, others requiring assistance, one woman with a precise crimp of copper colored hair seemingly so ancient, so wrinkled and shrunken despite her hopeful perky dress, it appeared she might wither away to dust before the rite ended. Still, she managed an impish, almost girlish grin and even a daring pose when she noticed Celia pointing the camera in her direction.

Soon, the service got underway. Celia, as unobtrusively as possible, knelt silently near the dais and began by focusing her lens first on the guest of honor, a tall, lithe, pretty girl who seemed suddenly struck rigid and serious as she read from the Torah, the Rabbi looking on with pride, beaming through a spiky salt-and-pepper beard. More shots followed of her with her parents, with her grandparents, and then with various friends.

When the service was over, everybody migrated to a large space next door, which had been transformed into something resembling a vintage disco, complete with a DJ spinning the latest singles, a large dance floor under a glittery mirrored ball, and at one side, a massive buffet groaning with platters of all sorts of delicious-smelling food. She photographed the dancing, the adults expertly twirling through masses of teens, the girls towering over the few awkward boys who would dance (most of the boys were over in a corner conspiring about something or scrunched intently over their phones while partnerless girls danced with themselves). Some time later, the father of the Bat Mitzvah girl noticed Celia photographing food and asked if she'd eaten.

"Actually, um...no," Celia answered.

"Then please, take a break. You must come sit."

She protested that she needed to keep working. Suddenly, she was seeing photo ops everywhere as if she was looking at the world through a new set of eyes, and she didn't want to miss a thing. But he was having none of it. He insisted, escorting Celia to a large round table with a mass of flowers in the center, sitting her down between his ultraglamorous, cryptically smiling wife—all sharp angles, sparkly jewelry, and a perfume that smelled of the exotic—and that ancient woman she photographed earlier, who was now tucking into a plate with the hearty appetite of a woman far younger. "You like?" she said as she daintily sliced what appeared to be a dumpling in two, speared one half, and held it out.

"I don't know," Celia said, unsure if she'd ever even tasted one.

"You try."

Celia bit into the dumpling. The dough was thin, soft and billowy as an old balloon, the inside bursting with a fragrant mushroom, meat, and cheese mixture that was indeed delicious.

"Vernykys," the old woman said. "It's good, yes?"

"Yes!"

"Always good to try new things, yes?" the old woman continued. "Do one thing new every day, and you will live a long life."

"I'll try!" Celia answered.

The woman smiled and clapped hands so bony Celia was afraid they might shatter.

Then the father set down a plate in front of her, this one with a roll of stuffed cabbage and a crisp brown disc of Chicken Kiev, which provided a small, pleasing explosion of hot butter when she broke into it with a fork. She wound up cleaning her plate before getting back to the business at hand.

Later, after the event wound down, Celia, exhausted, sat in her mother's Wagoneer in the Temple parking lot and, with a critical eye, scrolled through the shots. She found them decent, acceptable, with a few that had potential to be rated a notch higher. She headed back to her mother's in a fog, fell into bed, and because her brain had been working overdrive slipped into a deep dreamless slumber.

IN THE WEEKS THAT FOLLOWED, she began to look for a place of her own. Nothing quite fit. There were newly constructed apartments in the city, skinny towers that knifed through the sky with lofty wide-open spaces that seemed ice cold. There were brownstone studios in Brooklyn up too many flights of creaky, narrow, possibly even dangerous stairs. A drafty sagging cottage with weathered gray shingles and green shutters out by the churning Atlantic held promise but ultimately felt too remote. Meanwhile, she com-

pleted the Bat Mitzvah job, printing out bound albums of
photos for the family and friends. Payment was wired into
her account. When the money first dropped, she just stared
at the amount. It wasn't that it was so sizable—it was that,
somehow, she had pulled the job off, made the whole thing
work, and because of that, she felt an enormous jolt of pride.

She uploaded sample photos to her page on the app,
and soon she was pinged with a couple of job inquiries. No
done deals, yet, but leads that were solid. Sonya pitched in
again, convincing higher-ups at work to hire Celia to do
some product shoots for a roll-out on the company website.
This was an unchallenging gig—there was no real way to jazz
up pharmaceuticals—but it paid well, and Celia insisted on
treating Sonya to an expensive dinner in the city the night
they finished the shoot. They ate too much steak, drank
too many martinis, and danced like mad at a nearby club,
so she slept late the following morning. When she finally
stirred, the house smelled of her mother's fresh-brewed coffee, sizzling bacon, and toast. Still, she could barely drag herself from bed, so she just laid there for a while, enjoying
the warmth under the covers and the quiet. Until she heard
Daisy doing her morning tidying up downstairs, humming as
she dusted this and that, singing but mangling lyrics to one
of her favorite oldies as she ran the vacuum.

The doorbell rang.

She heard murmuring between Daisy and a man, and
then her mother called: "Celia? Sleepyhead? Do you know
what time it is? Are you up yet?"

"Barely," Celia shouted back.

"You'd best get down here."

There was something in her mother's tone, a touch of the bemused and mysterious. She threw back the covers, climbed out of bed, and headed for the stairs. She joined Daisy at the front door. A large truck had pulled up to the house. The driver was standing there, eager to complete the delivery, and somebody needed to sign for it. "I didn't order anything," Celia said. "Did you?"

"No," Daisy answered. "Not that I can remember, anyway."

This earned her a sidelong glance from Celia. She turned back to the driver. "What is it?"

"I couldn't tell you, ma'am. I didn't load the truck. I just drove it here. Sign for it, and we can open her up."

She was curious, so she scribbled her name on the little screen he held out. She and Daisy walked down the driveway and waited while the driver unlocked the rear door of the semi. The door clattered up. When she saw what was inside, Celia gasped. And then she smiled.

IN THE TRUCK WAS THAT old Triumph, which had once belonged to Fionnula Gibbs' daughter, Mary Rose. But the car—a veritable wreck the first time Celia had laid eyes on it—had been transformed. Now it was a gleaming flame red with a brand new black canvas top. All the chrome had been buffed until it sparkled. Inside, the leather seats had been restored, so springs no longer poked out. The wood trim on the dash was polished to a shine. There was a flashy new sound system with Bluetooth and navigation, all the modern conveniences the original builders of the car never could have imagined. Mechanicals had been restored, too, so when Celia slipped in the key and turned over the ignition, the engine purred. She took it for a short spin; it rocketed forward in a smooth straight line, shifting from one gear to the next with an ease and fluidity that belied its years.

Dante had done the work with the help of Lester Brenneman, his father, as he now referred to him, using the repair manual that Lester had socked away for all these years in his cluttered old house. This she learned from the sealed note the trucker handed her when she finished the little test drive. Her name was scrawled across the front. She tore it open and began to read. Dante wrote that he hoped this note wouldn't take forty years to reach her. He wanted to give her the car, he went on, because his insurance had come through, and he had bought a new truck. He hadn't forgotten her mentioning she once wanted one just like it. Also, he still felt he owed her for helping out with the pictures of his food and his barbecue shack because business had taken off since they were posted on the new website Roberta constructed. Also, he missed her, he wrote, missed her bad. He asked her to come back to Hodges Creek. Finally, he wanted to marry her if she'd have him.

She finished the note as the driver of the truck said his goodbyes, closed up the back, climbed into the cab, and slowly rolled away.

"Why are you crying?" Daisy asked because tears puddled in Celia's eyes and started to roll down her cheeks. She wiped them away with the back of her hand, silently berating herself for being such a cornball.

"Because I think I'm going to have to leave you, for a while at least, and that makes me a little sad."

"You're going to go?"

"Uh-huh."

"Really?" Daisy asked, and Celia girded herself for another battle.

"Yep."

"Well. Finally!"

Celia gaped at her mother, who actually had a giant smile on her face. "Oh, that's nice," she said.

"I'm kidding! Jeez, lighten up! To be perfectly honest, sweetheart, I'd been trying to figure out how I was going to get rid of you. I mean the way you ensconced yourself in your old room, I was thinking I might even have to sell the house to get you out, and I don't really want to do that. I love this house despite the fact that it's falling to pieces on me."

"Thanks for the concern, Mother."

"What should I tell your sisters? Will you be back for Sunday Supper? This week, I am finally making my Oriental Casserole. I've been having such a taste for it, and I realized everything I needed is right in my pantry. Everything was all just hidden where I couldn't see it!"

"I don't know when I'll be back."

Daisy nodded and bit her lower lip. "Anyway, you don't need to worry about me. I'll be perfectly fine. Plus, Lois is just across the street. We've got each other's backs, you know, me and Lo. We always have."

Indeed, Lois could be seen peeking warily through her curtains as the truck left. Then her front door opened, and out she came. Of course, she also had to use a walker now, and Celia couldn't imagine how these two ladies – Lois sporting a bum leg and Daisy wrestling with an increasingly addled brain—could help each other if one of them really needed it, especially now as she watched Lois make her way across the street in a painfully slow way. "You'd be dead by the time any help arrived if you really needed it. You understand that, don't you?' Celia said to her mother.

"Such a worry-wart," Daisy answered with a blithe wave. "You should try to get over that, dear. In fact, it's probably what's been upsetting your tummy."

Indeed, over the last few days, she'd been having heartburn. Well, she'd been under stress, with a new business to figure out and with a whole new decade now less than a year away to fret over. Every night, she'd lay in bed and think about that, about how the time would pass quickly, so fast it would make her head spin, and before she knew it, here would be another birthday. Well, also there was that vegan lasagna Daisy had made, and they'd been picking at for days. Too much fiber?

Lois finally reached Daisy and Celia. She needed a moment to catch her breath, another bad sign, Celia noted. All three women took a step back and admired the car.

"That's one fine-looking ride," Lois said. She sounded almost like a teenager, as if that's what a car like this brought out in a person—a lust for rebellion and danger.

"Word," added Daisy.

Celia worked hard to contain her laughter.

Both women demanded a spin. Celia took them individually around the block because she couldn't fit both at once, each one waving at neighbors they knew and dangling their arms out the window to catch the breeze. By the time she was done, she had formed a plan. She would drive down to Georgia. She'd pay Dante for the car because she thought it was beautiful—a work of art really, unlike anything else on the road—and she did indeed want to keep it. And that would be it.

Or maybe she would stay. At least a little bit. Or not. She didn't bring a lot with her, just threw together a few tops and pairs of well-worn jeans. She packed the new camera and all its paraphernalia. She sent texts to Bernadette and Rosalie that she'd be missing from this Sunday's supper, but she'd be in touch. She kissed her mom and hugged her as hard as she could, just drank in that familiar mom smell that could be found nowhere else and never duplicated. She promised she'd see her soon even if suddenly the future seemed like one big question mark. She found this scary and exhilarating.

In the Triumph, she cranked up the new sound system as she merged into heavy traffic on the thruway. She pointed the car south and revelled in the open-air as the morning sun warmed her skin.

It was farther along into this journey—traffic had thinned and the road narrowed—when Celia noticed something in a car she fast approached and then veered around to pass. It was an SUV with what looked like a mom and dad up front and a bunch of kids in the back. Framed in one window was a young girl. She was gazing at Celia with a faraway, dreamy expression. Celia's hair was blowing in the wind. She had tunes cranked. She smiled when she saw the girl staring at her because she recognized something in that face, looking at her as if she had the answer to some mystery.

Who knew if the kid could hear it or not, but she said out loud, right to her, as if she could, "It's going to turn out all right."

She downshifted to give herself more speed. The Triumph torqued forward as it gained momentum. And then Celia was gone.

Acknowledgments

No book comes into existence on its own, and this one is no exception. In fact, you probably would not be reading it right now without the hard work and dedication of the folks at indie publisher Writing Bloc. Massive props to Michael Haase, founder and fearless leader of this organization of dedicated authors. I first came to know Michael when we were involved in another publishing venture, and I read one of his stories, *An Adventure With Dada*, which I found both hilarious and, in parts, a tug at the heartstrings. I remember thinking: *this is a person I'd like to get to know better.* When Writing Bloc was in its infancy, and there was talk of putting out an anthology of short stories, I did not hesitate to submit, and I'm so glad I did. *Escape!*, the debut publication, is a wonderful collection of eclectic tales that covers escape of all kinds. *Deception!* the next anthology to come from Writing Bloc, promises to be equally as absorbing. Writing Bloc has grown to include podcasts, a newsletter, and of course, it is all over social media. It's a cooperative effort among like-minded folks, and thank you, Michael, for being the spark.

Editing can make or break a book. I am sincerely grateful to Cari Dubiel, Becca Spence Dobias and Kendra Namednil. Each one of these fine editors made my writing so much better. I am deeply indebted to them all, and hopefully one day I will learn the proper use of a comma, and stop using the word 'then' as if it was going to be snatched out of my vocabulary for eternity! (Did I get that comma right?) But to the entire Writing Bloc team, thank you all again.

Rosa Entertainment's Sidney Sherman has stood steadfast behind my efforts for a very long time. Much gratitude for keeping the faith.

Few shout-outs to family and friends. To the Late Carol and Norman. To my sister Jane (and Whit), my brother John (and Irina), all six nephews (and latest addition to the fam, Maddie!), to intrepid traveler Marlene Raynor, to all my cousins and their children, to Paula Diamond, whose ties to the book world have always been a fascination, and to Marcia Parlow Pomerance, for similar and other reasons...thank you all.

Everybody should have a friend like Sal Ladestro in his or her life. I know of few people as kindhearted and generous, and I value our friendship enormously. Kate Funk was an early supporter of *Women Like Us*, having read just a few chapters and encouraging the idea of pursuing publication. Props! Joe Smith, too, for early and steadfast support.

And, of course, to Sam Destro, who's been there for me for way more years than I want to admit right now. And, finally, to our animals, cats and pups past and present, who have been our loyal companions. I can't imagine life without them either.

About the Author

Jason Pomerance was born in New York City, grew up in Westchester County, and graduated from Middlebury College. He lives in Los Angeles with his partner and their beagles. His first novel Women Like Us was published in 2016, and his novella Falconer debuted that same year on Nikki Finke's Hollywood Dementia. Mrs. Ravenstein, a short story, was part of Writing Bloc's Escape! Anthology, and his story Violet Crane will be included in the publisher's anthology, Deception, coming this fall. He has also written film and television projects for numerous studios and production companies, including Warner Brothers, Columbia Pictures, FremantleMedia, and Gold Circle Films.

Photo credit: Steven Murashige

9 781699 212318